IT'S
ALL YOUR
FAULT

IT'S
ALL YOUR
FAULT

PAUL RUDNICK

 SCHOLASTIC PRESS / NEW YORK

All rights reserved. Published by Scholastic Press, an imprint of Scholastic Inc., *Publishers since 1920.* SCHOLASTIC, SCHOLASTIC PRESS, and associated logos are trademarks and/or registered trademarks of Scholastic Inc.

The publisher does not have any control over and does not assume any responsibility for author or third-party websites or their content.

Library of Congress Cataloging-in-Publication Data
Rudnick, Paul, author.
  It's all your fault / Paul Rudnick.—First edition.
     pages cm
  Summary: Seventeen-year-old Caitlin Singleberry is a proper Christian teenager and member of a family singing group, but today she has been given a truly impossible assignment—keep her cousin Heller Harrigan, Hollywood wild child, out of trouble for the last weekend before her first big movie debuts.
  ISBN 978-0-545-46428-4 (jacketed hardcover) 1. Cousins—Juvenile fiction.
2. Teenage actors—Juvenile fiction. 3. Motion picture actors and actresses—Juvenile fiction. 4. Singers—Juvenile fiction. 5. Humorous stories. [1. Cousins—Fiction. 2. Actors and actresses—Fiction. 3. Singers—Fiction. 4. Humorous stories.] I. Title. II. Title: It's all your fault.
  PZ7.R8792It 2016
  [Fic]—dc23
                                    2015015697

10 9 8 7 6 5 4 3 2 1   16 17 18 19 20

Printed in the U.S.A.   23

First edition, February 2016

Book design by Abby Dening

For John

one

May God and Everyone Else Forgive Me

I am a good Christian girl and I am so ashamed.

Up until forty-eight hours ago I had never tasted alcohol, kissed a boy, worn anything sleeveless or sung a song in public at the top of my lungs using suggestive and inappropriate lyrics. I had never kidnapped anyone or held up a convenience store at gunpoint or stolen a convertible. I don't even have a driver's license.

In a very few minutes I am going to have to leave this jail cell and try to explain everything to my parents, my eight brothers and sisters, Reverend Benswelder, all of the lawyers everyone's hired, the police, the mayor of Parsippany, New Jersey, and all of those journalists and their camera crews plus all of those people from those things on the Internet that I have never been allowed to read or follow or click on or whatever those procedures are called.

I have no idea what I'm going to say.

two

Oh No

It's happening. I can feel my chest getting tighter and my hands starting to clench and soon I won't be able to breathe because I'm having a panic attack. I was diagnosed with a severe anxiety disorder when I was eight years old and couldn't go on escalators because I knew I would fall and the escalator would chew me up. I've had therapy to try and control the attacks through medication and deep breathing and behavioral modification but right now, unless I list the names of my brothers and sisters in order, three times, all of them will die. Carter Corinne Caleb Callum Carl Castor Calico Catherine. Carter Corinne Caleb Callum Carl Castor Calico Catherine. Carter Corinne Callum Caleb . . . NO NO NO that was wrong and I have to start again only now I have to repeat the names six times because I have to protect everyone and I know this sounds crazy but I can't stop. Carter Corinne Caleb . . .

three

Who I Am

My name is Caitlin Mary Prudence Rectitude Singleberry and if you live in the middle section of New Jersey you might have heard of or maybe even listened to my family. My parents run a small grocery store but they also, along with my siblings, have been making records and performing since before I was born—at seventeen I'm right in the middle.

I have always loved being a Singing Singleberry and I've always hoped that I would someday get married and have children who would join our family onstage and off, but I don't know if this is still going to be possible. I don't know if anyone let alone a wonderful Christian boy with firm morals, an openhearted smile and neatly pressed khakis will want to hear me sing ever again, let alone fall in love with me, not after the way I've behaved. On top of that I'm supposed to be going to college next year but that's probably never going to happen. I've been so worried I won't get accepted anywhere that I've applied to twelve schools and I've compulsively rewritten my essays and spell-checked them more times than I can count but now, well—what college on earth would even consider accepting someone with my criminal record?

I don't believe in blaming other people for my shameful actions because that is not what a Singleberry does. But may God forgive me because I do blame someone else for all of the unspeakable things that have happened. I blame my cousin Heller Harrigan.

I know that Jesus tells us to turn the other cheek but with all due reverence, while Jesus suffered many dreadful things, he never met Heller. If he had I sincerely believe he would've added, "Turn the other cheek except when it comes to Heller Harrigan. You're allowed to smack her as hard as you can. Tell her I said so."

I HATE HELLER HARRIGAN.

four

Aunt Ecstasy

I should start with this past Friday morning when my aunt Nancy came to our house for the first time in four years, since that other terrible day. I'm sorry but right now and maybe forever I'm too upset to even think about what happened on that earlier day, let alone discuss it. I've tried to never allow myself to remember it but every time I see Heller's name or her picture or oh my Lord, one of her disgusting videos, I can't help myself. Everything that happened on that day and everything that turned two families into strangers is all because of Heller and me.

When I heard Aunt Nancy talking to my mom downstairs I was shocked. My mom called my name so I tiptoed downstairs to our living room.

"Caitlin!" said Aunt Nancy. "Look at you! Carol, why didn't you tell me? She's a total hottie!"

I instantly started back up the stairs until my mom said, "Catey, it's okay. We need to talk to you. It's an emergency. Nancy, please try and be more sensitive."

"I'm very sensitive!" said Aunt Nancy. "I was paying her a compliment! I mean, under that blazer and that sweater and all of that weird long hair, it looks like Catey's got a rockin' bod goin' on. And Carol, for the one millionth time—it's not Nancy, it's Ecstasy."

"Nancy . . . ," my mom said, taking a deep breath.

"Look," said Aunt Nancy, "I know that you think I changed my name because of the party drug but that's totally not it. If I wanted to name myself after a drug, I'd just call myself Advil or Motrin or Penicillin. Actually, Penny Sillin' might be kind of cool, if I was a rapper. But I changed my name years ago, after I met that amazing man in Calcutta who finally managed to give me a triple orgasm, I mean boom boom boom! It was like—what's that incredibly difficult thing that figure skaters are always trying to do in the Olympics? The triple lutz? That was exactly what that gorgeous Amri Kapoor managed to do— he performed a triple lutz on my—"

"Nancy!"

"What? I should've held up a paddle with a score of one hundred and ten percent! Instead, I decided to honor my phys- ical happiness and my emotional rebirth by changing my name to Ecstasy. Caitlin, you understand, don't you?"

I froze and I started to panic and I looked around desper- ately for someone else to answer the question.

I should also mention that since I'd last seen her four

years ago, Aunt Nancy's electric-blue dreadlocks had grown almost to her waist and she was wearing one of her usual get-ups including a T-shirt that said I Want To Kill Everyone I Don't Love, skintight jeans with holes in them and thigh-high pirate boots.

"Speak up, Caitlin," Aunt Nancy said. "You don't have a problem calling me Aunt Ecstasy, do you? You're seventeen now, just a few months younger than Heller, so you know your way around a triple orgasm, don't you?"

"M-M-M-Mom!" I finally blurted out.

"Nancy," said my mom, who was wearing a nice crisp white blouse and a denim wrap skirt like a mom should. "As usual, you're being deliberately provocative just to upset Caitlin. That's not why we're here, is it?"

Aunt Nancy got very quiet, which as you might imagine was something that almost never happened. Aunt Nancy is one of those people who like to keep talking about anything that pops into their heads; she has two speeds, full chatter or unconscious. Maybe that's why she drinks and takes drugs, just to slow herself down. If Aunt Nancy was being quiet, something huge was definitely about to happen.

five

A Girl Made of Sin

Caitlin," said my mom, "we know that years ago, you and Heller were very close. I hope you've understood why it's been in both of you girls' best interests to remain . . . apart."

"Because of—" Aunt Nancy began, but my mother glanced at her sharply.

"We all remember what happened the last time our girls were together," my mom said. "Caitlin, even though we try to keep you kids away from all of those trashy magazines and those gossip shows and all of that sludge on the Internet, I'm sure you're aware that Heller has become something of . . . a celebrity."

Of course I knew that Heller had turned into a celebrity. Everybody in the world knows that. It was all Heller had ever wanted. Because in my opinion, Heller doesn't have a soul.

"But Heller isn't just some reality show idiot," Aunt Nancy said. "Heller is a star."

When we were little Heller and I would watch shows on the family-approved channels and a lot of the shows were about girls. Sometimes the girls were just nice girls and sometimes they were secretly witches or rock stars or geniuses. Heller loved those shows because the girls always wore fun outfits and sang and danced and lived in big, brightly colored houses and had nice parents and sometimes a snarky little brother. The stars of these shows always had a best friend who was either shy and nervous or fun and wisecracking. But while I knew those shows were just empty calories and that watching them could destroy important brain cells, Heller was studying them.

"I can do that," Heller would say and then she'd imitate the girls on her favorite shows by either flipping her hair or doing a dance move. Sometimes, when Heller would make us dance together or sing silly songs, I'd get confused because Heller would announce that we were on *The Heller Harrigan Show* or sometimes she'd call it *Here Comes Heller*. I'll admit it, back then it was exciting to be around Heller because she was so, I'm not really sure what to call it, but I guess I'd say that Heller was always really eager to have adventures and jump around and stand right next to school crossing guards and try and make them dance with her.

As for me, back then I was happy to be either Heller's best friend or to be playing the role of Heller's best friend. I once caught Heller staring at me and then she said, "On our show, I don't think that you should be called Caitlin. I think you should be K-Bop." I let Heller call me K-Bop mostly because I couldn't stop her. It was fun to hang around with Heller because we were so little and because we hadn't gotten into any trouble yet and because my parents hadn't explained to me about how dangerous Heller could be. How evil.

I know what you're wondering: Wasn't the fact that she was named Heller a warning sign, like a Parental Guidance Suggested sticker? When I was little I thought "Heller" was just another name, like Susan or Caitlin, but then my sister Corinne told me that being named Heller was like being named The Devil. Back then I wasn't sure who the Devil was, so I asked my mom.

"Well," my mom had said while we were setting the table for dinner, which can take a long time for a family with so many people in it. "Your aunt Nancy has her own ideas about raising children," my mom continued, straightening up the knives and forks after I'd put them next to the plates. "I actually had to talk her out of naming Heller something much worse."

"Like what?"

My mom sighed and then she laughed. "She'd made a list. Until I put my foot down she was trying to decide between Heroin and Hurricane."

six

Heller's Rise

I'm so worried," said Aunt Nancy in our living room. "I love Heller more than my own life and I raised her to be whatever she wanted to be and to explore every possibility and never to say no to any new experience. I just wanted her to be free and open and creative." Then she looked right at my mom and said, "Because those are all really good things, no matter what anyone says."

"But there's a difference," said my mom, "between freedom and anarchy. Between running around being creative and forgetting to get an education, in order to become a decent human being."

"Jesus, Carol," said Aunt Nancy. "I was doing my best."

"And look what happened," said my mom in a very calm voice, as if the sisters were playing chess and my mom had just announced "Checkmate."

While Aunt Nancy had always been scattered and she'd had all of these different jobs and none of them for long, Heller had been determined. She'd used her mom's computer to do research on agents and auditions and acting classes and she'd convinced Aunt Nancy to sign her up for all sorts of things and to drive her into New York City to audition for anything that needed a Girl, Ages 7–10, or a Happy Little Kid, 8–12, or a Beam of Sunshine, Must Be Able to Skateboard, Ages 8–11, No Older, We Mean It. The first thing Heller had booked, when she was nine, was a TV commercial for Nut Hut Extra Creamy Peanut Butter. In the ad Heller had snuck into a kitchen, climbed onto a countertop, grabbed a forbidden jar of peanut butter from a high shelf and then shoved her fingers into it. Her TV mom had caught her with peanut butter all over her face and hands and Heller had insisted that "Nut Hut Peanut Butter isn't just extra creamy! It's extra dreamy!"

This commercial had been on TV for what seemed like twenty-four hours a day for two years and it had led to Heller getting more commercials and then a few smaller roles on TV shows, a TV pilot that didn't get picked up and finally, the lead on a show called *Anna Banana*.

Almost every girl in America and around the world had wanted to be Anna, who was this sweet good-hearted girl in middle school who was also secretly a top fashion model. During the day Anna would wear jeans and T-shirts and pull her hair back into a ponytail but on weekends and at night she'd wear makeup and designer gowns and get flown all over the world for photo shoots.

The strange thing about Anna Banana was that when Anna was at home or at school, no one ever recognized her or realized that she was also Gloriana, the world-famous model. When she was just Anna she'd spend her days studying and playing soccer and hanging out with her friends and no boys ever wanted to go out with her; the mean kids would call her Anna Banana to make fun of her. But when she was Gloriana she'd go to clubs and parties and she'd appear on magazine covers and huge billboards, and rock stars and princes and Olympic gymnasts would be after her.

Even though my parents had spent the last four years making sure Heller and I never saw each other and that Heller's name was never mentioned in our house, they were the ones who arranged for this whole past weekend. I'm trying really hard not to hold them responsible for ruining my life and for pretty much guaranteeing that I'd end up in this jail cell, sitting right near a girl wearing a leather biker vest over her bare skin, who's just asked me if she could lift up the bandage on my arm and take a look at my tattoo. My TATTOO? WAIT! WHAT?

"You really don't know?" says the girl. "Whoa. Maybe it's like a laughing clown with his tongue pierced. Or maybe it's like Satan eating an ice-cream cone only when you get real close the ice cream is all screaming babies."

I'm going to try counting the bars on the cell because I can feel the panic rising. My therapist has warned me about counting because once I start I can't stop but right now I'm in jail and I have a horrible unknown tattoo and I'll start counting in one corner although if I end on an odd number the panic will only get worse but I don't know what else to do and if the girl in the vest interrupts me I'll have to start again. One, two, three, four, five, six, seven . . .

"What are you doing? Your lips are moving—are you counting the bars?"

One, two, three . . .

seven

Tentpole

F or the past year," said my mom in our living room, "Heller has spiraled out of control. She's become addicted to alcohol and to all sorts of drugs and she's had at least one secret marriage that we know of, although I'm not sure if it was legal. She's been arrested for drunk driving and shoplifting, but her lawyers made a deal with the court, so she's been in rehab. She's being allowed out for the first time. Later today."

I'd known that Heller's life had gotten wild but I'd had no idea she was in so much trouble. For a second my heart went out to her, but only for a second. Because I'd warned her. When we were little I'd told her that if she kept skipping school and using bad words that terrible things would happen. While I didn't want to act superior and snitty and tell Heller and everyone else I told you so, well, I TOLD YOU SO.

YOU'RE WELCOME.

"She's being allowed out because I hope she's been getting well, and because of her movie," said Aunt Nancy.

"*Angel Wars*," I said, and suddenly everything was starting to make sense.

If you're a female between the ages of ten and assisted living, or even if you're a guy or even if you're too embarrassed to say it out loud, the *Angel Wars* books are your bible. They're not my bible because the real Bible is my bible but even though I've been homeschooled and not allowed to watch regular TV, I know all about *Angel Wars*. Fine, I'll admit it, I've read all of the books in the trilogy, which have sold more copies than there are people in the world because a lot of girls have hoarded multiple copies of each book and hidden the backup copies under their beds or in their lockers or in hollow trees, in case there's a nuclear holocaust.

"*Angel Wars*?" asked my mom as if she'd never heard of the books before. I love my mom but I just have to say it: She was lying.

The three books, which are called *Angel Wars: First Flight*, *Angel Wars: Devil's Dominion* and *Angel Wars: Aloft*, were written by a nice preschool teacher in North Carolina who first self-published the books online along with selling stapled-together xeroxed copies out of the trunk of her Toyota Camry at yard sales. After a year the books became a cult phenomenon and once they were republished by a regular publisher and translated into over eight hundred languages, the sales wouldn't stop. Here's how I know how popular and addictive the *Angel Wars* books are: I was allowed to read them only after I caught my mom reading the second book in the toolshed out behind our house. She didn't hear me open the door to the shed because she was so absorbed in her book, which she was reading by flashlight. She begged me not to tell Dad, so we made a deal: I'd keep my mouth shut as long as I could borrow the books.

That's another reason why I love my mom: While she tries really hard to be a good person every single second of the day, sometimes she just has to give in, eat three cupcakes in a row, and read *Angel Wars*.

Since the *Angel Wars* books were so overwhelmingly successful, a studio decided to make at least four movies out of them and Heller was cast as Lynnea, the Chosen Winglet, for one simple reason: The studio didn't know what Heller was really like because the studio wasn't her cousin.

eight

Here It Comes

The *Angel Wars* movie seems to have cost over two hundred million dollars to make," said my mom. "It premieres next week all over the world."

"The studio is going insane," said Aunt Nancy. "They've tried to keep everything that's happened to Heller as quiet as possible; they've been paying all sorts of people to hush everything up because there's so much riding on this movie and because people love those books so much. And because this movie could turn Heller into a major movie star."

My mom has always told me that Hollywood is a very dangerous place and that it can turn people into monsters. I'm not saying that Aunt Nancy is a monster but for someone who talks a lot about solar power and tantric energy and rediscovering her birth self, Aunt Nancy also knows a lot about what she calls the entertainment industry.

"Heller becoming a movie star isn't really our concern here," said my mom. "What I'm worried about is Heller herself, and what's happened to her. Because Heller is still a member of our family and we love her very much."

My mom and Aunt Nancy exchanged a look—checkmate again.

"So the studio, the people who made the *Angel Wars* movie," said Aunt Nancy, "they want someone to stay with Heller every second for this whole weekend before the movie opens. She's all booked up with an enormous press junket and a whole schedule of appearances and then the world premiere in Manhattan. They want someone who'll be a cross between a chaperone and a sober companion and a bodyguard. I would do it but the studio doesn't trust me. There was only one person I could think of who knows Heller and who's also, well, who's not some skeevy character like everyone else in Heller's world. Basically, the studio is looking for someone who understands Heller and who's also a stick-up-her-ass, uptight teenage nun. But in a really good way."

"Meaning you," said my mom, and she took my hand.

It was starting with my legs, which were shaking and numb. I clutched my mom's hand really hard and I squinched my eyes shut. My whole body was trying to curl up into a tight little ball to escape the panic as if maybe I could roll out of its path. I had to say something, I had to do something, I had to stop this whole situation from getting any more real.

"NO!" I said. "I . . . I . . . can't! I won't! Please don't ask me to do this! I . . . I . . . I can't!"

"Sweetie, Catey, it's okay," said my mom, putting her arms around me. "You don't have to do anything you don't want to. We'll completely understand."

"I . . . I . . ." I was doing the deep breathing and trying to unclench my fingers. My mom's hug was helping but the dread wasn't going away.

"Catey, I totally get it," said Aunt Nancy. "I shouldn't have come here."

I was instantly back in that last day, the last time I'd seen Heller. The day I'd almost died. People who've been in car accidents and plane crashes sometimes can't remember the details; they just remember waking up days later in the hospital. I remembered almost everything, especially the fear. My therapist had me rate my attacks on a scale between one and ten, but why does the scale stop at ten? Ten is nothing. Ten is being alone in our house on a dark night and hearing the screen door slam. This attack was already somewhere near a thousand. This was Heller.

"Catey, Catey, I'm right here, nothing bad is going to happen," said my mom, who was hugging me very tightly because I'd started to rock back and forth, and open and shut my eyes very quickly to blot out the world.

"It's just . . . ," said Aunt Nancy. "No. Things will work out. They have to."

"What?" I asked and opened my eyes. "What were you going to say?"

"I know that you hate Heller," Aunt Nancy said. "And I know that you have a very good reason to hate her and I'd never deny that. It's just—and I have no right to say this but it's all I keep thinking—Heller needs you."

Heller WHAT? Heller had never needed me. Heller didn't need anyone. Heller was the most independent and confident and reckless person I'd ever met. Heller was the total opposite of me, in every way. But now—she needed me?

"What . . . what do you mean? Why does Heller need me?"

"Well," said my mom, "you are so sweet and so disciplined and so conscientious. Your father and I are so proud of you. You're a role model, and a fine young woman. I'm just going to say it, right out loud—you're a Singleberry. You could set an example. Just maybe—you could change Heller's life."

Oh my God. Literally. OH MY GOD. God was speaking to me. God was saying, Caitlin, you're a very good girl but that isn't enough. You have to help others. You have to reach out. If you're a truly good person, you have to help the most difficult and the most undeserving and the most disgustingly evil people in the world.

You have to help Heller.

How could I help her, when I hated her guts? When she'd never listen to a word I'd say? When she'd be drunk or high or having sex or doing something even worse than all of those things put together, something so putrid and rancid and revolting that my brain was too pure to even conceive of it?

My mom was right. There was only one way to help Heller. I was going to Singleberry her.

I stopped rocking and I smoothed my skirt and I raised my chin high, because I was accepting the Lord's challenge. Just like Lynnea, from *Angel Wars*, I was going to descend into the bowels of the underworld and I was going to save the planet, or at least Heller Harrigan. Maybe I wasn't an angel or a saint or Joan of Arc. Or maybe I was.

"I'll do it," I said proudly, although I was also trying to sound selfless and humble because that's who I am. "I'll go."

nine

The Highway to Heller

Within half an hour my mom had packed my suitcase for the weekend while Aunt Nancy dithered, saying things like, "Doesn't Caitlin own anything with a little shimmer?" and "Does she really need that many pairs of kneesocks? Aren't kneesocks just chastity belts for your shins?" My mom finally shut her up by saying, "Nancy, we'd like Caitlin to be herself and not some hormonal Hollywood creature. And it won't hurt Heller to see what underwear looks like."

My whole family clustered around me as this huge black limousine pulled up in front of our house. I'd traveled before, as far as Branson, Missouri, for concerts with all of us packed into a reconditioned school bus. My dad had bought this bus years ago at a county auction and he'd installed seat belts and he'd painted the outside in our family colors of burgundy and gold. He'd painted a musical staff running along both sides of the bus and he'd inscribed each of our names on the musical notes, adding more notes and names as each new Singleberry arrived. We called the bus the Singleberry Express and sometimes the Singlebus, although Heller had once commented, "That thing looks like it's taking mentally handicapped students to choir camp. Which I guess it pretty much is."

I'd certainly never been inside a limousine and when it pulled up my brothers and sisters surrounded it, as if it was a piñata filled with treats, or explosives.

"This is so cool," said Carter, who's seven and who loves pretty much anything on wheels.

"Is this whole car just for Caitlin?" asked Corinne, who's Carter's twin sister. "Does it have a bathroom?"

"Kids, don't touch the car," said my dad, although I could tell that he wanted to. My dad is really good at doing anything mechanical so I'm sure he was dying to pop the limo's hood or to see what driving a limo might feel like, especially on the turns.

"Caitlin is only riding in this car because she has a job to do," my mom explained to everyone.

"Oh man, limos," said Aunt Nancy, getting misty-eyed. "The first time I ever had a three-way was in a limo."

"What's a three-way?" asked Carter.

"A three-way is like a turnpike," said Calico, to head off that particular conversation.

"Sweetie," said my mom, hugging me especially tightly, "we are all so proud of you, but we want you to be extra careful about everything and we want you to call us every hour on the hour for an update."

My dad handed me a cell phone, which was the first time I'd ever touched one. I'd seen other people with cell phones and my parents had them but the Singleberries had a rule: As my dad always said, "No one under the age of eighteen needs a cell phone unless they're a surgeon, a drug dealer or a prostitute." The first time he'd ever told me this, Heller had piped up with. "Wouldn't it be incredible to be all three?"

"Ms. Singleberry?" said a tall woman in a spiffy black uniform, who was the limo's driver. "I'm April, and I'll be with you for the entire weekend." April, who I later found out had won many women's bodybuilding titles, including Ms. Olympia, Ms. Universe and Ms. Number One Tri-State Delts, opened the limo's rear door for me.

"Oh, April, please take good care of our little girl," said my mom.

"Of course I will," said April, and I trusted her already because she was almost six feet tall with really broad shoulders and a great smile and she looked like if another car ever tried to cut her off or steal her parking space, she'd just pick that car up, spin it a few times and toss it into a nearby river.

"Caitlin? We're late," said a man, probably in his twenties, sticking his head out of the backseat. "Wyatt Markowitz. I'm Heller's manager. Her new manager. I'll fill you in about everything on the way."

Wyatt was nice-looking and everything about him, including his hair, his eyeglasses and his tight blue suit, looked perfect and expensive. As we left for Manhattan, he said, "Your family, they're for real, right?"

"What do you mean?"

"I saw some videos of your family singing online and I thought you were great but for a second I wondered if maybe you were an improv troupe, you know, doing a take on that sort of music, with the matching outfits and all. I think you were all wearing these maroon polyester blazers, right? And the guys had flared pants and the girls had those knee-length skirts and kneesocks. I mean, I hadn't seen kneesocks in maybe, like, ever. Oh my God, you're wearing them right now."

"Of course," I said, looking down at the white socks, with a mustard-colored stripe at the top, which I'd worn my whole life. "My mom and my sister Catherine make almost all of our clothes, which makes us feel really special, and we order our kneesocks in bulk from this company in Ohio. I can give you the company's address if you want some."

Wyatt tried to speak but for a moment he couldn't.

"No no no, thank you, I'm good. And thank you so much for helping us with Heller, because she could use a friend, a real friend. I've only been working with Heller for the past six months and I had to clear out a lot of people. I'm not sure why but Heller seems to attract a lot of, well, questionable hangers-on. Why are you staring at me?"

"I'm so sorry! I wasn't staring! Or I didn't mean to! I'm sorry!"

Wyatt smiled and said, "Okay, Caitlin, be honest, because I know that you've been homeschooled and that you've led a very sheltered sort of life with that humongous family of yours,

which is why you're perfect for Heller. But tell me the truth—
have you ever met a Jewish person before?"

I blushed so hard that my face probably matched my
maroon blazer. Wyatt was right because I had been staring at
him and I'd never met anyone Jewish; the closest I'd come was
probably a Lutheran with brown hair.

"I'm sorry! I think it's wonderful that you're Jewish! But I
don't want to say anything wrong and insult you!"

"You are incredibly sweet," said Wyatt, "and I don't think
you could ever insult anyone. But okay, if you're going to hang
out with Heller in the world of showbiz and beyond, you're
going to meet all sorts of people." Then he laughed and said,
"Oh my God. You are such a total über-goy."

"A what?"

"A goy means a non-Jewish person, in Yiddish, which is
sometimes the universal language of show business. Okay,
repeat after me: meshuggeneh."

"Meh-shoog-en-ah," I said slowly. "What does that mean?"

"It means crazy. It means Heller. Okay, now say facacta."

This word was even trickier so I sounded it out:
"Fa-cock-tah."

"Which means ridiculous. Which also means Heller, no,
not Heller herself, because she's amazing and she can break
your heart, but everything around her can get major facacta.
Okay, just one more, because it's gonna come in truly handy,
trust me: oy vey iz mir. It's pretty much all-purpose, for whenever everything starts going wrong. It's a combination of 'Watch

out,' 'Woe is me' and 'Just wait until your father gets home, mister.' I mean, what do you say when everything in your life just blows up in your face and it feels like the entire world is about to end in some terrible intergalactic mega-disaster?"

I thought about the worst moments of my life, like that day with Heller and now waiting to hear back from all those colleges, and those times when everything would be fine and then out of nowhere I'd feel like something awful was going to happen to one of my brothers or sisters because of me and I wondered: What if Wyatt's Yiddish words could help? What if when I started freaking out I could just say or think some Jewish abracadabra and I'd start to calm down?

"Oy vase is more," I said, trying to get it right. Wyatt was staring at me and then he said, "I love you so much that I may have to try on your blazer. One more time: oy vey iz mir."

"Oy vaze his smear," I said, and Wyatt couldn't stop laughing.

"What?" I said. "Was that really bad? Am I just hopeless? I mean, at being Jewish?"

"No," said Wyatt, wiping his eyes. "You're doing fine and I love you for trying and I think you're a complete breath of fresh air, and just what Heller needs. It's just, and I say this with only the greatest affection and respect, but you are the whitest, most Christian human being I have ever met. You're what we call a super shiksa."

The limo left the tunnel we'd been driving through and suddenly we were right in the middle of New York City.

"Oy vays gosh . . . ," I whispered to myself.

By the time we got to Heller's apartment building, Wyatt had filled me in on Heller's schedule for the next four days, which would be my schedule as well. That night there was going to be a party at a downtown club, thrown by the studio that had produced the *Angel Wars* movie. On the next day, Saturday, Heller and I would be moving into her midtown hotel to do a full day of interviews and photo shoots for magazines, websites and entertainment TV shows all over the world. There would also be a huge press conference where Heller, her costars, the movie's director and Sarah Smilesborough, who had written the *Angel Wars* books, would all be interviewed together in a big ballroom and they'd be taking questions from hundreds of the most dedicated *Angel Wars* fans, who'd won a lottery.

It sounded to me like the whole weekend was going to be all Heller, all the time. Which I suppose made sense, but still—no wonder she was in so much trouble, if the world constantly revolved around her. Thankfully, on Sunday Heller and I would be welcoming a little girl with leukemia who'd requested Spending a Day with Heller Harrigan through the Make-A-Wish Foundation. Heller and the little girl would be shooting a public service spot to raise money for cancer research.

I wondered if even meeting a little girl with cancer could change Heller. I was just going to have to double down, to force Heller to lead a more pious and decent life, like mine. I would even get her to finally apologize for everything she'd done to me. "I'm truly and sincerely sorry," she would say. "I almost killed you and there's no way I can ever make up for that. You have behaved perfectly and I am inhuman garbage."

If Heller had trouble saying this, she could consult the series of notecards I'd prepared.

On Monday there was going to be a red carpet and the gala premiere of *Angel Wars* and a big party afterward. I was going to be one of the first people on earth to see the *Angel Wars* movie! But that wasn't why I was here, I reminded myself: I was here to do God's work. I was here to fix Heller. I was going to lead her into the light, even if I had to chain her up and drag her, kicking and screaming. For a second, I wished I'd brought a gun.

"Do you think you can handle all that?" Wyatt asked, handing me a packet filled with credentials, tickets, and printed-out copies of the schedule.

"I'll try," I said. "I'll do my very best, with the Lord by my side."

Wyatt took a quick look to see if there was anyone else with me, and said, "If you have any questions I'll be right here, along with plenty of other people from the studio. Never let Heller out of your sight. She can't drink anything even approaching alcohol or take anything stronger than an aspirin and I mean just one baby aspirin every twenty-four hours. If you see her talking to anyone who looks sketchy or skanky or on the make, just get rid of them or call me to do it. Don't be afraid to stand up to people and get tough with them. This is your ironclad assignment, Lieutenant Caitlin, no, Corporal Caitlin, no,

Commander in Chief Caitlin: When it comes to Heller, absolutely no booze, sex or drugs. I know that's a lot to ask."

I was tingling. It was finally happening. After all those years of listening to Heller and following her around and doing everything she told me to do, even if I knew it was wrong, I WAS IN CHARGE.

Stay humble, I warned myself, even as there were invisible fireworks bursting all around me, along with a thousand-piece marching band and a gospel choir, all wearing kneesocks.

"Teamwork makes the dream work," I told Wyatt, which was something my dad liked to say. I raised my hand and gave Wyatt a brisk salute.

Wyatt was looking at me and shaking his head the way people do when they first see an adorable puppy or an especially cute baby. He looked as if he was about to say "Aww . . ." or "Ooohhh . . ."

"Okay," he said instead, only now he was looking more than a little worried. "Let's go see Heller."

ten

The Heller Hilton

How long has Heller lived here?" I asked Wyatt as the limo approached a big industrial-looking building in a downtown area called Tribeca.

"She's had this place for almost a year," said Wyatt. "Although most of the time she stays at either her house in LA or her Malibu place, and she's also got an apartment in London."

"Heller has . . . four houses?"

"Oh please—the London flat is microscopic, it's like three bedrooms. Tops."

HELLER HAS FOUR HOUSES. There are eleven of us in Parsippany and we all share bedrooms and one tiny bathroom with one sink. I'm not complaining because our house is really cozy and so many people in the world don't even have a house or a roof over their heads, while HELLER HAS FOUR HOUSES. THERE'S ONLY ONE OF HER.

The sidewalk in front of Heller's building was lined with those movable metal fences that the police use for crowd control. "Is there going to be a parade?" I asked as I saw a group of grubby men and women, some of them wearing army jackets and all holding heavy, complicated cameras with zoom lenses, standing behind the metal barricades. "No," said Wyatt. "Well, it's sort of a parade, or at least it's a public event. It's Heller."

FOUR HOUSES. At what point after she had the first three houses did Heller start to think, gee, I'm so cramped, I can barely breathe, I think I need FOUR HOUSES?

April drove the limo into a parking garage underneath the building, which, as Wyatt explained, "lets Heller get in and out without being mobbed." Wyatt used a key, not just to get into the building but to unlock the elevator that brought us to the penthouse fourteen floors up. The elevator opened onto an enormous room filled with haphazard clumps of furniture, racks of clothes, and piles of partially unpacked boxes, as if someone was either moving in or moving out.

"What is all this stuff?" I asked.

"Heller wasn't sure what she'd need for this weekend so she brought a lot of options, and her assistants are still unpacking things."

"Her assistants? How many assistants does Heller have?"

Wyatt shut his eyes and counted on his fingers: "One, two, no, Avery quit, and there's Becca, but she's back in LA, and Kyle, and Nina, and Fiona for shoes . . . six. Right now, at the moment, Heller has six assistants."

Six. Assistants. For. One. Person. One seventeen-year-old person.

Calm down, Caitlin. Deep breath. This is only the beginning. This is the first trickle of evil, before the tsunami.

"Hello?" Wyatt called out, but no one answered. Then a woman—Nina? Fiona?—appeared from somewhere else in the apartment carrying garment bags and a wig on a Styrofoam head. "I don't know where she is," said the woman as she rushed off into another room. Then a really tall, incredibly skinny guy in a tank top and a chef's hat came through carrying a wooden bowl of something. "The kale needs to breathe," the guy said as he also went off into some other part of the loft. "I haven't seen Heller, but she needs kale!"

"Hello?" Wyatt said again, and I followed him through what looked like a bedroom and then a bathroom and then another room that might have been a library because there were bookshelves with no books and then we went through a few guest rooms and a room with an enormous flat-screen TV on the wall, a lot of audio equipment and tons of Moroccan-type leather cushions on the floor. I had now been through more separate rooms than there were in our entire house. OUR ONE HOUSE.

"Hel?" said Wyatt even louder once we were back in the main room. "She's supposed to be here. She's not supposed to go out, not without supervision, it's part of her probation. HEL?"

I could never shorten Heller's name because it sounded like a curse word. Or a destination. I would always say "Heller," although even that made me feel wicked, as if I would someday have to explain to God that I had no choice, although God would most likely smile and tell me, "Caitlin, you always have a choice."

YOU COULD CHOOSE TO HAVE, FOR EXAMPLE, ONLY TWO HOUSES.

As Wyatt started to frantically call different numbers on his cell phone, I didn't know what to do. I hadn't even started my assignment and I'd already failed. I was going to take control of Heller's life and turn her into a completely different person, into a much, much better person, into someone like me. But now she was already gone who knows where, and what if she was at a bar or buying drugs in an alley or deep-kissing a dangerous ex-husband? I hadn't even seen Heller yet but I was starting to hate her even more because as usual, even by disappearing, she was making everything about her.

"Caitlin, this is very upsetting," said Wyatt. "I hope nothing has happened. I'm gonna head back downstairs and grab April and we'll check out the neighborhood to see if Heller's on the loose. Can you just wait here and call me the second she turns up?"

I nodded but after Wyatt left I didn't know what to do. There was a sort of French chaise and some Lucite chairs but I didn't know if I was allowed to sit on anything. I was alone but there were SIX ASSISTANTS somewhere in the loft and maybe they had their own assistants and I could hear the distant sounds of blow-dryers and blenders.

God was testing me. He'd given me a sacred task and I'd thought it would be easy. I thought I'd just show up and that the mere sight of me would make Heller fall to her knees and beg my forgiveness, and then beg for my help in becoming a responsible, sensitive human being. That wasn't how evil worked, especially evil the size of Heller. Evil was strong and unstoppable and devious. I wasn't worthy to do battle. I wasn't ready. Heller was going to win, the way she always did.

Unless for the first time ever in the history of the universe, I didn't let her.

I had an idea. I remembered that when Heller was eleven she'd gotten this huge crush on smoking. She'd steal cigarettes from her mom and at first she wouldn't light them but she'd sit on the picnic table behind our house, cross her legs and wave the cigarette around while imitating her mom by saying things like, "Darling, can I get a light? I'd sell my soul for a ciggie!" or "I'm going to quit, I swear I am! From now on I'm only going to smoke pot, which is really a health food!"

One night when Heller was sleeping over, we'd snuck outside and actually lit a cigarette and smoked it. I was hopeless because I kept coughing and because when I tried to dangle the cigarette off my lower lip, the way Heller had demonstrated, the cigarette kept falling onto my chest and burning holes in my pajama top. Heller, on the other hand, was a natural smoker, maybe because she was already an actress so she was using the cigarette as a prop. The first time she'd inhaled she'd thrown her head back and blown the smoke out through her nostrils as if she'd been doing it all her life. "Mmmm . . . ," she'd said as if she'd just licked a frosting bowl, "K-Bop, you're my very best friend but this cigarette is a really close second."

I went through the different rooms of the loft looking for an open window. I found one and crawled out onto a fire escape, which went up to the building's roof. I pulled myself onto the roof, which was covered with wooden decking and landscaped with trees and flowers in big ceramic pots. I'm not good with heights so I started touching my neck and then my arm, back and forth, in sets of three, which helped me be less afraid.

At the opposite side of the roof someone was sitting on the ledge and dangling her feet over the side of the building as she tilted her head back and exhaled cigarette smoke into the night sky.

For a split second I wanted to erase everything and call her name and start over.

It was the person I'd shared everything with, including the most fun I'd ever had in my life.

It was the person who'd almost killed me, the person I'd hated so much since that day four years ago, I'd done almost nothing with my life except hate her.

It was my very best friend forever and my biggest enemy and my mission from God.

It was Heller.

One, two, three . . .

eleven

Two Girls on a Rooftop

Get the fuck out," said Heller, without turning her head.
I felt like Heller had slapped me.

"I mean it, leave. Right now."

Heller still hadn't looked at me, but I wasn't leaving. I stood
there, getting used to seeing Heller again, or at least the back of
her head, after four years. I'd seen photos of her everywhere
and I'd seen her online and on TV, but this was different. This
was scarier. This was real. One, two, three . . .

"Hello, Heller," I said, trying to keep my voice even and
calm, as if I was talking to a wild animal or a crazy person.

"I know why you're here, but I don't need a bodyguard or a
chaperone or a babysitter. I'm fine. Just go. Scat!"

I steadied myself. "Heller, this isn't your decision. Our parents and your studio have asked me to come here. There are a
lot of people depending on you. And from what I've heard, you
can use some . . . support."

"By support, you mean that you're here to spy on me 24-7, and report back at fifteen-minute intervals to the gestapo. Everyone's afraid I might start using again and dive-bomb right off the deep end and ruin their little movie, no that's wrong, and ruin their great big multi-zillion-dollar potential franchise, including *Angel Wars* backpacks, workout gear, and those sunglasses with the little wings on them. I don't know why everyone's so worried. I mean, what do they think I'm gonna do?"

She stood up, balancing right on the narrow ledge. She lifted one foot so she was waving her arms and teetering. I was yards away but I started to get dizzy. One, two, three . . .

"Wouldn't it be terrible if two seconds after you got here, I jumped off the roof? You would have a ton of trouble getting another babysitting job."

Heller began hopping on one foot and all I could think was, oh my Lord, she's going to do it. I only just got here and now I have to somehow grab Heller or talk her off that ledge.

"This could be so cool," Heller said, still on one foot and leaning out even farther. "It's such a perfect idea."

"What's a perfect idea?" I asked, trying to keep it together. Heller knew how I felt about heights. More than anyone, Heller knew that once I got higher than the second floor of any building I'd start to shiver. Heller knew that the last time we'd seen each other we'd climbed up very high and the worst thing in either of our lives had happened. Heller knew all that and here she was, daring me to come closer and trying to make me feel like I was still thirteen years old.

"Oopsie!" said Heller, lunging even farther.

One two three one two three one two NO!

I was shaking and furious but I couldn't let her win, not on the very first night. I grabbed a nearby railing with both hands and gingerly peered over the side of the building. Down below there were now at least a hundred people pushing against the metal barricades, including more photographers and even more fans clutching posters of Heller along with Anna Banana dolls and Anna Banana comic books; there were also a lot of young girls wearing Anna Banana T-shirts and there were whole families of *Angel Wars* fans with every member wearing little plastic angel wings on their backs and headbands with bobbing plastic halos.

"If I jump, all of those paparazzi will have to make a decision," said Heller. "Will they run out of the way so I won't fall on them, will they try to catch me and save my life, or will they figure if they move really fast, they can take the picture of a lifetime, of me coming right at 'em. They could make a fortune."

The crowd spotted her and started calling her name and the fans began holding up their phones to take her picture: "HELLER! HELLER! HELLER!"

I felt dizzy and nauseous and really far away from Parsippany. I wanted to run back downstairs and all the way home but I didn't want to give Heller the satisfaction. I was seventeen and I was in charge so I stepped a few feet back from the railing and I clapped my hands briskly, like a schoolteacher quieting a classroom of unruly kindergartners, and I told Heller, in my most no-nonsense voice, "Heller Harrigan! Get down from there! Right now!"

I clapped my hands again and Heller froze. For the first time she turned to face me head-on. "Jesus Christ," she said, staring at me as if I was the crazy person. "Who are you, fucking Mary Poppins? Oh my God—what are you wearing?"

Heller jumped down from the ledge and started circling me. "Are you still wearing all of that Singleberry polyester? And those kneesocks? And they let you across the border?"

"What I'm wearing isn't important. Although I am dressed in a practical, respectful and dignified manner. Unlike some people."

Heller glanced down at her own outfit, which consisted of bikini panties, bare feet and a skimpy T-shirt that read Right Outta Rehab!

"Do you love this?" she asked, tugging on her T-shirt to make sure I could read it. "I also have one that says Angel Whores but I promised Wyatt I wouldn't wear it."

"I think that is . . . a very mature decision. I would like you to come downstairs immediately so we can discuss the weekend's schedule and your wardrobe and your many responsibilities."

I was feeling stronger, as if I had the upper hand. I'd gotten Heller off the ledge, I hadn't let her intimidate me, and now I was going to get started on changing her completely. I'd stopped counting, at least for a few minutes. I gestured toward the fire escape.

"No."

"No?"

"I'm sorry, that was rude. What I meant to say was, 'Fuck no.'"

Heller sat down on a wooden chair and crossed her legs.

"I'm gonna lay this out for you. Isn't it wacky, I don't hear from you, or any of your family, not a Singlepeep, for all that time. Now, boom, all of a sudden, right before I'm opening in the biggest movie of all time, here comes little Caitlin Prissypants Singletoons, knocking on my door and my roof. I'm not saying that you want something, and I'm not saying that all of a sudden you'd like to be—shazam!—best buds again, and I would never ever, God forbid, use the words Singleberry and starfucker in the same sentence, but doesn't this all seem just the tiniest bit suspicious? Just a smidge? Just a Singlesmidge?"

Heller leaned back and took a satisfied drag on her cigarette. She reached inside the stretched-out neckline of her T-shirt and scratched herself. She'd challenged me and said terrible, untrue things, with that smirk on her face. She'd mocked everything sacred. Everything Singleberry. How DARE she?

"Heller," I said, standing straight and tall, because good posture can defeat dishonesty. "You're right—we were friends, once upon a time. I haven't contacted you for reasons you're well aware of. But I am not here because of your fame or your money or your FOUR HOUSES and your SIX ASSISTANTS. I am here as a Christian, because you are in need. You have committed felonies, you have been arrested, you have abused countless substances and you have . . . behaved in an overtly sexual manner."

To illustrate this last transgression, I wiggled my hips provocatively. This felt sinful, but I wanted to shame Heller.

"I'm here," I continued, "to guide you into the light of truth, decency and perhaps pants."

Heller snorted and took another deep drag on her cigarette. It was time to talk turkey. I lowered my voice.

"I'm here to make sure you behave yourself, because if you mess up one more time, then your career and your life are over and you know it, you stupid, thoughtless, spoiled little spawn of Satan."

Heller's eyes widened. We were now on equal footing. No—I had definitely pulled ahead.

Heller stubbed out her cigarette on the arm of the chair. She looked thoughtful. She was taking me seriously.

"Well, K-Bop . . ."

I quivered with rage.

"Do not call me K-Bop!"

"Well, K-Bitch, here's what I have to say to you and the big scary studio and to everyone on earth who's so damn worried that Heller Harrigan is going to detonate her own life and take everyone down with her . . ."

Heller grinned, which made me take a step back, because it was always her grin that had gotten us into the most trouble. When Heller grinned, she looked like a little girl who was about to jump into a snowbank or a pile of leaves or onto her own birthday cake.

"Let's go to a party!" said Heller, and then she was gone, running down a hidden stairwell while I tried to keep up and while I yelled the same way I had since the very first time I'd met Heller when we were toddlers:

"HELLLERRRR!!!"

twelve

Who Are These People???

We went to the party in three black minivans with tinted windows, as if we were going to rob a bank or overthrow a government. One van was filled with bodyguards and studio people while Heller's assistants rode in the next one and Heller, Wyatt and I were in the last van with April driving. When I got into the van Heller was using her phone and without looking up she asked, "What are you still doing here?"

"You know why I'm here. Who are you calling?" I asked, because I needed to monitor Heller's social contacts.

"Hit men. There's this guy I know and he says that for two grand, he can have you shot and buried in an unmarked grave."

"Heller is just kidding," Wyatt assured me. "She's testing you."

"Now I'm on Craigslist," Heller said, still without looking up. "I've got the price down to three hundred plus french fries, and they can make it look like an accident."

As we got under way, everyone in the van stayed on their phones and even April had an earpiece.

"Guys, you know what I think could be really fun?" I said. "What if we all just put down our devices and talk to each other?"

No one answered because they were still using their phones, and I heard Heller say, "No, don't worry, no one will miss her. If you could see what she's wearing you'd understand."

As Heller kept pushing more buttons on her phone, she opened the clear plastic case that was on her lap. The case was divided into little compartments, each filled with a very few pieces of different treats, including M&M's, candy corn, Life Savers and miniature candy bars. It was like the case where my grandmother keeps her carefully labeled medications. Heller picked out three pieces of candy corn and then put one piece back.

"Heller?" I said, because I was confused by this. Heller sighed dramatically and finally looked at me as if I was a small, not especially bright child.

"Do you know how many calories there are in one piece of candy corn?" Heller asked. "It's weird because the package says that candy corn doesn't have any fat but that's not true because it's all sugar, and I always wonder if the little yellow stripe is more fattening than the little white stripe. I'm taking two pieces because it's a big night and I need energy."

"Heller," said Wyatt. "You can have three pieces of candy corn."

"No," said Heller firmly, and then, "Stop staring at me like that, K-Bop. Do you have any idea how many photographers are gonna be out there this weekend, just dying to get a picture of me with a muffin top or cellulite or my ass hanging out? Maybe you can snap one yourself. Those pictures sell for the most money because they can put them on the front page of the tabloids with a headline like 'Heller's Weight Is Off the Charts!' or 'Heller-Belly!' or 'She's a Heller-potamus!'"

"But, Heller," I said, "you still require proper nutrition, including each of the four basic food groups . . ."

"Which in Hollywood are cigarettes, vodka, bottled water and air. I have all of these dresses that all of these designers are giving to me for free and they've all been altered so they fit me within an inch of my life. So I don't need a piece of candy corn poking out of my stomach."

Heller paused and looked at me, as if she was daring me to question her logic. She'd changed into a tight, sleeveless black velvet top and a tiny sequined black skirt. I'd seen thousands of pictures of Heller looking perfect in fancy dresses but I'd never thought about the work involved and the dieting and the denial. I wondered if Heller had an eating disorder or, worse, if she wanted to have one.

"Heller," I said, "what if you wore something less revealing?"

"Said the girl in the plus-size rubber blazer."

"It is not plus-size!"

"It's a shower curtain."

"You should eat something!"

"Shut up. Fuck you. Welcome to my world," she said, and then she was back on her phone.

The club was in a downtown warehouse with mobs of people waiting outside. We stayed in our van until everyone else had gotten out of their own vans and then the rest of the group surrounded us and we all moved into the club together, like we were smuggling Heller across state lines. The club was incredibly dark and packed with people and the music was really loud and thumping, and I was having trouble breathing.

I tried to keep my panic in check by keeping Heller and Wyatt in sight. I just have to say one thing: I don't understand that kind of music. It never sounds like a song but more like a broken garbage disposal that won't stop burping and chugging and spitting, and if there are ever any lyrics they're just the same thing repeated over and over again saying something like "smack that thang" or "bump that thang" or "bounce that thang," but I don't know what the thang is.

Someone from the club led us across the dance floor and past some guards with really thick necks and into a roped-off area where Heller and I sat at a little table.

"Where are we?" I asked.

"We're in the VIP section," said Heller, rolling her eyes as if she couldn't believe how dense I was. "It's for celebrities and models and rich people and their crews. And their super-repulsive neo-Nazi FBI informants."

"I am not an FBI informant!"

"You might as well be. Can you please stop eyeballing me like I'm about to overdose, just so you can kneel over my corpse and start singing some gospel song called 'Jesus Is My Drug Mule'?"

"Excuse me, but from what your mom told me, you do have a history of extremely dangerous and self-destructive behavior . . ."

"And you probably have permanent ridges on your shins from the elastic in those kneesocks."

"I do not! Not if I wear the correct size!"

Heller stood up for a second and waved, and hundreds of people screamed and held up their phones and took her picture.

"They need you," Wyatt told Heller, and then he brought her a few feet away to a raised platform where she stood in between a huge blown-up poster for the *Angel Wars* movie and a prop can of Angel Power, the *Angel Wars* energy drink. The can was taller than Heller. The music stopped and Heller was in a spotlight.

"Hey, y'all!" said Heller. "How are ya?"

The crowd screamed again as Heller grinned and for a second I thought that if Heller told all of these people to follow her into the street and burn down the building, or to spray-paint her name across the front of the White House, or to rip off my arms and use them as golf clubs, they'd do it in a heartbeat.

"Welcome to the official opening event of *Angel Wars* Weekend International!" Heller said, and the crowd screamed even louder and I thought my eardrums were going to burst.

"I know that we all love the *Angel Wars* books and I hope you like the movie! Tonight everybody here is going to get a free can of Angel Power, the energy drink that's so packed with power you'll feel like you're flying!"

A row of models wearing white spangled minidresses and little golden wings started tossing cans of Angel Power into the crowd as the music thumped back up and Heller waved and came back to our table. She looked at me triumphantly, as if she'd just demonstrated how famous she was, and she handed me a can of Angel Power. I took a sip and then spewed every bit of it all over the table.

"K-Bop!" said Heller, who couldn't stop laughing. "Where are your manners?"

"That tasted horrible! What's in that?"

"Who knows? Probably caffeine, cat vomit and motor oil. Or maybe it's angel poop."

"But . . . but . . . your picture is on the can!"

"I didn't say it was *my* poop. Please, it's just business. When I signed on to do the movie I agreed to do all of this promotion and all of these appearances; it's just part of the deal."

I was starting to understand why the studio was so worried about Heller. She wasn't just starring in the *Angel Wars* movie— she was the *Angel Wars* ambassador. If she messed up, everything would fall apart. I wondered what it would feel like to have my face on posters and cans of soda and everything else—would it be exciting and a nonstop ego boost or would it feel weird, like I was trapped in some alternate universe on the planet Caitlin?

"Hey, Hel," said a really tall, good-looking guy. "Who's your friend?"

"She's not my friend," said Heller. "She's a narc crossed with an Amish surveillance drone. She's here to make sure that I don't get drunk or high or have sex with you on top of this table. K-Bop, this is Mills Stanwood."

"Hey, K-Bop."

I was about to tell him my real name but as he smiled at me and his narrow blue eyes crinkled I felt like the most wonderful tractor-trailer in the world had just run me over because, oh my God, OH MY GOD, it was MILLS STANWOOD!!!

He was on the *Angel Wars* poster standing next to Heller because he was playing Tallwen, the high school quarterback who falls in love with Lynnea! Tallwen is one of the Stelterfokken, a celestial tribe assigned to secretly protect the Chosen Winglet! MILLS STANWOOD WAS TALKING TO ME!!!!

Calico, who's two years older than me, has the biggest crush of all time on Mills and in our room, underneath her mattress, she's hidden a stack of magazines with his picture on the cover where sometimes he's wearing a tank top and smiling and pointing his forefinger right at you and sometimes he's looking off into the distance because he's thinking about you.

As far as I could tell from the magazines and from everything Calico had shown me on the computer when our parents were out of the house, Mills was the star of a cable TV show called *Blood Stud*, where he played a really unhappy but totally cute vampire named Dane Belmont. Calico had told me that

"Dane never wanted to become a vampire but his first girlfriend ever had turned him into one so that he would never leave her, but then they broke up. Dane hates having to kill people by drinking their blood so that he can stay alive, so he only kills criminals and dictators and bullies, and he travels the world seeking the enchanted moonstone, which has the power to make him human again. While he's searching he helps people because his special vampire tears can heal broken bones."

"But you know, don't you, that vampires don't really exist," I'd told Calico. "They're just made up and they're silly and dumb. Why are you wasting your time over some TV actor who wears plastic fangs and who can't keep his shirt buttoned?"

As Mills Stanwood kept smiling at me, I completely understood why Calico had written his name in secret vampire script with a magic marker on the bottom of her foot where my mom would never see it. While my dad is handsome and some of my brothers are perfectly nice-looking, although I would never tell them that, I'd never seen anyone who looked like Mills Stanwood. Maybe that was another reason why some people become famous: They actually look like their posters.

"Close your mouth," Heller said to me. "And stop drooling. Or wear a bib."

"I think that K-Bop has a beautiful mouth," said Mills as he sat down next to me, and although I'm horribly ashamed to admit this, at that second I wanted him to bite me in the neck and turn me into a vampire so that we could go to a twenty-four-hour IHOP and have pancakes and talk or we could just pretend to talk while I watched him pour syrup and then smile at me some more.

"K-Bop likes you," Heller told Mills. "Her gills are inflating."

"Please do not call me K-Bop! It's insulting and demeaning and juvenile!"

"K-Bop's parents are named Calvin and Carol and they have eight hundred children who all have names starting with C, like Cucumber and Cockatoo and Colostomy . . ."

"I only have eight brothers and sisters and my parents like the letter C because it stands for Caring, Cooperation and our Creator."

Heller mimed choking herself.

"Yo, Hel, welcome back," said someone else, a guy wearing a little hat pushed back on his head, along with a worn leather motorcycle jacket and a limp T-shirt. "Here ya go. Your favorite. I remembered."

As this guy started to hand Heller what looked like a bottle of imported beer I stood up and grabbed the bottle. "NO!" I said, as loudly and firmly as I could. "Heller has no interest in drinking any form of alcoholic beverage and will you please leave this restricted area immediately! Or I will . . . I will . . . I will call your parents!"

Everyone was staring at me and Heller covered her face with her hands.

"You're kidding, right? Hel?" said the guy, so I said, "NO! I am not kidding! Take that bottle of beer and . . . and . . .

recycle it! I'm warning you! Because I am . . . a fully authorized warning person!"

"Okay, chill . . . ," said the guy as he backed off and blended in with the people on the dance floor.

"Nicely done," Wyatt told me. "I can see why your family sent you here."

Heller stood up and she was so furious she could barely speak. "I . . . CAN'T . . . BELIEVE . . . YOU . . . DID . . . THAT!" she sputtered.

"I'm not going to apologize," I said. "That person was offering you a poisonous and life-denying substance—"

"Hey, Hel," said a very skinny, unbelievably beautiful blonde girl who was wearing a dress the size of an oven mitt. "Look what I got." The girl opened her hand and she had a little cellophane packet with some pills inside, resting in her palm.

"ARE THOSE NARCOTIC PILLS?" I demanded as I stood up again, speaking even louder because that seemed to be effective. "Heller has no need for those pills, thank you very much! She does not need to go on a drug trip or get high or . . . or . . . become the sort of person who would take those pills and go on a murderous rampage and end up in a maximum-security prison with other such criminal pill takers!"

"Okay . . . ," said the beautiful girl, backing away into the crowd as Heller mimed banging her head on the table.

Wyatt grinned at me and said, "That was Ticey Shandles."

"Who?" I asked.

"She's on the cover of Italian *Vogue* this month," he said, "and she's the face of Multresse hair-care products."

"I don't care who she is," I said, "although if she's on the cover of an Italian magazine, why is she speaking English?"

"THIS IS A TRAIN WRECK!" said Heller, leaping up from the table and heading out onto the dance floor.

"You're amazing," Mills said to me as his knee touched mine under the table, and I wondered if just maybe our knees had somehow gotten instantly glued together, which would be crazy and medically impossible and maybe the best idea I'd ever heard in my entire life. But I had a job to do and Heller was getting swallowed by the crowd.

"Heller!" I called out. "I don't think you should be dancing! Dancing can lead to . . . inappropriate touching! And shared bodily fluids!"

"I HOPE SO!" yelled Heller over her shoulder and now I almost couldn't see her. I'd been starting my crusade by keeping Heller away from beer and drugs but now I was about to lose her.

Mills grabbed my hand and I'm not completely sure but I may have blacked out and left my body and floated over the crowd and looked down at myself holding hands with Mills Stanwood. I zoomed back into my body when I heard Mills say, "Come on! We can find her!"

As Mills took me onto the dance floor I noticed several things: first, that Mills had an earring, and second, that I'd just completely changed my mind from thinking that boys who have earrings are gross. I saw that the blond highlights in Mills's hair were fake and I decided that the fake blond highlights in Mills's hair were God's finest achievement since creating Mills in the first place.

"There she is!" said Mills and then we were both smushed right up against Heller on the dance floor and we were all doing something that I couldn't really call dancing because it was more like bobbing up and down and moving our shoulders a tiny bit, which was the only sort of dancing we could manage because we were packed in with so many other dancers. I looked around frantically to keep the exit signs in view but people were waving their arms and my shoulders were starting to tense up and I was beginning to worry about falling down and having drunken people step on my head and how if my obituary said that I'd died in a nightclub people would think I was a terrible, out-of-control, substance-addicted person. People would think I was Heller.

"Heller!" I yelled, trying to be heard over the music, which had grown even louder.

Heller mouthed something that looked like it involved my name and an f-bomb and she started moving through the crowd while I struggled to follow her, and as the crowd closed behind us we reached an exit. I couldn't see Mills Stanwood anymore and while I was planning to use my phone the minute we left the club to check in with my mom, I wasn't sure if I should tell her that I'd held hands with Mills or that while I was trying to turn Heller's life around, she wasn't cooperating. I was drowning in an ocean of degenerate clubgoers, secondhand smoke and Angel Power energy drinks!

thirteen

I Am Not Going to Have Sex with Mills Stanwood!!! Shut Up!!!

Once I got outside Heller was standing by the van as Wyatt and April tried to calm her down. As I got closer I could see that Heller was vibrating with anger and had shut her eyes and put her fingertips to her forehead.

"What are you doing?" I asked.

"I'm trying to make your head explode with my mind. I'm trying to splatter your tiny little prayer-monkey pea brain all over the street."

This was something Heller and I had tried to do when we were kids, only we'd always aimed it at other people. I shut my eyes and put my fingers onto my own forehead.

"I'm using my mind to thwart your evil plan," I said. "I'm calling upon our Lord to deflect your violent thoughts and channel them into cleansing you of unholy impurities."

"Ladies," said Wyatt, "I have a thought. Why don't we stop using our mind power and hop in the van and go someplace quiet, where we can have a bite and maybe work through our differences. April, do you know Hutterman's Diner in Brooklyn?"

"Got it," said April. "I'm going to use my mind power to levitate Heller and Catey into the van."

Once we were traveling Heller got even more frustrated. "What is going on here?" she said, holding her phone out an open window. "I can't get a signal!"

"We're getting near the bridge," said Wyatt. "It's a dead spot."

"Why do you need to use your phone every second?" I asked. "What will happen if you don't?"

"If I can't use my phone then I will be forced to admit that I am sitting inside a van next to you!"

"Why is that so bad? Why can't we talk, so I can help you overcome your deeply rooted emotional and spiritual problems?"

"My problems? My PROBLEMS? You are my problem! Even if I did have a problem, what would you know about it? What's your average day like? You probably wake up at five A.M. and go milk something, like a cow or a goat or your neighbor's garden gnome, and then you pray for the next five hours, and then you get homeschooled in how to, I don't know, churn butter or make beeswax candles or crochet your own armpit hair into a scarf!"

"You are so ignorant. Just because I'm homeschooled it doesn't mean that I'm backward. Our parents make sure that we keep up-to-date on scientific discoveries and politics and current events. At least I have an education."

"That's not an education! That's a crafts project!"

"Well, next year I'll be going to college!"

This shut Heller up. While Heller had never liked school, college might be a sore spot.

"Where did you apply? Middle Earth? Hogwarts? Obedience school?"

I was tempted to tell Heller a tiny bit of the truth, about how I'd applied to twelve schools because I was convinced that I wouldn't get in anywhere. I'd gotten good scores on my SATs and I'd written my essays on the benefits of being homeschooled and singing with my family, and I'd talked about all of the volunteer work I did in Parsippany, but what if it wasn't enough? There was so much competition and I constantly worried about my applications getting lost or hacked or sabotaged. I'd picture the applications arriving on the admissions directors' computer screens scrawled with obscenities or photos of me on the toilet.

"I've applied to . . . several schools," I told Heller. "I'm still waiting to hear back. At least I don't spend every night drinking and doing drugs at some filthy nightclub. How can you stand places like that? With all of that noise and temptation and all of those disgusting, morally compromised people with sideburns?"

"I like those places! It's just like you being homeschooled! I've been going out since, I don't know, since I was doing *Anna Banana!*"

"You were going to nightclubs when you were THIRTEEN? They let you in?"

Heller's life made no sense. Since that last day, when she'd left Parsippany, I'd tried to imagine how Heller lived, but I couldn't. I would picture her waking up at noon when a maid brought her a glass of orange juice and maybe a marijuana cigarette on a silver tray, and then Heller would scratch her back using a crucifix, but that was as far as I could get.

"Out there, in the clubs in LA, they'll let anyone in," said Heller. "They'd let a newborn baby in, if the baby was in the business."

"If the baby had a manager," added Wyatt.

Heller leaned back against the van's leather seat and shut her eyes. She looked really young, like she was still thirteen, but she also looked ancient, like a thirteen-year-old who'd been placed under a magical spell, or maybe a curse, so she'd stay young forever. She looked exhausted, as if she'd been writing college admissions essays for the past four years.

"I loved going out. Maybe it was because I was working so hard, like eighteen-hour days, even on weekends. Don't get me wrong, I was doing exactly what I wanted to be doing and I loved every second of it, but I was a kid and I would get so scared that if I didn't work even harder, it might all go away. So even when I had some time off I'd just sit in my house and worry and study my lines and sort of vibrate. I started going to clubs just to blow off steam and get out of my own head. You'll think it sounds ridiculous and you'll never get it, but I would go to places like that to relax."

This did sound ridiculous. That was the first nightclub I'd ever been to and it had been the opposite of relaxing.

"Why were you so worried? *Anna Banana* was a big hit, wasn't it?"

Heller turned to me with a look of unholy glee.

"Did you watch it? K-Bop, are you a closet Bananafan?"

"I think I saw the show maybe once," I lied.

"Just once?" Heller asked, and I could tell she hadn't believed me. She started to sing, under her breath, one of the most absurd songs from the show, called "Lonely Banana":

"SOMETIMES WHEN IT'S LATE, I WISH YOU
WERE HERE
SOMETIMES I CAN'T WAIT, AND I WISH YOU
WERE NEAR
BUT I'M ALL BY MYSELF, ALL ALONE ON
THE SHELF . . ."

Without even thinking, I joined in with Heller:

"I'M JUST A LONELY BANANA
WON'T YOU BE A BANANA WITH ME?"

"I knew it!" Heller shouted. "You only saw the show once but you know all the words to that song!"

"I was just guessing! And it's a disgusting song!"

"I didn't know you back then," Wyatt told Heller, "in your Anna Banana days. Were they wild?"

"Oh my God, you have no idea. I was out in LA with my mom, which was already a pretty loony situation, but there was so much happening and it was really fun and really exciting but the whole time I just kept, I don't know . . ."

"What?" asked Wyatt.

We were driving across a bridge and Heller looked away,

out the window. "When I was doing *Anna Banana*, there were all of these grown-ups around and a lot of them were really nice but I couldn't, you know, talk to them about how I was feeling, about everything. That girl from the show, the one who played my best friend, Nicky, she was nice but she could be sort of too nice, you know what I mean? It's like, I once heard her talking on the phone to someone and saying that she wasn't just Anna's best friend, but that she was my best friend in real life too. Which wasn't true because we didn't have all that much in common, plus when she was on the phone I figured out that she was doing an interview and kind of bragging about being my best friend which was just sort of, I don't know, yucky. Because I kept thinking, she's not my best friend."

Heller glanced at me for a split second and then she looked back out the window.

"I don't have a best friend," she said.

I don't know why but Heller saying this hurt me so badly that I almost started to cry. We'd been best friends a long time ago, when we were babies. After what Heller had done to me I could never be her friend. I was only sitting in her fancy limousine as a favor to Aunt Nancy and my mom and because . . . because I was doing the Lord's work. So why was I so upset? Why did I want to hurt Heller right back?

"I have a best friend," I said. "My sister Calico."

"Your sister? The one with the squinty eyes and the mustache? Who looks like a really unpopular lobster? Is that the best you can do?"

"At least she's not some fake friend on a TV show!"

"You are pathetic!"

"Your show was canceled!"

"At least I had a show! At least I don't have to sing with my parents at a shopping mall, next to the Cinnabon and the neck pillow kiosk!"

"At least I have parents!"

Heller reached out to slap me but I raised my arm to stop her. She used her other hand to get around my arm but I slapped it away. She slapped me on the side of my head and we went at it, slapping each other as hard as we could.

"You little bitch! I thought you were supposed to be a Christian!"

"I am a Christian! Stop using the b-word!"

"Which word would you like? The c-word? The m-word? The k-word?"

"What's the k-word?"

"Kneesock!"

Heller tried to yank my left kneesock down, which made me so mad, I started yanking her hair.

"Stop it! Those are extensions! They cost a fortune!"

Wyatt leaned over from the front seat and pulled us apart.

"Girls, young ladies, people, dueling crustaceans, whatever you are!" he said. "Play nice! From what I've heard, you used to be very close. Instead of all this sniping and slapping, why don't we work on that?"

"BECAUSE I DON'T WANT TO!" Heller and I both said at the same time, and then we both jerked our heads away to look out opposite windows.

fourteen

Brooklyn Is Just Hollywood with Plaid Flannel Shirts

Once we were in Brooklyn, which was across the river from Manhattan, we arrived at this old-timey diner called Hutterman's, although as Wyatt explained to me on our way inside, "The owners actually found this place in upstate New York and they spent millions of dollars to update the plumbing and the electrical and then they brought it out here on a flatbed truck, and spent a few more millions to have it re-antiqued to look like it had always been here."

"Why did they do that?" I wondered, since if it was in Parsippany, the diner might get condemned by the board of health.

"Because this is Brooklyn," said Wyatt, "where everyone is cooler than cool and they like to pretend that they hate anything that isn't quirky and raw and authentic. Just watch, when Heller walks in, everybody will recognize her but they'll all try super hard to act like they don't care."

Wyatt held the door open and as Heller entered the diner I could tell that Wyatt was right. The diner was crowded with people in their twenties and thirties and all of the guys looked like really skinny lumberjacks with big bushy beards and ribbed wool hats, although I didn't know why they were wearing their hats indoors, and all of the girls were also really skinny and wore outfits that looked like old-timey thrift-store clothes, only expensive.

A woman carrying menus came over and murmured "Hel" and she and Heller almost kissed and hugged but not quite; they just leaned in the general direction of each other and made kissing noises. As this woman brought us to a booth, I could tell that everyone was pretending to talk but that they were watching Heller and, underneath their tables, they'd all started to use their phones, probably to tell other people that they'd just seen Heller Harrigan and were ignoring her.

"I love this place," said Heller as we sat down. "It's like LA only even prissier. If you asked these people if they'd ever heard of *Angel Wars* they'd all say no but believe me, half of these people are trying to write another trilogy just like it and the other half want to direct the movie."

"Hel?" said this completely cute guy, coming over to our booth. He didn't look like one of the super-cool people but more like he'd just trotted off a soccer field, with his face shining and his hair clean but a little messy. I guess what I mean is that this guy looked genuinely friendly instead of like he wanted something from Heller. I realized that this guy had also been on the *Angel Wars* poster at the club, standing on the other side of Heller opposite Mills Stanwood.

"Billy!" Heller said, hugging him like she meant it.

"Hey, Hel," he said, "who's your friend?"

"She's not my friend! Why do people keep saying that! She's . . . she's . . . she's trespassing!"

"Billy Connors," the guy said to me. "I really like your socks. Can I sit down for just a second?"

Okay. Okay. I WAS NOW SITTING ACROSS FROM MYKE, who was the boy who made ceramic pots in the town where Lynnea lived and who was in love with her. In the *Angel Wars* books, while Tallwen can be brooding and intense because he's trying to save Lynnea from the Darkling Creeper, Myke is completely open and warmhearted because he grew up with Lynnea and every morning he leaves a flower in this tiny clay pot that he'd made when they were kids and that Lynnea keeps on her doorstep, and sometimes Lynnea likes to turn the pot over to see where Myke had written both of their initials in the clay on the bottom. Later in the books after Myke has been imprisoned by the Darkling Creeper, who forces him to make pots to hold demon breath, Myke uses the bottoms of these pots to send secret messages to Lynnea and the other members of the Angel forces.

"Are you making fun of my socks?" I asked Myke, or Billy— just like with Mills, it was hard not to think of these boys as if they were their characters because of course they looked just like them.

"No!" said Billy. "I think that your socks are really cool.

Everybody else in this place is kind of dressed the same, but you're the only one wearing kneesocks. So I'll always remember you."

"Whoa!" said Heller, and then she started mimicking Billy. "'Oh, Catey, you're so hot! I wanna suck on your kneesocks so I'll always remember you!'"

"Shut up!" I hissed at Heller, but I wasn't looking at her because I was looking at Billy and he had such shining brown eyes and a slightly crooked front tooth and I was trying really hard not to reach out and touch his hair, to comb it a little because it looked so soft.

"How're you holding up?" Billy asked Heller, putting his arm around her—not in a pushy, she's-mine sort of way but more like an older brother who was looking out for her. I could tell by the way that Heller leaned her head on Billy's shoulder that she trusted him.

"I'm doing okay," said Heller, and then she nodded at me. "Except for my choke chain. The studio sent her. Every time I start to have any fun at all she yanks me back. She's like a Mormon prison guard."

"I am not a Mormon!" I said, and as a waitress came over and asked if we'd like to order drinks I told her, "Why don't we all just have some nice cold glasses of fresh whole milk?"

"Fresh whole milk?" asked the waitress. "Is that the name of a new cocktail? I can ask our bartender."

"No," said Heller, "but I think that Catey's absolutely right. Let's get four glasses of fresh whole milk. We can pour them over Catey's head."

"Heller!"

"Just water to start, for everyone," Wyatt told the waitress. "Catey, water's okay, right? Fresh whole water?"

"Ignore them, Catey," said Billy. "Where are you from?"

"Parsippany."

"In New Jersey?" asked Billy, delighted. "I'm from Tenafly!"

"Which is practically right next door to Parsippany!" I said, and that was when I started to think about what Billy and I would name our first baby but then I felt terrible because the first name I thought of was Mills! What was happening to me?

"Yo, are you Heather something?" said another guy, who was now standing at our table. He wasn't dressed like all of the other guys in the diner because he was wearing a pink shirt and a navy blazer and neatly pressed jeans and he had a tan, only it didn't look like a real tan, the kind you get from being outdoors. It looked more like spray paint, if you needed to paint something the orange of a highway safety cone.

"Oh, gosh, ordinarily Heller would love to chat," Wyatt said to the guy, "but we're on a tight schedule, and we're eating."

"It's just gonna take a sec," said the guy in the blazer. "I want a picture with my girlfriend, she's a big fan."

"I am not!" said the guy's girlfriend, who was wearing a very short skirt, very high heels and the kind of complicated hairstyle that looks like it needs blueprints and a construction crew. She was very tan as well and carrying a tiny rhinestone purse.

"You always say you love Heather Hannigan!" said the blazer guy.

"No, I said that I used to love her but that I don't think she has any business being Lynnea," the girlfriend said, and then to Heller, "No offense, but I think Lynnea should be prettier."

Heller didn't seem offended; instead, she looked at everyone else and raised an eyebrow as if she was telling us, "You see what happens?"

"Um, I think that Heller is really beautiful," said Billy, "and wait until you see her in the movie, she's incredible."

"Oh my God!" said the girlfriend. "You're Billy what's-his-name! You're Myke! But you're too short!"

"Guys, we appreciate your interest and we hope you love the movie," Wyatt told the couple, "but we really need to order some food, so if you'll please excuse us?"

"Nah nah nah," said the guy, "not so fast. Sure, we're gonna go see that movie, even if it sucks, so we're payin' this Heather chick's salary so she can goddamn well take a picture with me and Amanda. Heather, I got some blow in my Lotus, 'cause I know you're into that, so we can do the picture outside."

"Excuse me!" I said, standing up. "Ms. Harrigan is about to have her dinner and she has no interest in whatever you just offered her, which I believe indicated drug usage. So if you would please excuse us, we would like some privacy."

"Who's this bitch?" asked the guy.

"I am Caitlin Singleberry and I am in charge of . . . of Ms. Harrigan's physical and spiritual well-being."

"What did you say your name was? Captain Dingleberry?"

No. No. Please dear Lord, NO. Not now. I was having trouble swallowing and the room was spinning. I wanted more than anything to turn and run but my therapist had told me that

sometimes I could stop my panic attacks by confronting whatever I was scared of head-on. She'd said that if someone was
afraid of flying the only effective treatment would be for that
person to wrangle their fear and get on a plane. I always wanted
to ask her, But what if that person was right all along and the
plane crashes?

"My . . . name . . . is . . . Caitlin . . . Singleberry," I said
very slowly and clearly.

"Nah nah, that's not what you said, it's Dingleberry! Hey,
everybody, get a load of this smart-mouth bitch! She's a goddamn dingleberry!"

The guy and his girlfriend started howling with laughter.

Heller stood up.

"What did you just say?" she asked. "You total asshole with
a spray tan that makes your face look like a redwood picnic
table?"

"Oh oh oh," said the guy. "I thought so! Everybody loves you
because you're some big movie star, but right underneath you're
just another goddamn bitch, hangin' out with your little buddy
the dingleberry."

"She's not my buddy," said Heller. She glanced at me and
turned back to the guy. "But she's not a dingleberry."

I was stunned. Heller was, sort of, standing up for me.
Because I'd been homeschooled I'd never had all that much
contact with name-calling. But when my family would do our
concerts we sometimes ran into people who liked to call us the
Dingleberries. When I was little I hadn't known what this word
meant or why it had made my dad clench his jaw. Finally my

brother Carter had explained to me what a dingleberry was and it was completely disgusting and it had nothing to do with our wholesome singing family.

If you don't know what a dingleberry is I'm not going to tell you because it's too gross and involves an especially unpleasant and moist area of the body. If you really want to know then just look around and pick out the most immature person you see, who might be a teenage boy who's wearing his baseball cap backward and who smells like one of those body sprays that certain teenage boys use all over themselves instead of taking a bath. If you see or smell one of these boys, just ask him what a dingleberry is and after he finally stops snorting with teenage-boy laughter he'll be more than happy to fill you in.

"I will give you exactly one second to take that back," Heller told the blazer guy. On one hand I knew that I should try to jump up and get in between Heller and the guy, because I was supposed to be keeping Heller from getting into trouble. On the other hand, right that second I was shocked and, I'll admit it, secretly thrilled because Heller had remembered just how much I hated the word "dingleberry."

"Take back what?" asked the guy. "That your buddy is a first-class a-hole dingleberry? Of course she is. Look at her fuckin' kneesocks."

Billy stood up and took a swing at the guy, but the blazer guy was fast and well built and he landed a punch right in Billy's stomach and Billy crumpled.

"You hit Myke!" said the girlfriend, who sounded very excited by this. "You took him down!"

As the guy started to pump his fists over his head in a victory dance, Heller punched him right in the face and he fell backward onto his girlfriend, who started screaming because he'd broken one of her nails.

"I'm gonna kill you, you Hollywood bimbo!" the guy yelled as he stood back up, which was when I had an idea.

"Everybody!" I said to the whole diner. "This guy and his girlfriend! They work for the Darkling Creeper and they're trying to hurt Lynnea!"

Everyone in the diner jumped out of their seats and began piling on top of the guy in the blazer while his girlfriend shrieked, "No we don't! We're Angel people! And she's not Lynnea! She's too fat!"

I heard police sirens, and Wyatt grabbed Heller and me and dragged us out of the diner to where April was waiting with the van.

"Excellent move!" Wyatt told me, and he sounded grateful as April started driving us away from the diner very fast.

"Heller?" I said, because I was still having trouble believing that Heller had defended me.

"I had to do something," Heller said. "He called you a dingleberry. Which you are, because you sure have been hanging around my ass, but that guy was being a total dick."

I was torn between wanting to yell at Heller for using that many disgusting words in a single sentence and wanting to thank her for hitting that guy. I couldn't believe Heller's life: Everywhere she went, total strangers either wanted to grab her, as if Heller's stardom might rub off on them, or insult her and punch her because she was a star and they weren't. For the first time I started to understand why she might need to drink and take drugs. I still hated her, but a tiny little part of me wanted to hug her. I'd also noticed that Heller had stopped calling me K-Bop.

"Heller?" I asked. "Are you okay?"

Just then my phone went off and it was my mom and I'd never heard her so upset, maybe not since that terrible day four years ago.

"Caitlin," my mom said, "there are pictures of you and Heller all over the Internet! It looks like you've been involved in a terrible backroom riot, with brawling and bad language and men in plaid flannel shirts! What in the good Lord's name are you doing?"

fifteen

I Don't Know What I'm Doing!

As I started to try and explain to my mom about what had happened at the diner, Wyatt snatched the phone out of my hand. "Carol?" he said. "Caitlin and Heller are doing just fine. They were minding their own business at a quiet little out-of-the-way bistro when they were attacked, out of the blue, by a deranged fan. Our girls both behaved impeccably and everyone is on their way home safe and sound. Yes . . . yes . . . oh, completely . . ."

My mom's voice rose higher and higher and Wyatt held the phone a few inches away from his ear. I could hear the words "violence," "underage," "thoughts and prayers," and "teenage Armageddon." Finally Wyatt put the phone back to his ear and said, "Carol, you are absolutely right and this sort of thing is directly related to both those shows on cable television that feature vampire incest and to the crisis in the Middle East. I

will make absolutely sure that our girls never get anywhere
remotely near another situation like this, if I have to lock them
in those cages people use to carry their pets onto airplanes . . .
Of course I'm kidding . . . Yes, I know they don't make large
enough cages . . . Yes, it is sad . . . As for those photos you're
seeing online, I'm sure they've been Photoshopped beyond
belief, because Heller would never deliberately punch anyone in the face and Caitlin would never jump on anyone's
back . . . Yes, I know for a fact that Caitlin has at least two
extra pairs of kneesocks with her at all times, because you
never know when, um, when you're going to run out of
kneesocks . . . Of course I will . . . Bless you . . . bless us all . . .
Godspeed . . . amen . . . hallelujah . . . She'll call you first
thing in the morning . . . You too."

"This is so cool," said Heller, showing me a series of photos
on her phone. I tried to look away but I kept peeking at the
shots of me from the diner, including pictures where I looked
like a drill sergeant barking orders and other shots where I was
just staring at Billy and playing with my hair. Then came a picture of Heller punching that guy, which made me feel very
strange because in the picture it almost looked like Heller and
I were on the same team.

"You're famous," said Heller, and I wasn't sure if she was
mocking me or complimenting me.

"I don't need to be famous!"

"Bullshit," said Heller. "You just need to learn the rules. See
how you look almost decent in this shot? That's because it's

your right side. Everyone's face has a good side and a bad side, you have to figure it out. In this other picture, from the left, your jaw is too long so you look like a pterodactyl having a bad hair day."

"I do not look like a pterodactyl!"

"But from the right side you're almost hot. For Parsippany."

"I don't need to be hot! I don't want to be hot!"

"I'm trying to help you."

Heller was looking right at me and the weird thing was—she wasn't making fun of me. It was as if, while we spoke completely different languages, she was trying to communicate.

"If you're going to be photographed everywhere you go, hot is better. When I started doing *Anna Banana* it took me almost a year to figure out my best angles, but now whenever I see anyone holding a phone or a camera or even an ice-cream cone that might be a hidden camera, I put my chin down, I keep my eyes up, and I give them three-quarters from the left. Look at the pictures of any star and you'll see, they always pick one angle and stick to it. If anyone tries to grab a picture of your bad side, just cover that side with your hand or throw your coat over your head."

Heller scrolled through a batch of photos from different premieres and awards shows, and she was always photographed at a three-quarter angle from the left and she always looked fantastic. She held up another photo and while she looked a little dazed in it, she also looked stunningly beautiful. "What is that?" I asked. "Is that from a modeling shoot for a magazine cover? Who took that picture?"

"It was my first mug shot," said Heller happily, "from two years ago, for possession. I ended up doing thirty hours of community service and wearing an orange vest and picking up garbage along a highway. But look at that picture—worth it!"

sixteen

A Morning Person

I woke up the next morning at my usual time, which is 6:15 A.M. I always give myself fifteen minutes to become fully conscious so I won't accidentally do or say anything I don't intend to. Back home I always like to be the first person up because I like the quiet and, if I'm being honest, I also like being the most alert, ready-to-go, responsible person in the house. I love watching everyone else stumbling into the kitchen all bleary-eyed while I've already set the table and I'm wearing an apron and holding a pitcher of milk and a pitcher of orange juice. While my parents are always incredibly grateful that I'm so on top of things, one morning my mom stared at me and said, "Stop it, Caitlin. Go back to bed."

Later my mom apologized and told me that in a big family each person likes to carve out their own identity, the way Caleb is a terrific athlete and Carl, who's twelve, is already painting amazing portraits. "And Caitlin," my mom said, "I think you like to be Can-Do Caitlin, who always does her homework and chores without being reminded to and who the rest of us can rely on for just about anything. It's wonderful that you're so good with schedules and mowing the lawn and keeping track of all of our vitamins, but sometimes I worry that you'll drive yourself crazy. Or that you think we won't love you if everything isn't perfect."

"Which is just Mom's nice way of saying that you're really bossy," said Callum, who'd been eavesdropping.

"Mom, what's Callum's role in our family?" I asked.

"He's a medical experiment," my mom explained. "Your father made him out of old newspapers and a broken toaster."

"HE DID NOT!" Callum yelled as my mom and I started laughing.

When I left the guest bedroom at Heller's loft at 6:30 A.M., I was showered and dressed and I fully expected to be the only person on the move. I was surprised because three of Heller's assistants were standing by the front door, sipping coffee and standing beside a rack of garment bags and a pyramid of carefully labeled plastic boxes. Wyatt was on his phone in the kitchen and while all sorts of other people were running around, everyone was silent. Wyatt put his phone against his chest and whispered to me, "You do it. Wake the beast."

I nodded briskly and headed into Heller's bedroom, which was so strewn with opened luggage and mounds of clothing that at first I couldn't find the bed. I heard moaning from beneath a pile of mismatched bedding. After last night I was more determined than ever, not just to save Heller but to prove to her that there was another way to live, a healthier and happier and more God-fearing way.

My way.

"Good mornin'!" I said in my best up-and-at-'em voice. "Big day ahead! Best get a move on, missy!"

The bedding still wasn't moving so I sat down beside it and asked, "Who's ready for the most wonderful, big bright sunshiny morning? Because she gets to tell the whole gosh darn world all about that amazing new *Angel Wars* movie?"

Very slowly, Heller's head appeared, with her hair spiking in every direction and her eyes still sealed shut. "Am I having a drug reaction?" she mumbled. "How much did I do?"

"No siree bob!" I said. "You are going to have the best day of your entire lucky ol' life! Do you know why? Because from now on, every day is going to be the best day of your lucky ol' life!"

"Did I vomit?" Heller asked, still without opening her eyes. "Did the vomit turn into a person?"

"Heller, yesterday we may have gotten off on the wrong foot. I know we're not friends, and we don't have to like each other, but we do have to work together—on you."

Heller opened her eyes and smiled warmly, which terrified me. "I understand why you're here," she said. "I get that you're trying to help. I think it's great that you're so shiny and peppy and inspiring even right now in the middle of the night. I'm just going to ask you to do one thing for me, one eensy-weensy tiny little favor, if you can."

I couldn't believe my ears. My efforts were paying off. I was getting a peek at a brand-new Heller Harrigan. Good for me!

"Just name it! Can I grab you a glass of fresh-squeezed OJ or maybe a nice bowl of flax flakes with skim milk and sliced strawberries for additional fiber, or should I go turn on the shower so you can scrub yourself all squeaky-clean-tastic?"

"No, you don't need to do any of that, although you're very kind."

I was even more encouraged by Heller's use of decent language. Was it possible? Were my own personal goodness and decency contagious? Was Heller about to thank me and admire me and apologize for every disgusting and vicious thing she'd ever done, especially to me? I put my hands on my hips, bursting with pride.

"What would you like me to do for you? How can I be of service on this brand-spankin'-new rarin'-to-go Manhattan morn?"

"K-Bop? Catey? Singlesweetness?"

"Yes, ma'am?"

"I need you to go fuck yourself."

All righty then—if this was how Heller was going to keep behaving, I was going to prove that I was every bit as tough as her. Even while she whined and screamed and called me names involving sex acts with family members, I dragged her out of

bed and an assistant brought her some sort of fancy coffee with
lots of foam on top and even though Heller was still in her paja-
mas, Wyatt wrapped her in a long gray cardigan and knelt down
and slid her feet into a pair of ratty *Anna Banana* slippers,
which were shaped like grimy, furry yellow bananas, and everyone carried Heller to the elevator and into April's van and we
drove over to the hotel where the morning's press junket was
being held.

"Is she always like this?" I asked Wyatt on our way over.

"It's not so much that she's not a morning person," said
Wyatt, "it's that she's not a late afternoon or even an early evening person. When she's working it's a different story, because
no matter what kind of shape she's in, Heller is always prepared
and she's on time and she knows her lines. She's a professional.
But on her days off she's kind of in a coma."

"Sometimes we just put her in the trunk of one of the cars,"
added April.

"Oh dear Lord!" I said.

"No," said April, "you don't understand. Getting into the
trunk was Heller's idea. She says it's peaceful and no one can
find her. Although she can still text us her coffee order."

The hotel was a gigantic modern palace in Midtown and the
police had blocked off traffic for three blocks around to accom-
modate the mobs of Angel Warriors. From their sleeping bags
and pillows I could tell that many of these fans had spent the
night camping out on the sidewalk to make sure they could

grab a front-row view of whoever was entering or leaving the hotel. We took the elevator up sixty-three floors to a penthouse suite, where we only stayed for a few seconds before Wyatt announced, "Heller's got a wake-up yoga session. It's part of her rehab. Caitlin, have you ever done yoga?"

I'd heard of yoga but my family was bigger on group runs and jumping jacks and volleyball games as our program for staying healthy and fit.

"I've never done yoga," I told Wyatt. "Is it sort of like the Yiddish thing?"

"No," said Wyatt. "But just wait until you get to the more advanced poses. The greatest yogis, the spiritual masters, can pass a clean linen cloth into their noses, down through their intestines and then out their mouths and the cloth stays spotless. They also advocate drinking your own urine so no bodily fluid goes to waste."

"Oy vey iz mir," I said.

The hotel gym had been roped off for the use of Heller and other *Angel Wars* staff members. When we walked into the high, mirrored space with rubber mats on the floor, Mills Stanwood and Billy Connors were already there, both sitting cross-legged.

"Hey, Catey," said Mills.

"So great to see you," said Billy. "I'm sorry about last night with all the fighting."

"I wish I'd been there," said Mills. "Maybe I could've protected you."

"Or maybe you would've gotten punched," Billy told Mills.

"Whoa, bro!" said Mills, punching Billy on the shoulder, and then Billy tousled Mills's hair because Mills really liked his hair and had spent plenty of time styling it so it would look as if he'd never touched it. They reminded me of my brothers, when they'd start swatting each other around the dinner table until my mom had to order them to sit perfectly still with their hands on their heads, a sight that my sisters and I loved.

Mills was wearing a washed-out *Angel Wars* T-shirt with some holes in it so I had little glimpses of his tan skin. He was also wearing baggy sweatpants but they were baggy in a way that made me wonder if he was wearing underwear, which made me so embarrassed that I turned to look at Billy, who was wearing one of those old-fashioned undershirts without sleeves, which showed off his nice shoulders and arms, and he was wearing sweatpants that he'd hacked off into shorts and because I didn't want to check on his underwear situation I just kept blushing and turned to Heller, who was lying flat on her back on a mat beside me with her eyes shut.

"Are you checking out the dudes?" Heller said. "Because they both got into incredible shape for the movie."

"Well, I did," said Mills.

"That was almost a year ago," said Billy. "Now Mills is cross-training for the role of a guy who only eats ice cream and plays video games."

Mills and Billy started swatting each other again and Heller, still on her back, said, "Guys! I'm trying to sleep! Why don't you just do rock-paper-scissors to see which one of you gets to have bad morning sex with Catey?"

"HELLER!" said Mills, Billy and me all at the same time, and I didn't know where to look but luckily our instructor walked into the room carrying her own personal rolled-up yoga mat in a special sling over her shoulder, and the sling also had a strap to hold a bottle of water. She was in really good shape but there was something strange about her. She had long, straggly hair pulled up with a rubber band on top of her head and while she was skinny, her skin was sallow and her eyes bulged.

"It's yoga," Heller whispered to me. "They all look like that. They're supposed to be like the healthiest, most centered people on earth but they all look ten years older than they really are and like they haven't slept for months. It's probably from all the brown rice and urine."

"Namaste," said the woman. "I'm Razen and I'll be leading the group today in my signature blend of power yoga, gentle yoga, urban pilates and something I've invented and trademarked called muscle-medulla flesh-meld. It connects your mind with your body by drawing on your reserves of lactic sense memory."

"Catey?" Heller whispered. "Do you have any heroin? Like, on you?"

"Pay attention," I whispered back, and Razen asked me, "Is there a problem? You're the cousin, right? Are you ready to do some important work in and on your mind-body electrosphere?"

I had no idea what Razen was talking about and if her name hadn't been printed on the schedule I would've thought she was called Raisin. As usual Heller had just managed to get me into trouble, so I decided to become the nicest, most hardworking and most cooperative person in the class. "I'd love to work all over myself, Razen," I said. "Thank you so much for helping us today."

"Namaste," Razen repeated.

"Namaste means stop being such a little suck-up ass-kisser, in Hindi," Heller whispered, "or maybe it means look at Razen's camel toe in her flesh-colored yoga pants," which made me snort, which made Razen look at me again even more sharply.

"All right," said Razen, "I'd like everyone to begin with a downward-facing dog."

I copied Heller, who was dragging herself into this position, with her hands and feet on the floor and her butt in the air. Actually, I'm never sure what to call that part of the body because all of the different words people use are so embarrassing, including "bum," "keister," "booty," "buttocks" and "rear end." Personally I think that God deliberately put that part of our bodies in a place where we wouldn't have to see it or think about it.

"Get your ass toward the ceiling, Catey," Heller told me and once I'd done this I was looking through my legs directly at Mills and Billy, who were both doing the downward-facing dog and smiling at me upside down, as if they were having a contest to see which one could be the cutest even with the blood rushing to their faces. This made me so flustered that I collapsed, although luckily I was wearing my usual exercise outfit, which was a clean, sturdy, gray sweatshirt and matching sweatpants with no emblems of any kind.

"That's a really flattering ensemble," said Heller. "You look like a vacuum cleaner bag."

"Let's all move easily and gracefully into a side plank," said Razen.

A side plank, it turned out, meant that I had to balance on one hand with my legs stretched straight out and my feet stacked and I ended up facing Mills and Billy, who were both doing side planks. Mills winked at me and Billy saw him do it, so Billy used his free hand to nudge Mills in his lower back, which made Mills fall onto his face, which made me gasp because Mills had such a handsome face and I didn't want his face to get smushed or damaged in any way, so I said, "Billy! Don't do that!" Which made Billy look really sorry, like a little boy who's just been punished and who knows that if he makes his lower lip quiver then he'll be forgiven for anything. Which was when Mills nudged Billy's stacked feet and sent him toppling over too.

"Back row?" said Razen. "Is there a problem? Are you having trouble with your mind-body flow?"

"We're good!" said Mills.

"We're flowing!" said Billy.

"We're going to transition into a headstand," said Razen as she effortlessly stood on her head with her legs shooting straight into the air and her fingertips barely touching the mat for balance. While I know that yoga people are supposed to be peaceful and serene, just at that moment I was starting to feel like Razen was showing off, and I wondered if her last name was Bran.

"I'll spot you," said Heller as I struggled to get anywhere even close to a headstand. Heller stood up and held on to my ankles as I wobbled. I was now looking directly into Billy's incredible brown eyes as he was managing a pretty good headstand, although I think he was holding his breath from the effort. Out of the corner of my eye I saw Mills, whose headstand was even better because I think Mills had been a gymnast in high school. Both boys were trying to hold perfectly still and as I watched them I knew: They were trying to impress me, just like how in the *Angel Wars* books, Myke and Tallwen battle over Lynnea.

As the blood filled my head I wondered: How did I get here? I'd never been on a date and I'd barely even talked to any boys except for my brothers and here I was, standing on my head while two of the cutest boys ever, the boys who so many other girls from all over the world were swooning over, those boys were both trying to make me smile at them.

"Look, Catey, no hands," said Mills, who took his hands off the floor so he was now balancing only on his head.

"He can only do that because his head is flat," said Billy, who had now lifted himself into a handstand and was walking back and forth balanced only on his hands.

"Catey, you're doing great," said Mills.

"You even look pretty upside down," said Billy.

I farted. Only it wasn't me! It was Heller, who'd hidden her face behind my feet and then made an especially juicy and revolting fart noise, and I could tell from the looks on Mills's and Billy's faces that they thought I'd done it, when I hate farting more than anything! Once when I was praying, I'd promised God that I would seriously think about joining the Peace Corps or a convent if only God would help me to never make any farting or burping or other embarrassing noises in public ever again and now here I was, and then Heller made another even louder and more completely disgusting fart noise! Heller was trying to sabotage me not only in front of Mills and Billy but before God!

"Jesus, Catey," said Heller, now using her hand to fan the air in front of her face. "Mexican breakfast?"

Mills and Billy both collapsed onto the floor, rolling with laughter.

"That wasn't me!" I insisted, and I tried to stand right side up, only Heller wouldn't let go of my feet.

"Flatulence is completely natural," said Razen. "It's a healthy release of sulfurous toxins and stored gastro-related tension."

"And guacamole," said Heller, finally letting go of my feet.

seventeen

No More Farting!!!

I am going to kill you!" I told Heller after I'd run back to our hotel suite in shame and humiliation.

"Oh, calm down," said Heller.

"I can't believe you did that! In front of Mills and Billy!"

"It was pretty fabulous . . ."

"It was HORRIBLE! It was DEVASTATING! Now I can never see them ever again! It's all your fault!"

"Jesus Christ! It was a joke!"

"Heller! Once and for all, you must stop taking the Lord's name in vain! It degrades your spirit and it hurts my ears!"

"I know."

Heller said this in a genuinely sad tone of voice, looking at the floor. She seemed sincerely upset, which made me deeply suspicious.

"You need to make an effort to stop using such terrible language!"

"You're right. It's a disgusting habit, and I really need to improve."

"Do you know what I do? When I'm hurt or angry and I'm on the verge of using—one of those offensive or blasphemous words? I substitute the name of a town in New Jersey. For example, if I stub my toe, I might say, 'Oh, Lake Hopatcong!' If I'm cooking and I burn myself, I'll say, 'Weehawken!'"

"That is a seriously great idea. Let me do one."

"Very good. Let's imagine you're caught in the rain without an umbrella. What do you say?"

"Um . . . Trenton?"

"Why not? That's excellent. You're at the beach, and a jellyfish stings you."

"Hackensack!"

"You're getting it!"

I was feeling good about this. I'd taken the yoga class trauma and transformed it into a teaching tool.

"You're at one of your filthy nightclubs, or at a degenerate Hollywood party. Someone approaches you and offers you an illegal substance. What do you say?"

Heller thought about this, furrowing her brow.

"Go Teaneck yourself, you Dunellen piece of motherfucking Mount Kittatinny!"

"HELLER!"

Soon Heller was standing in one of the suite's four bedrooms. She'd showered and was wearing her first interview outfit of the day, which was a blue-and-white-striped minidress with matching boots made out of the softest possible leather. Heller's stylist, a tiny woman named Nedda, was on her knees with pins in her mouth, hand-stitching the hem of the dress, while Kenz, Heller's hair and makeup expert, was removing the coffee-can-sized rollers from Heller's hair and back-combing. "This look is very flight-attendant-from-the-future," said Nedda, although her words were muffled by the pins, "with nautical accents. Mallory, I need the ruby anchor necklace from Cartier!" Mallory was an assistant who could move like lightning on very high heels.

"Heller," I said, "I'm supposed to be an authority figure and people are supposed to listen to me and they won't do that if you keep making farting noises! Mills and Billy think I'm some sort of—fart machine! With no manners!"

"Oh please," said Heller, who was now holding her arms straight out as Nedda fussed with her sleeves. "I have no idea why, but Mills and Billy are both totally hot for you. They loved, hearing you fart. It was like a rectal symphony."

"Look up," instructed Kenz as he began to outline Heller's eyes with eyeliner.

"Mills and Billy are not hot for me!" I insisted, and everyone in the room, including Heller, Nedda, Kenz and at least five assistants, all said, "Oooo . . ."

"But they're not!" I said. "No one's hot for me! I'm . . . I'm . . . I'm from Parsippany!"

"Was that a curse word?"

"No!"

"Catey, are you a virgin?"

Everyone was staring at me and I turned bright red even though I had no reason to be ashamed.

"Of course I am!"

"Catey, listen to me. I love Mills and Billy, and we totally bonded while we were making the movie, but you have to understand something about both of them—they're actors."

Everyone in the room said "Uh-huh" and Kenz added, "Sing it, sister."

"Of course they're actors," I said. "That's why they're in the movie."

"Here's the deal," said Heller. "There are only two types of people in the world: regular people and actors. Guy actors are the worst because they're so adorable. That's why they become actors in the first place, because everyone in their tiny little Omaha town kept telling them, 'You are so adorable, you should be a movie star.' They've known since practically before they were born that they're adorable, even when they try to act all macho or geeky, which they secretly know only makes them more adorable. All of which makes you want to slap them, only then they smile, or ride a horse, or take their shirt off and show you their abs, which only makes them more mega-off-the-charts-stop-that-right-now adorable."

"I hear you," said Nedda.

"There oughta be a law," said Kenz, "you can have a killer smile or a killer six-pack, but not both."

"Guy actors have only one goal above all else," said Heller.

"What?" I asked.

"They want to make you fall in love with them. They want to make the whole world fall in love with them. That's their job, on-screen and off. They can't leave a room until everyone in that room is willing to sign a notarized affidavit saying that they're in love. If you don't fall in love or if you hesitate because you're, oh, I don't know, reading a book or saving a baby from a forest fire, they get frustrated and try even harder. When you showed up, this innocent little homeschooled geekster space android from the planet Parsippany, it was like Mills's and Billy's brains practically exploded. You're like the entire global viewing audience poured into one God-fearing, wide-eyed, sometimes-I-wear-three-pairs-of-panties-to-muffle-my-farts Singleberry who doesn't use a speck of makeup or pluck her massive bloated caterpillar unibrow."

"I can help with that," Kenz murmured.

Maybe Heller was right, but she was still being so snarky and condescending and besides, the most I'd ever worn was two pairs of underwear.

"What you're saying," I decided, "is that I could be anyone, and Mills and Billy just want to make sure that I join their fan clubs and scream and cry whenever I see pictures of them."

"Bingo," said Heller. She paused and then, grudgingly, as if it was killing her to admit it: "Fine. Jesus. Fuck me. Newark me. There is one more thing. Mills and Billy are probably tired of hot girls and top models and neurotic actresses. Of needy, please-hold-my-purse, ultra-high-maintenance, motor-mouthed girls like me. You're the opposite. Of course they're both falling in love with you. At least a little bit."

"With me?"

Heller smiled and said, without sneering, "With you."

Wyatt stuck his head into the bedroom and announced, "We've got Tally Marabont from *Heads Up, America*. Are we ready? Nedda and Kenz, can we do something with Caitlin? In case she's ever on camera we don't want anyone to say, 'Oh my God, there's a terrorist with one big eyebrow and a blazer! She's going to force Heller to make a birdhouse out of Popsicle sticks and sell it at a Christmas bazaar!'"

Kenz coaxed me into trimming an inch off my hair and parting it on the side. He added a tiny swipe of blush and dabbed on a very natural-colored lipstick. I allowed him to shape my eyebrows but when I caught him reaching for some eye shadow I yelled, "Stop!" I'd never worn makeup before and I could feel it on my face. I'd never understood why anyone would want to wear makeup because I considered it a form of lying. The Bible says that harlots wore kohl around their eyes and I'd always wondered if Aunt Nancy had considered naming Heller Harlot instead, which would have been perfect.

Kenz told me, "Get over yourself, baby doll. Eye shadow isn't a lie, it's just a higher truth. If God didn't want you to have longer and fuller eyelashes then why did he give us this amazing new twenty-four-hour latex-luster volumizing liquid mascara with fiber-optic micro-beads?"

I could tell that Nedda was itching to get me into a designer outfit, but we finally agreed on a simple dark skirt and a striped blouse along with my Singleberries blazer and a fresh pair of navy-blue kneesocks, although Nedda groused, "You still look like the loneliest girl at boarding school. In Nebraska. In 1957."

When I stepped into the suite's main living area it had been transformed into a TV studio. Heller was sitting on a couch in front of two huge *Angel Wars* posters, one of which featured her in flight, with her wings, and the other a close-up of her face with the halo, which glowed as it floated over her head. There were large industrial-looking lights on metal stands with complicated reflectors, all aimed at Heller. There were men with video cameras strapped to their chests and balanced on their shoulders and Heller was wearing a small microphone clipped to the neckline of her dress. She looked beautiful, with perfect hair and makeup. She looked like a flawless gorgeous movie star playing the role of Heller Harrigan. She looked like a very expensive lie.

"What?" said Heller, who caught me staring at her.

"Nothing! It's just—you look different."

"You mean I look like they found my body yesterday and they've been embalming me all night."

"Yes! No!"

"I'm a movie star. This is how people expect me to look."

A way-too-skinny, way-too-tan, way-too-blonde woman, probably my mom's age, was seated near Heller. "That's Tally Marabont," Wyatt whispered to me. "She's the most popular entertainment-show host in the country and she's a bitch on wheels."

As I was about to ask Wyatt if he could avoid using

the b-word, and as I was wondering how you'd attach wheels to a B, someone counted, "Five . . . four . . . three . . . two . . . one, and we're live! Tally?"

"Hi, I'm Tally Marabont," said the way-too-everything woman, looking into one of the cameras. Wyatt turned my head toward a video monitor, where I saw that the on camera Tally looked perfectly nice and ten years younger, instead of like a puddle of melted crayons. "It's called lighting," Wyatt whispered in my ear. "When she's off camera Tally scares children."

"We're here today with the hottest young star in America," said Tally, "and possibly on the entire planet, and she's about to get even hotter, because she's starring in one of the most anticipated movies of all time. Let's say hello to the popular and gifted and at times wildly controversial Heller Harrigan!"

"Did she really need to say 'wildly controversial'?" Wyatt muttered.

"Hey, Tally," said Heller, with a grin, which made me notice something. In real life whenever Heller grinned, it was as if she couldn't help herself because she was having such a great time and because she'd just come up with some horrifyingly wicked idea and couldn't wait to share it. Now her grin looked more careful, as if she'd practiced it and as if she knew that millions of people, and especially Tally, were demanding to see it.

"There's that billion-dollar grin," said Tally. "I bet that everywhere you go, people want to see that movie-star smile."

"That *Angel Wars* smile," said Heller.

"Good girl," Wyatt murmured. "Sell the movie."

"But, Heller," said Tally, "you've now reached a very highly pressured and potentially nuclear moment in your life. The *Angel Wars* books have sold more than a hundred million copies all over the world, and when you were first cast as Lynnea, while many fans applauded, there was also a huge public outcry. There are still websites called everything from We Hate Heller to Boycott This Movie, and worse. Far worse. How do you feel about so much hate?"

Heller paused and I could see her mentally counting to three and keeping herself in check, a system that I approved of. "Well, Tally," she finally said sweetly, "first of all, I completely understand why so many people of all ages love the *Angel Wars* books, because I love them. When something's precious to you, you don't want to see it changed or betrayed or destroyed. I would just like to assure everyone, but especially all of the Angel Warriors, that we have made this movie with only love and respect. I'd like everyone to know how honored I feel, and humbled, to have been allowed to play such a memorable and exciting character. All I'm asking, all I'm hoping for, is that audiences will give me, and this amazing movie, a chance."

"Yes," Wyatt murmured, "perfect. Every bullet point, on the nose."

"That's a great answer," said Tally. She put her fingertips together and her face got harder looking, as if playtime was over. "But there's something else I need to ask you, something that's been burning up the Internet."

Heller sat up straighter and her smile stayed in place.

"After you shot the movie a year ago, your personal life went off the rails. I've heard well-substantiated stories of substance abuse, sexual misbehavior, a criminal arrest and more. I'm told that you've just spent several months in court-ordered rehab at a private facility in Arizona. And you're still just a teenager! While you're here promoting this potential blockbuster in your pretty designer clothes, do you intend to address these stories?"

"You can do it," Wyatt whispered, "you can handle it, stay on point . . ."

"Tally," said Heller, and I knew that whenever Heller used Tally's first name she was trying to keep the conversation friendly and down-to-earth. "I'm seventeen years old. I've been working in this business since I was a kid and I've been working hard. I'm incredibly grateful for all of the opportunities I've had. As for my private life, well, I think that I'm just gonna say this . . ."

Heller grinned strategically.

"My name is Heller. But now I'm playing an angel. Let's just leave it at that."

"Good girl!" said Wyatt, as we grabbed each other's forearms because we were both so nervous.

"That's all very charming," said Tally, "and really fun, but you still haven't answered my questions. You were Anna Banana and now you're Lynnea. Which makes you a role model for young people and especially for young girls everywhere. Do you sincerely believe that those girls should follow the example of someone who's twisted her life into a sad and disturbing Hollywood catastrophe?"

Heller's face got very tense and her eyes narrowed. She was such a good actress that anyone watching her could instantly tell what she was going through. Heller had been monitoring herself and following a game plan, but now she was furious and gripping the arm of the couch while taking short, sharp breaths, like a tiger about to leap onto a jeep filled with giggling tourists who'd snapped one photo too many.

"You know something, Tally," said Heller, "before we get into my life, which I'm happy to do, let's talk about yours. Is it true that right before your divorce, your husband, who I think was your fourth husband, came home unexpectedly and caught you in bed with a pair of—"

"Oh, shit . . . ," Wyatt muttered, digging his nails into my arm.

I started panicking, only the weird thing was, for maybe the first time ever I wasn't panicking about me, but about Heller. At first I thought, don't try and save her. Whatever Heller had been through, including all of the sex and drugs and felonies, was her own fault. She'd wanted to be a big star and answering tricky questions was part of her job. Four years ago Heller had teased and bullied and coaxed me until I'd almost died, so I certainly didn't owe her anything. Watching Heller getting ripped to pieces on national TV might be satisfying and a kind of justice.

But Heller was getting picked on in front of millions of people. I stopped thinking and I stopped panicking and I

jumped, I literally jumped in front of the cameras as if I'd rico-
cheted off a trampoline, and I sat beside Heller.

"Hi there, Tally!" I blurted out. "I'm Heller's cousin, Caitlin
Singleberry. I'm one of the Singing Singleberries and we're a
fun, wholesome, all-American Christian family. I'd just like to
say something and I am so excited and downright thrilled to be
here on . . . on this program, which I love even though I haven't
ever technically really seen it. But I think you're so pretty and
so . . . super-pretty and you're, like . . . a super-pretty blonde . . .
pretty person and Heller has been telling me about how much
she admires you as a journalist and a powerful woman and . . .
and because you're so creepy thin."

One of the cameramen made a little choking noise but pretended it was a cough.

"What I'd really like to say is . . . that I'm just a regular girl
from Parsippany, New Jersey—hey, Parsippany! Of course I
love Heller because we're related so my mom says I have to, but
more than anything I love *Angel Wars*. I'm probably the number
one *Angel Wars* fan in the whole world, even more than my
mom, who I once caught kissing an apple and saying, 'Tallwen,
we musn't.' When I heard Heller was going to be Lynnea, at
first I was really upset because I didn't know if Heller was the
right choice for the role. I was so upset that I, like, vomited. I
hate vomiting. I hate it worse than farting. Oh my Lord I can't
believe I just said the word 'farting' because doesn't just saying
the word 'farting' sound like farting? Please pretend I didn't
just say farting. Can we erase the part where I said farting?
Wouldn't it be wonderful if scientists developed a way to erase

farting forever? Like we could have fund-raising triathlons and bake sales and carnivals to find a cure for farting?"

I could see Wyatt behind the camera with his eyes popping out and his mouth hanging open.

"I mean, I know that Heller has quite a reputation," I said because I knew that I had to keep talking and I also knew that I desperately needed to stop saying the word "farting." "Because Heller has gone to parties where there was most likely the kind of wild premarital dancing that can lead to the worst sort of deep-kissing and maybe she's even drunk an entire beer and I'm not talking about lite beer or root beer, and I wish I didn't have to say this but I bet Heller drank that beer right from the bottle like . . . like a hyena. But do you know what, Tally? By the way, I love your name, is Tally short for something like Tallyho or Talleyrand, the French diplomat who obtained peace with Austria in the 1801 Treaty of Luneville? I learned about Talleyrand because I'm homeschooled and I know that some people think that homeschooling is weird but it's not weird at all I mean look at me I'm not one little bit weird am I? AM I?"

I could tell that everyone in the room, including Tally and Heller, was staring at me as if my hair was on fire but I knew that I had to keep going, only I had no idea where I was headed.

"Okay, let's get back to Heller being Lynnea," I said because I knew I was supposed to be promoting the movie. "Lynnea had a rough life too, just like Heller. People made fun of her because she wanted to be a forest ranger and . . . and her back ached because her wings were growing in and she had trouble finding a comfortable position to study in although personally I like to study while sitting on a straight-backed chair at the kitchen table. Plus Lynnea found out that the people who she thought were her parents weren't her parents at all plus she found out that she was the Chosen Winglet and that she had to save the world, which sometimes made her afraid and even downright grumpy, which I completely understand because I'm sure that having to save the world would make a person extra, extra anxious, don't you think? I'm so glad that I don't have to save the world although shouldn't we all be trying every day to save the world in our own little ways, maybe by, for example, using our old shoelaces to tie up flattened cardboard boxes for recycling because when you recycle you can save a river or an ocelot or a hungry dolphin from disappearing forever? When you see a hungry dolphin don't you just want to hug it and buy it a sandwich, unless a sandwich would kill the dolphin?"

I knew I was sounding certifiable and that I had to either finish talking or yell "Save the hungry dolphins!" and jump out the window. I tried to pull everything together by saying, "So all of this means that Heller is in fact the perfect person to understand Lynnea because Heller *is* Lynnea. Tally, just wait until you see the movie because after I saw it I . . . I had to pray to our Lord so that he would let me see it at least ten more times as a form of daily worship. I'd just like to say to everyone out there who's watching this show and I bet that you're all the most wonderful people . . ."

I faced one of the cameras, the one with the glowing red light on top.

"When you see this movie with my cousin Heller in it you're

going to fly right up to heaven! Oh no, not because you'll be dead but because you're going to be blessed and saved and washed in the holy spirit of . . . of . . . *Angel Wars* the best movie ever! Yay!!! Yay vase meir!!! Amen and shalom and whatever Mormons or Muslims or Seventh-Day Adventists like to say! YAY!!!"

I stopped because I'd run out of things to say so I hugged Heller to show how supportive I was and then I put my hands in my lap and smiled like an idiot.

"Well!" said Tally. "There we have it, the very first exclusive rave review for *Angel Wars*, straight from Heller Harrigan's cute-as-a-bug cousin, Camden! What an unexpected treat from a girl who sounds like she might've had one cup of coffee too many! She must be telling the truth because just look at those kneesocks! That's all the time we have!"

"Cut and out!" said someone from behind the cameras, and then the lights got less blinding and Tally stood up, smoothed her skirt, flipped her hair and held out her hand, not to Heller, but to me. "Thank you, young lady," she said. "You've just given us a completely fresh, up-close-and-personal take on your famous cousin, which I bet America is going to eat up with a spoon. Well played, Heller."

"Thank you, Tally, and it's so great to see you," said Heller, "and thank you so much for having us on the show."

eighteen

Since When Is My Name Camden?

You are out of your mind," Wyatt told me once he'd dragged Heller and me off into a corner while the crew was setting up the room for Heller's next interview. "I can't believe you did that and I can't believe Tally went for it!"

"What . . . the . . . hell . . . were . . . you . . . doing?" said Heller, in a tight, quiet, dangerous voice.

"I was helping you. I was healing you. I was getting you back on track," I said, feeling proud of myself.

"I was handling it!" Heller exploded. "I was doing fine and I didn't need you to chime in and start babbling like a chimpanzee on crystal meth!"

I was baffled. Why didn't Heller understand that I'd only been trying to help, because she'd been in trouble? That I wasn't the enemy?

"But . . . but . . . ," I said. "You were about to ruin everything!"

"I was not! I've been practicing for months! You're an amateur!"

"I saved you! You should be grateful! You should thank me!"

"I should thank you? For what? For horning in on my interview? For hogging the camera? For talking about hungry dolphins? You're just like everyone else. Are you that jealous?"

"I am not jealous! I was doing my job!"

"You don't have a job! Wearing kneesocks so you don't have to shave your legs doesn't count as a job!"

"Ladies, children, people, interviewees," said Wyatt. "Reel it in a few hundred miles. Heller, you were doing fine, but there was a moment when you let Tally rile you. You let her provoke you. Which is why Catey stepped in. Catey, thank you for lending a hand, but in the future maybe you should consult with me before you—take action. I think we can all agree that the interview was a success and we're all on the same page and we don't need to keep attacking each other in a manner that could seriously affect our professionally applied hair and makeup. Agreed?"

"Just keep her off camera," said Heller. "Where she belongs."

"Fine," I said, trying to keep my voice from trembling. "For the rest of the weekend I'll . . . I'll just let you keep destroying yourself."

"Why, look," said Wyatt. "Here's Tom Farling from *Entertainment Edition*, our very next delightful interview. Heller, you know Tom . . ."

The rest of the morning stayed tense, but Wyatt had me stand out of camera range so Heller couldn't see me. I was really angry at her for being so ungrateful, although I have to admit, I was buzzing from my moment on camera.

I'd never been interviewed before and I'd certainly never appeared on TV and the whole experience had made me dizzy and off-balance and excited. It was like the aftermath of a panic attack when I'm still out of breath but the danger has passed. I couldn't believe I'd acted so recklessly and saved the day or at least the interview. That's why Heller was so upset: because I'd acted like her. She was trying to be poised and polite and good-girly while I'd taken a huge risk. Heller was the jealous one.

As I watched, Heller was interviewed by grown-ups from newspapers and magazines and entertainment TV shows, by teenagers from all of the *Angel Wars* websites, blogs and Twitter feeds, by eight-year-olds who had their own YouTube channels and by so many other people that I lost count and the faces began to blur, especially because everyone asked Heller the exact same questions: "What was it like to grow up as Anna Banana?" "Did you ever dream that you'd be playing Lynnea?" "What do you have to say to all the Heller haters?" "Are you married?" "Do you have a boyfriend?" "Are you dating anyone special?" "How did you get in shape to play an angel?" "Are you a Hollywood bad girl?" "What music do you listen to?" "Can I take a selfie with you?" and "Why is that girl over there wearing kneesocks—did she burn her legs?"

Even though Heller was doing all the smiling and answering the same questions over and over again, just watching her do it was exhausting, especially because with every interviewer Heller had to keep pretending she was being asked each question for the very first time, which she did by pausing and pretending to think about whether she liked working out or whether she was a strict vegan or whether Meryl Streep was her idol. "People wonder why movie stars get paid so much," Wyatt told me. "It's not for acting. It's for doing this."

We were almost down to the last scheduled interview when an assistant rushed over to Wyatt and said, "We've just had a request from someone called Henry Firenze, who says that he has over eight million Twitter followers and he's a huge Heller fan. He wants to know if we can squeeze him in."

"Who?" said Wyatt. "Henry what? I've never heard of him and we're booked down to the last second. It sounds suspicious—Henry Firenze? Call security."

"I'll talk to him," said Heller. For the first time all morning, she seemed genuinely happy. "It's okay."

A guy only a few years older than Heller and me came into the room. He was Asian American and really handsome, with great cheekbones and an easy way of moving; as if he was comfortable in his own body and not at all daunted by entering a suite filled with strangers. He had a white streak in his otherwise dark hair and at first I thought it was one of those trendy touches that would grow out if he didn't keep bleaching it but the streak looked real and I remembered reading once that a white forelock can be a genetic trait.

"Henry Firenze," said the guy, right to Heller. "Thanks so much for seeing me. I'll be quick. Big fan."

"No problem, Henry," said Heller, and by the way she said the guy's name I could tell that something was up.

"Two minutes, Henry," said Wyatt. "That's all the time we've got."

"I understand," said Henry. "So, Ms. Harrigan, this is a very stressful time for you because people must be asking you all sorts of questions. How are you holding up?"

"I'm . . . doing okay," said Heller, and from her voice I knew that she'd considered her answer instead of being automatically cheerful and dutiful like with all of the other interviews.

"Have you seen the movie?" asked Henry.

"Not yet," said Heller, which was odd because up until right now Heller had been telling people she'd seen the movie countless times and that it was amazing and completely faithful to the book and she loved it.

"I know the movie is going to be great," Henry told Heller. "I know how much it means to you and how hard you've worked. Don't drive yourself crazy, okay?"

"Um, do you have any actual questions, Henry?" asked Wyatt.

"Just one," said Henry. "But first I've been wondering— who's that?" He was pointing at me.

"No one knows," said Heller. "She just showed up and she keeps scarfing mini muffins from the buffet and she shoved three crullers down her shirt and she won't leave."

For the record I'd only eaten two mini muffins and I'd wrapped a cruller inside a napkin in case of an emergency.

"Heller?" said Henry.

"She's my cousin," Heller admitted. "From New Jersey. She's here to make sure that I don't get drunk or high or steal a car and drive it right into a busload of Angel Warriors. She's an Olympic-level buzzkill. If I even think about having a cigarette or dropping an f-bomb, her head splits open and this nasty humpbacked lizard wearing an apron pops out. See, there it is."

"That's not true!" I said. "I'm just here as . . . as . . . a volunteer! I'm a devoted family member and a sacred sounding board!"

"She's . . . she's helping," said Heller. She looked at me and then looked away.

"It sounds like you're both doing just fine," said Henry, smiling and nodding at me, and that was when I knew: Once they'd met Henry for even ten seconds, guys like my brothers, and Mills and Billy, would think that Henry was the coolest guy on earth and they'd try to imitate his loping walk and his crooked smile and probably his white forelock, only they'd end up looking like dopey teenage zebras. Henry was cool in a completely offhand way and he was cool because he seemed to truly care about Heller, something he'd proved by not asking any pushy or disgusting questions. He looked like he wanted to put his arms around Heller and tell her that everything was going to be okay.

"Here's my question," said Henry. "Heller Harrigan, you're a total megastar. Everyone's watching you every second to see if you're going to mess up. A lot of people are hoping you'll mess up because they think that might be fun to watch, the way crowds gather around car accidents and plane crashes. But let me ask you something. I know this would never happen, but what if—everything does fall apart? What if the movie tanks and everyone blames you and all of those Angel Warriors target you with their golden crossbows? If, God forbid, that happened, what would you do?"

Henry was looking right into Heller's eyes and she was looking right back, as if they were daring each other to do something, but I wasn't sure exactly what.

"I'd deal with it," said Heller. "It wouldn't be my most favorite experience ever and it might take a while to yank all of those golden arrows out of my head, but I wouldn't . . . go off a cliff. I wouldn't die."

When Heller said that she wouldn't die she didn't sound like some silly girl saying, "OMG, when so-and-so looked at me from across the cafeteria I thought I would die!" She sounded like someone who might have come very close to dying or who'd seriously thought about it. There was a pause as Heller and Henry Firenze, or whatever his name really was, kept looking at each other. Heller wasn't using her trademark grin but another kind of smile, something braver and smaller and a little scared.

"Thank you, Henry," said Wyatt. "Please tell all of your followers that Heller loves every one of them and that they're all going to worship the *Angel Wars* movie and that they should keep tweeting!"

After Henry left, Heller was on her lunch break and we were alone in one of the suite's bedrooms, surrounded by racks of outfits—Heller had changed her clothes, her makeup, her hair and her accessories at least twelve times during the morning because, as Wyatt had explained to me earlier, "Heller is also a fashion icon. She can't look the same in all of her photos and video chats because the fashion bloggers need tons of new Heller looks to analyze, criticize and then copy. The magazines like to print collages of Heller's outfits so that readers can vote for their favorites and argue over how many times Heller's repeated the same belt or bag, and whether this means that the repeats are Heller's favorites. We'll have plenty of tips for where to buy Heller's favorite belts and bags and where to buy much cheaper versions that look almost the same, even if they may fall apart or give you a rash after you've worn them a couple of times."

An assistant brought salads for Heller and me. We hadn't spoken since the Tally Marabont interview because we were so mad at each other, but after a few minutes of watching Heller nibbling on a single lettuce leaf I couldn't take it anymore.

"You have to eat the whole thing!" I said. "Then you should have another salad and a protein shake. You're working very hard and you need your strength."

I was sounding like my mom, which was just fine.

"People who are going to be having their picture taken in high def wearing a white catsuit are not allowed to eat," Heller said. "I'll be able to eat in two more days."

"You can wear the white catsuit with a nice down-filled vest," I suggested, and then because I couldn't wait one second longer I broke down and asked, "Who was that guy? With the white forelock? Henry Firenze?"

"Why should I tell you? So you'll feel really on top of things? So you can give pretend interviews to your stuffed animals? So you can tell all of your little friends the inside dirt about Heller Harrigan? If you even have any little friends?"

"Because if you don't tell me I'll call your mother and ask who he is. Is that what you want?"

Heller stared at me and then she finally said, "That wasn't Henry Firenze. He made that name up because he knew I'd recognize it. Firenze is the Italian word for Florence, which that guy always told me was the most beautiful city in the world and where he wants to live someday. With me. So that wasn't Henry. That was Oliver. Happy now?"

Heller looked at me skeptically. It occurred to me that maybe Heller was the one who didn't have any friends. She knew thousands of people, but from what I'd seen, most of those people either worked for her or wanted something from her or thought she was crazy, or all three.

As for me, since our parents had separated us four years ago I hadn't had many friends either. Since I was homeschooled I mostly hung out with my brothers and sisters and my anxiety issues made me limit contact with outsiders. I'd had a best friend but terrible things had happened, which made me even more wary of having any friends at all. As far as I could tell, having a best friend was dangerous because a best friend knows everything about you. No one can hurt you like a best friend.

"Heller," I said, "we were friends but now we're not. We're not anything. I'm here to check up on you because you need

that. But I will guarantee you one thing: If you tell me something in confidence and if you ask me to keep it a secret just
between us, then I swear I will never tell anyone."

"Okay," said Heller quietly. "I still won't tell you about
Oliver, not everything, because . . . because if I told you everything I might, I don't know, I might start remembering too
much, which could send me right into the volcano. I'll tell you
how I met him."

I couldn't tell if Heller had decided to trust me, at least a
little bit, or if she had to talk to someone.

"The really humongous trouble started right before I got
cast in *Angel Wars. Anna Banana* was over and I was sixteen
and I was having trouble getting work. There were a few offers
but they were mostly just crappier versions of *Anna Banana*,
like what if Anna moved to Switzerland and became the
babysitter to a pair of rich, spoiled twins or what if Anna moved
to New York and enrolled in fashion school and became an
unpaid intern for a bitchy designer with a pair of rich, spoiled
twins. I didn't want to do that because I knew it would be a
step backward. Whenever I auditioned for movies or plays or
grown-up TV shows, the casting people and the directors would
take one look at me and go, 'Oh, right, you were some sort of
drippy teen princess on TV, you can't possibly do anything else,
next, please.'"

Back in Parsippany I'd wondered about what Heller had
been doing after *Anna Banana* went off the air, but all I'd
ever been able to find online had been pictures of her looking
out of it at the openings of nightclubs in other countries and a

few shots of her as some rich guy's guest on board his yacht in the Mediterranean, where she'd been wearing a bikini and sipping champagne with a lot of other people who were sup- posed to be famous only I'd never heard of them.

"I was getting desperate and I had my old creepy manager who kept asking me if I wanted to be on a reality show where I'd get dropped onto an island with a bunch of other people who used to be teen idols, but who'd gone to jail or found Jesus. When I said no he told me that I could make a lot of money if once I turned eighteen I made a sex tape called *The Really Big Banana*, only I'd have to pretend that it was private and act all upset and outraged once it was for sale online. When I tried to explain to him why making a sex tape wasn't such a good idea either, he just said, 'Well, you're broke.'"

"You were broke? How? Didn't you make a lot of money from doing *Anna Banana* and the *Anna Banana* movie and all of your records? Everyone in Parsippany had one of those *Anna Banana* backpacks." I hated myself for asking these kinds of questions because it made me feel like I was Heller's accountant.

"I did make a lot of money but I was still a minor and so my mom was in charge of everything and she was supposed to be putting most of what I was earning into a protected bank account and I know she was trying her best and I know that she didn't do it on purpose, but, well, she'd never had to deal with that kind of money before. Then one of her boyfriends, this total sleazebag with a ponytail—I mean sleazebag alert—he said that he was this big-time private sector Wall Street financial advisor even though he didn't seem to have any clients. He'd say that he was representing such big stars that he had to respect their privacy. My mom, of course, was crazy about him and she gave him all of the money I'd made because he told her that he could triple it by parking it offshore and by investing in, what did he call it, a diversified portfolio. Which meant that three weeks later, without telling anyone, he'd sold our house in LA and our car and he'd disappeared off the face of the earth, along with every penny I'd ever earned."

"But, but—didn't you call the police? Couldn't they arrest him and get all of your money back?"

"They tried. But he had a fake passport and the last time anyone had seen him he was in Ecuador, where they won't extradite sleazebag embezzlers with ponytails to the United States. There was nothing anyone could do. My mom was a total mess and she kept crying and apologizing, which meant that I had to comfort her and tell her that it wasn't her fault and that I didn't care about the money as long as she was okay. Which was pretty much true because I was way more pissed off about the way that guy had treated my mom, but still—I was broke and I was over and I was seriously thinking about showing up at your house and seeing if maybe your parents wouldn't notice one extra kid and I could just be another Singing Singleberry."

"You should have! My parents would have understood!"

The second I said that Heller shot me a look because we both knew that was a lie.

"Then the studio that owned the *Angel Wars* books announced that they were looking for someone to play Lynnea. I was insane for those books and I identified with Lynnea because she had to fight for anyone to take her seriously as the girl who could defeat the Darkling Creeper. I knew that if the director would just let me audition I could prove myself. But for months he wouldn't even see me and so I bombarded him with letters and emails and texts and I put myself on tape reading from the books and acting out my favorite scenes. My scuzzball manager kept telling me it was hopeless and that the director was screen-testing every other actress my age on the planet and that this one or that one had the inside track, so I should just give up and endorse some rubber diaper with batteries in it that was supposed to give you a great butt while you slept. I'm not kidding—it was called the Snooz-Booty."

"Oh my Lord!"

While I still would never feel sorry for Heller, I was starting to wonder if back then, when she'd been alone and struggling, I'd let her down. What if I'd called her? What if she'd had some support? What if I hadn't been so focused on hating her?

"Finally I was at the end of my rope and I was pretty much living in my car and I told myself that even if I didn't get the part, I had to at least be sure I'd tried my very best. So I find out where the director is having his final callbacks for his top choices for the part and it's on a soundstage in the Valley. I figure out a way to sneak in by bribing the guy who's doing maintenance on the soundstage, who luckily had a twelve-year-old daughter who really needed an autographed copy of Anna Banana's autobiography; remember, it was called *I, Banana*."

I did remember this book because I'd found it at the library. I'd read it to see if there was anything about Heller's childhood in the book, which meant I was secretly reading it to see if there was anything about me, or about what Heller had done to me. There hadn't been a word about that part of Heller's life because Heller's network had hired someone to write the book for her, since it was Anna's story and not hers. It had been all about how much Anna loved doing homework and helping others and it had included tips for outdoor exercise and healthy snacks like apple slices or little bags of almonds and grapes. It had ended by saying, "We can all be our own best banana."

"Right after they'd auditioned the last girl I had the maintenance guy shut off all the lights in the building and when they came back on a few seconds later, there I was at the far end of this huge, empty soundstage and I'm dressed like Lynnea, you know, with the braids crossed over my forehead and I'm holding this crossbow, which I'd found at a yard sale and spray-painted gold, and I'm pointing the crossbow right at the director so he can't move. I do that big speech from right before the end of the first book, when Lynnea faces off in the Netherdome against General Vlad Corpsemonger."

"The Darkling Creeper's first lieutenant!" I gasped. "Who created that child army by stealing the souls of all the kids who were killed by the genetically engineered Darkling Plague-Spores!"

"Exactly. So I tell General Corpsemonger that he will never prevail and that I will use the power of prayer to retrieve those children's souls from the Gravesend Receptacle. As I announce that I'm the Chosen Winglet, I'm walking slowly but steadily toward the director, and just as I pull back my arm to send a golden arrow flying right between the director's eyes, I put down the crossbow and I say, 'Heller Harrigan. Thank you for seeing me.'"

"Oh my gosh!"

"And I got the part!"

Even though I knew that not only had Heller been cast as Lynnea but that she'd already made the movie, I wanted to hug her and congratulate her, but I didn't because we weren't friends anymore. If we were friends I would've already known the story because Heller would've called me and told me all about her audition right after it had happened, and we would've shared the whole thing. I would've been part of Heller's adventure. Instead I'd been back in Parsippany, trying so hard not to think about her. I just nodded, as if a stranger had told me this story on a bench at a bus stop and I was being polite and a good listener.

"Once I heard the news I was over the moon because the director was giving me a chance and I was going to be Lynnea. But the second that the studio made the announcement, it started. The war against Heller Harrigan. I completely understood it because everyone loves the *Angel Wars* books and I was Anna Banana, which meant I was a joke. The web just detonated, there were all of those websites about how I had no talent and about how I was this washed-up has-been and about how I was too fat and too short and too ugly and about how anyone else, even the dog from *Anna Banana*, would be a better choice to play Lynnea. There was that one girl, Ava Lily Larrimore, who runs Angel Warriors International, which is the biggest fan site of all; I mean, she has over forty million followers and she hates my guts. I still don't know why, but not only did she not want me to play Lynnea, she wanted to slaughter me, she thought that I should be arrested because I'd damaged the precious *Angel Wars* legacy. She sent the studio a petition signed by her forty million followers saying that if I was Lynnea then all of those followers plus their friends and families, none of them would go see the movie."

I'd read things about Ava Lily Larrimore online. She was this grim-looking sixteen-year-old girl and as far as I could tell she truly believed that the *Angel Wars* books had been dictated by God and were a divine prophecy and that they were real. I loved the books as much as anyone, but I'd never gone that far.

"Which was the first time I really fell apart," said Heller. "Even after I'd lost all of my money and when I couldn't get a job, I was still okay because I was thinking, I'll buckle down and I'll work even harder and I'll turn things around. But I wasn't ready to have so many people, to have the whole world think that I was nothing and that I was wrong and that I should be ashamed of myself. So I made up a schedule in my head. I would rehearse for the movie with the director and the rest of the cast for ten hours every day. Then I'd train in the gym for another two hours with a coach so I could do all of the stunts in the movie myself and I wouldn't need a body double, not even for the flying or the battles. I'd take another two hours every day to keep rereading the books until I'd memorized them. Finally I allowed myself one hour at the end of each week when all by myself on this little beach or in my car, I could drink."

"Heller?"

Heller was looking right at me, to see if she could trust me. I wasn't sure how to reassure her—I almost reached out to touch her arm but that felt fake, as if I was her minister or guidance counselor. I just nodded, which I hoped was enough.

"It was the only way I could deal with everything, with wanting to be so good and with working so hard and with so many people hating me. I would buy a bottle of Jack Daniel's because that made me feel like a tough guy, and I would sit there really late at night and I wouldn't stop until I'd finished the whole bottle and passed out. A few hours later I'd wake up and I'd take a shower and I'd get back to work. I made a deal with myself that I'd never complain about anything and I'd never tell anyone what was going on as long as each week, I had that one hour when I could just not think about anything. Because, believe me, if I couldn't drink, all I would do with any downtime would be to obsess over whatever else I should be doing to prepare for the movie and about how I could get Ava Lily Larrimore to like me."

Heller was scaring me, not just because of how hard she'd pushed herself and because of her blackout drinking but because I understood. While I had never experienced anything like Heller's kind of pressure, I knew what it meant to want to be perfect every second of every day. I knew about punishing myself for even the tiniest failure. I knew about freaking out because no punishment was ever enough.

"I was handling everything, I was holding it together because I had my goal to make the movie and I had my whiskey, so I had a secret friend. Until one night when I was sitting on the beach in the dark and I'd put away about half the bottle, my phone rang. It was the director's assistant, this totally nice girl, and she asked me if I could come in an hour earlier the next morning for a costume fitting. I said of course, but once I got off the phone I started going a little nuts because I had to reconfigure my schedule. I decided that I needed to get in an extra half hour at the gym the next day to make sure that all of my costumes fit perfectly. I got in my car and I really thought I was fine because my brain was buzzing. I'm a block away from the little apartment that I'd rented for me and my mom and I swear to God, I see one of the Darkling Creeper's Dastroids, those nasty little drones he uses to grab little kids out of their beds. I see one, a Dastroid, coming out from behind this parked car and I needed to destroy it, I had to crush it, before it got anywhere near some little kid.

"I steer my car right toward the Dastroid and I step on the gas and I get in a fender bender. Because of course it wasn't a Dastroid, it was just some guy trying to parallel park his Hyundai. I dented his car and I got a summons to appear in court and I couldn't tell my lawyer or the judge or the whole world that I was really fighting the dark forces, so I pleaded no contest to reckless driving. The judge let me off with probation and a warning but the studio got really nervous, so my manager told me that if I still wanted to be Lynnea, I had to go to rehab, for the first time. So I did. It didn't get in the tabloids or online because it was only for three days at this incredibly private clinic in Wyoming. Which was where I met Oliver."

"Did . . . did Oliver work there? Was he a counselor?"

"No. He was a drunk. Like me."

"Ladies?" said Wyatt, as he opened the bedroom door. "I hope you've finished your lunch because we have to get over to Madison Square Garden, which is already completely out of control. As my mother always says, you need to wait at least forty-five minutes after eating before you can battle the Darkling Creeper in an exclusive, fully staged, one-time-only, once-in-a-lifetime live performance in front of twenty thousand screaming Angel Warriors. Led by Ava Lily Larrimore."

nineteen

Angel Warriors Attack!!!

On the schedule the next event had been listed as "Madison Square Garden Live Performance," but I'd had no idea what a big deal it was. Wyatt and Heller explained it to me in the van on the way over:

"The *Angel Wars* premiere can't be just another movie opening," said Wyatt. "It needs to become an internationally celebrated holiday for Angel Warriors everywhere. Since we need to make sure that everyone is on board, we held a lottery and so twenty thousand fans get to attend the first ever, right-there-in-front-of-your-very-own-eyeballs, starring-Heller-Harrigan-as-Lynnea-herself Netherdome showdown."

"When we shot the whole Netherdome scene for the movie, in Morocco," said Heller, "it was amazing. They built this huge arena, just like in the book, and they used over five hundred different colors of sand to create the Netherdome mandala."

"Wait," I said, "are you saying that right now you're actually going to stage Lynnea's battle against Malestra and the Dastroids?"

In the *Angel Wars* books, there's an unseen world called the Otherlife that is ruled by three Hosts, including the Golden Lord, who seeks only peace and beauty for all humankind. The Golden Lord's sworn enemy is the Darkling Creeper, who feeds on ignorance and despair.

The third Host is Mistress Miracle, who judges every soul's behavior and determines where they'll end up; readers have claimed that Mistress Miracle reminds them of a mythical goddess crossed with a Rose Bowl parade float.

For the first time ever, Mistress Miracle convenes an AllSouls Universium. To avoid an all-out war she proposes that each realm select a single combatant: the Golden Lord chooses Lynnea while the Darkling Creeper and General Corpsemonger pick a merciless killing machine named Malestra.

"You're going to do the whole Netherdome battle?" I asked as we drove deep beneath Madison Square Garden, an indoor sports and entertainment stadium that filled an entire city block. I was getting used to April finding the most subterranean entrances to any building in order to keep Heller's whereabouts as mysterious as possible.

"We're doing a version of it," said Wyatt. "It's going to be spectacular. You'll see."

As I waited outside Heller's dressing room while she got into her costume I began to feel short of breath and at first I didn't know why, since I was only there as an observer. All I kept thinking was: I'm inside the *Angel Wars* books. My phone buzzed, which made me jump.

"Sweetie," said my mom, "we saw you and Heller on Tally Marabont and we were so impressed! You both handled yourselves so well! But I'm calling because we've just had the most wonderful news—you got an email from Parsippany Tech! They've accepted you! You're in!"

My panic expanded. Getting into college was the first step toward the rest of my life and "the rest of my life" was the sort of phrase that appeared on all of the college websites, where I'd tried to ignore it because thinking about the rest of my life made me feel like I was standing on a ledge fifty stories up and the ledge was sliding back into the building.

Parsippany Tech was a good school and the campus was only a few miles from our house so I could live at home. Parsippany Tech had an especially good business program so I could study accounting, which would be a really smart thing to do because the world is always going to need accountants. I was pretty good at math although not as good as my sister Catherine, so she could help me study.

If I only got into Parsippany Tech that would be just fine and the rest of my life would fall into place and I could finally stop obsessing and spell-checking and worrying about getting accepted anywhere else, and I could concentrate on how the famous poet Emily Dickinson had almost never left her house and she turned out to be—Emily Dickinson. Who wrote that poem with the words "I'm nobody! Who are you? Are you nobody too?" Which is my favorite poem.

I joined Wyatt in the greenroom, which was a waiting area with a kitchen and a pool table. I asked, "So Heller is going to perform the whole showdown in front of all these people? And Ava Lily Larrimore is going to be Malestra? I thought that Ava hated Heller—why is she doing this?"

"The marketing team has been polling the *Angel Wars* fanbase," said Wyatt as he inspected a table filled with snacks, from baskets of celery and carrot sticks to platters of power bars, muffins and doughnuts—from what I'd observed, being in show business meant that there was always lots of free food, but because everyone was on a diet, no one ate anything. "They found out that the fans are divided between the people who love Heller, and the people who listen to Ava because Ava's constantly tweeting and sending out mass emails and *Angel Wars* Alerts. I decided it was a good idea to keep your friends close but your enemies closer. It's risky but it's made the whole thing even more of an event—it's like the *Angel Wars* Super Bowl."

"Why is Ava so angry? Why's she on such a rampage against Heller?"

"Here's the simple answer," said Wyatt as he plucked the cashews, which were his favorites, out of a plastic bowl of trail mix. "Ava is a Killer Medium."

"A what?"

"Okay, because you were homeschooled I don't think you know about Killer Mediums."

"Killer Mediums?"

"There's a mistake people make because they assume that the mean girls are always the prettiest and most popular girls in school. That's not always true because the queen bees are usually very confident and so they can't be bothered preying on underlings. Then you've got the oddballs, the chubby kids and the stoners and the drama club fiends, but if they're smart, the oddballs hang out with their friends and create their own little worlds."

I'd never heard about any of these cliques but they sounded complicated and scary so I was glad that my parents had kept us at home. Just thinking about walking down a high school hallway while other people smirked and whispered about me and competed to see who could say the nastiest things was terrifying. In a way Heller's life was exactly like that hallway, times the population of the world.

"You've got the cheerleaders and the knockouts," said Wyatt, "who I call the Bigs, and you've got the outcasts, and they're the Littles. The girls you really have to worry about are the Mediums. They're perfectly nice-looking and they get decent grades, and they're polite, at least to people's faces. But once they get home and go online everything changes. Because the Mediums have opinions, about how everyone else should behave and about how the world should work. In their offline lives, most people won't listen to them. Okay, sometimes the Mediums have a few friends, but the Mediums keep telling them how to dress and who they should be dating, which is why after a while those friends start to drift away. Occasionally the Mediums will even have boyfriends but then the Mediums will start telling those boyfriends to tuck in their shirts and to drive more carefully and pretty soon those boyfriends start to drift away too, toward other girls who aren't quite so strict. While the Mediums are reasonably bright, they're never a whole lot of fun.

"All of this makes the Mediums deeply pissed off because they feel ignored. When the Mediums log on, watch out. They're suddenly all-powerful. They're in charge. If someone dares to disagree with them, well, that's what the delete button is for. A Killer Medium's favorite words are 'stupid' and 'boring,' or when they're really on fire, 'soooo stupid' and 'soooo boring.' When a Medium becomes passionate about something, a Killer Medium is born. A Killer Medium will take her obsessions very seriously and she'll tell her favorite pop star to lose ten pounds, and she'll critique her favorite TV star's kitchen, and she'll inform her favorite YouTube personality that she's using too much blush and looks like a whore. Once Ava Lily Larrimore had read and reread the *Angel Wars* books, well, just picture a Killer Medium with millions of Killer Medium followers, all primed to defend their turf. Sometimes I think that we should send all of the Killer Mediums to Afghanistan because al-Qaeda wouldn't stand a chance."

"I love the *Angel Wars* books," I said, "and I really hope that the movie is wonderful. Does that make me a Killer Medium?"

"No," said Wyatt, offering me a paper plate of Pepperidge Farm cookies. "You're too sweet and too anxious and too insane to ever become a Killer Medium. A Killer Medium would eat you for lunch. Don't get me wrong, I think it's fantastic that so many people love the *Angel Wars* books and see themselves in the characters. But Ava Lily Larrimore isn't just a fan— she's a dictator. She demands total obedience. Even Sarah Smilesborough, who wrote the books, has been freaking out. Sarah is a total sweetheart and she told me that at first she was incredibly flattered when Ava kept texting her and emailing her and sending her these thirty-eight-page handwritten letters about her favorite parts of the books, along with Instagrams of her guinea pigs, which are named Lynnea, Tallwen, Myke and Avianda."

"Who's Avianda?" I asked, wondering if I wasn't a proper Angel Warrior because maybe there was a character in the books named Avianda who I'd forgotten about.

"That's why Sarah got scared. Ava has sent her an outline for everything that Ava thinks should happen in a fourth *Angel Wars* book. She's demanding that Sarah create a character called Avianda, named after guess who, and Avianda is supposed to be even braver and prettier and more resourceful than Lynnea."

"But—doesn't Sarah Smilesborough always say that she's told the whole *Angel Wars* story and now she's working on a book about something completely new and different?"

"Yup, and she's been really clear about that. Which is why Ava Lily Larrimore has started showing up outside Sarah's house in North Carolina, dressed as Avianda, in order to make it clear that writing another *Angel Wars* book isn't really Sarah's choice. It's a direct command from the Grand Ultimate Take-No-Prisoners *Angel Wars* Authority."

"Oh my gosh!"

"Here's the ultimate key to the Killer Medium: She has absolutely no sense of humor. None. It's uncanny. If you say something funny to a Killer Medium or if you ask her to lighten up, she'll just stare at you and ask, 'Why did you say that?' Because on every level until the day she dies, the Killer Medium will never, ever get the joke."

"You guys?" said Nedda, appearing from inside Heller's dressing room. "She's ready."

twenty

Entering the Arena

When I walked into her dressing room, Heller turned around and I instantly became the biggest, most awestruck, most helpless, geekiest Angel Warrior who'd ever lived. I sailed light-years beyond Ava Lily Larrimore and her Killer Medium storm troopers. I was an *Angel Wars* love slave because I was looking at Lynnea.

In the books, at first Lynnea is an ordinary teenage girl who cuts her own brown hair, has to remember to wash her face and wears mostly jeans, plaid flannel shirts and her favorite hoodie; she's a cross between a tomboy and a pile of laundry. Once Lynnea's wings start to grow and she fully accepts her status as the Chosen Winglet, she's transformed. When she first flies into the arena and hovers a few feet off the ground, the crowd goes silent because, and I remember every word from the book: "Lynnea was now a creature of golden sunset and mystic starshine, a glorious Winglet newly born."

Thanks to Nedda, Kenz, and Heller's own gift for trans-forming herself, that's exactly what Heller looked like. She wasn't wearing her wings but her skin now had a golden glow, not like a suntan but more like the soft gleam from a polished piece of jewelry. Her hair was streaked with a thousand subtle shades of color, from the most innocently pale blonde to a bon-fire red, and it fell down her back almost to her waist, with Lynnea's two trademark narrow braids crossing right above her forehead like a crown. After a second I realized that Heller had to be wearing a wig but the effect was so natural and most likely expensive that it seemed real.

Heller was wearing Lynnea's fitted white linen tunic, braided golden belt and white linen pants tucked into high, white leather boots that didn't look fancy and fashionable but sturdy. Heller was also wearing Lynnea's necklace, which was a pair of golden wings that encircled her neck and that Myke had hammered and molded for her in his home workshop.

Heller was watching me very carefully, from inside Lynnea, which made me confused—who was she? Who should I talk to?

"Are you freaking out?" asked Heller. "Should I slap you really hard?"

"No! It's just, I don't know, I mean, look at you . . ."

"Guys?" said Heller, to Nedda and Kenz. "Could I talk to Catey alone, just for a second?"

After everyone had left, Heller held up her hands, center-ing herself. "Okay," she said, "I know that you hate me and you will never approve of anything I do, but this is a time-out, okay? Everyone else here, they're all great and I couldn't do any of this without them but they're all on my team so they're too close to tell me the truth. All of those thousands of Angel Warriors out there have their own ideas of exactly what Lynnea is supposed to look like and how she's supposed to behave. So tell me exactly what you really think—is this okay? Am I getting away with it?"

Heller was searching my face for an answer. I'd never felt so powerful. I could crush her.

"Heller," I said, "I'm not going to flatter you, or suck up to you, or try to make you happy."

"And . . . ?" said Heller, leaning forward. "Spit it out!"

"And . . ."

"Say it! Or I will rip your face off!"

"You don't look like Lynnea, the way I've always pictured her and the way everybody's always pictured her."

"Oh," said Heller, in a tiny, destroyed voice. "Fine. Thank you for your honesty."

"You ARE Lynnea."

"Really?" said Heller, as if she'd just died and then instantly bounced back to life. There were tears in her eyes and a second later there were tears in my eyes too. Neither of us wiped our eyes or even blinked or sniffled because neither of us would ever admit to caring about each other that much.

"Really, truly, yes in doody," I said without thinking, and then I remembered—this was something that Heller and I had said all the time when we were little, and it was something I hadn't said since that last day we'd been together, four years ago.

"Yes in doody?" said Heller, grinning. "Are you a Teletubby?"

"Get out there," I said. "And save the world."

As soon as Heller left her dressing room she was surrounded by her team, along with everyone's assistants and even more studio people and a pack of security guards wearing headsets and carrying all sorts of other tech devices.

Wyatt brought me to a front-row seat in what had been turned into the Netherdome. First of all, Madison Square Garden is the size of a football stadium; it's like a building where you could stack up airplane hangars and store them. When you fill up a place that enormous with people, the sound that all those people make, even before anything starts happening, is not only deafening, but enters every bone and organ in your body and makes them vibrate. On top of that, when all of those deafening, vibrating people are also the most passionate, vocal, overexcited Angel Warriors who've ever lived, the ultimate effect is very intense; it was like being inside the official *Angel Wars* website just a few seconds before the second or third books were released and everyone in the Angelsphere had logged on and they were all Skyping and texting and tweeting that THEY COULDN'T WAIT ONE MORE SECOND OR THEY WOULD DIE, THEY WOULD LITERALLY DIE, I'M NOT EVEN KIDDING!!!

"This is really something, isn't it," said Wyatt, who I didn't think was easily impressed. "Look at all of these people. It's like a combination of one of those mega-churches, a ticker tape parade and that intergalactic bar in *Star Wars*." Looking around, I could see what Wyatt meant, because the sold-out-to-the-rafters crowd included zillions of sobbing girls my age and younger, all clutching one another and standing on their seats and holding up their phones to take pictures of the arena and of each other taking pictures. There were the parents of the really little kids, and the parents were every bit as excited as their six-year-olds, and there were the most committed, serious Angel Warriors of all: These were adult men and women of every age, race and size, who were each either costumed as a character from the books or smothered in *Angel Wars* merchandise.

The stuff these people were wearing or holding included glow-stick halos mounted on *Angel Wars* baseball caps; oversized *Angel Wars* T-shirts silk-screened with the logo from the movie; *Angel Wars* tote bags filled with special triple-platinum editions of the books featuring three additional pages; plastic golden crossbows; and, of course, plastic harnesses, which were attached to the little sets of plastic golden wings on everyone's backs. These wings were making the people wearing them lean forward, which made them look even more eager and overheated. I don't want this to sound in any way mean because everyone looked amazing, but when a grown man wears a little set of plastic wings, getting him to actually fly might present an aerodynamic challenge.

"Check your phone," said Wyatt. "#AWLiveEvent."

Wyatt showed me how to do this and every split second there were tweets:

CANT BELIEVE IM HERE!!!

IF TALLWEN LOOKS AT ME IM GONNA
SKREAM!!!

ANGELS EVERYWHERE—AM I IN HEAVEN???

MYKE ROX!!!

TALLWEN ROX HARDER U STUPID HO!!!!!!!!!!!!!

I looked around the arena and I wished that I had my
own halo, tote bag and set of wings, because it was incredible. In the book, Mistress Miracle uses a monastery of one
hundred devout Buddhist monks to painstakingly create the
world's largest and most elaborate mandala, which is an impossibly intricate set of drawings made entirely from different
colors of sand.

I don't know who the studio hired to create the *Angel Wars*
mandala inside Madison Square Garden but it was magnifi-
cent: The entire floor, which seemed to go on for miles, was
covered with a perfectly smooth layer of truckload upon truckload of the finest grains of sand worked into pictures of all the
stars of the movie and moments from the major scenes. While
a painting that large and that specific would have been breath-
taking, the fact that all of these images were made entirely of
sand, and of sand that hadn't been glued into place, made the
whole arena seem precarious and sacred and magical and also
like the world's largest billboard for the books and the movie,

and I wanted to tell everyone to be really careful and to hold their breath so that we wouldn't disturb or destroy even an inch of the mandala.

OMG IS THAT ALL SAND???

LYNNEA IS BETTER THAN KATNISS OR TRIS!!!

HELLER SUX BUT LYNNEA RULES!!!

IM UP IN TOP ROW IM GONNA FLY!!!

SKYLER SIT DOWN!!!!!!

The lights in the arena changed dramatically, with lasers blasting out over the crowd's heads, which made everyone scream. Electronic music from the movie's soundtrack boomed, which made everyone scream even more, and I started to understand what this event was all about because it allowed the fans to be included in the whole *Angel Wars* phenomenon, through screaming. I've never been to a rock concert but I've heard that there's always lots of screaming and that the screaming sometimes drowns out the music but that no one minds because fans can always listen to the music once they're back home or in their cars. At a Singing Singleberries concert, we usually have more polite audiences who applaud at the end of each song and who'll only clap along with the beat if my dad raises his arms over his head and starts clapping first to let everybody know that it's okay.

"This is fabulous!" Wyatt told me, over the noise. "It's *Angel Wars*–palooza!"

> ITS STARTING SO EXCITED BUT I HAVE TO
> PEE!!!!!
>
> ---
>
> CAN U FEEL MAGIC EVERYWHERE????
>
> ---
>
> SO HAPPY! CANT BREATHE! BEST DAY EVER!!!!
>
> ---
>
> SKYLER JUST HOLD IT!!!!!!

All the lights went out and a huge face appeared on three Jumbotron screens that had been lowered from the ceiling. It was a woman's face, and her mane of white hair had a life of its own, streaming and curling with the tendrils forming yin and yang symbols, hearts and exclamation points.

"I am Mistress Miracle," said the woman, and everyone screamed again as the woman smiled. "Welcome to the AllSouls Universium. Today we decide the fate of all humankind, and I shall require the assistance of all in attendance. Are you ready to fully participate, in the triumph of goodness or the onslaught of evil?"

This caused the loudest screaming yet and I had no idea which side the crowd was on or if it mattered. What mattered was that Mistress Miracle was here and she was talking to us.

"That's Caroline McNaught," Wyatt told me. "She has three Oscars but no one here cares. From now on, she's Mistress Miracle."

"As you know," said Mistress Miracle, "each realm has chosen a combatant to represent their interests. Who shall battle on behalf of the Golden Lord and all that is righteous?"

A shaft of light burst from the heavens, and there was Heller, up near the ceiling, aloft on her glorious golden wings with a span of at least twelve feet. I could see the individual feathers fluttering. I knew that Heller must be on wires but those wires were so thin and transparent they became invisible and Heller really seemed to be flying and the crowd went ballistic, with everyone, but especially the girls, sobbing and hugging one another as Lynnea, who they'd read about and dreamed of and talked about for years, came to life. Even more amazingly, I could tell that the crowd wasn't just watching an astonishing special effect—they were watching Heller, because through her talent and her determination and her stardom, she was making them watch.

Heller gradually swooped to earth, landing at one side of the mandala with a gentle whoosh. As her wings gracefully folded and detached, allowing Heller to move freely, a radiant halo appeared over her head, and the halo seemed to be free-floating and followed Heller's every move.

"I am Lynnea, the Chosen Winglet, and I shall defend the Golden Lands," said Heller, and her voice had been amplified so that while she was speaking simply and clearly, she could be heard throughout the arena.

LYNNEA SO BEAUTIFUL AND BRAVE!!!!

I WANT LYNNEA BRAIDS!!!!

NAMING MY BABY EITHER LYNNEA OR
MACKENZIE CAN'T DECIDE

HELLER GAIN WEIGHT????

"Who will battle for the Darkling Creeper, on behalf of the Destervoid and all that is unholy?"

Another shaft of light appeared at the opposite end of the arena, only this light was tinted purple and contained a slashing black rain and I wasn't sure if this rain was water or black glitter but it was hurricane-force. A girl appeared near the ceiling and she seemed to be riding the rain as she slithered to the floor of the arena. This girl was dressed just the way Malestra is described in the book, in a tight black jumpsuit that gleamed like armor, with a stiff collar and a crown with high, jagged black spikes. A cobra rose from this crown, spitting and hissing at least ten feet in the air, right at the crowd, and then the cobra disappeared as everyone gasped.

"I am Malestra," said the girl, "and I serve the Darkling Creeper and his regiments of necessary doom!"

MALESTRA SO EVIL!!!!

AVA LOOKIN GOOD!!!!

IF MALESTRA WINS UNIVERSE IS DOOMED!
EEEK!!!!!!

LUV U AVA KILL HELLER!!!!!

The girl's voice, which had been amplified, made me realize the difference between how an experienced actress speaks and how a regular person comes across. While Heller had sounded straightforward, her voice had been filled with emotion, with pride and torment, as if Lynnea knew that she was doing something important but the responsibility was tearing her apart.

"Ava Lily Larrimore," said Wyatt, pointing to Malestra. Ava's voice was less passionate and even a little high-pitched and nasal, like a girl you might overhear at a restaurant complaining about her salad and asking to see the manager. Ava was perfect as Malestra because she sounded like she was about to stomp her foot and tell everyone in the arena to shut up because she was talking.

The crowd hissed "Malestra" and Ava raised her arms for silence, proclaiming, "You will all serve the Creeper! You will bow low!"

"I've never thought of this before," said Wyatt, "but doesn't the name Malestra sound like a new antidepressant that would make you feel even worse?"

"The first round!" said Mistress Miracle. "A battle of words! Malestra, should you prevail, what form will our world inhabit?"

"Our world," said Malestra, just like in the book, "will at last become a realm of constant deceit, of delicious inhumanity, and of joyous dread. There is an evil in every one of us, in every soul here tonight, and the Darkling Creeper shall nourish that evil and allow it to bloom within the horror of an eternal night!"

"Ava should know," said Wyatt.

"Lynnea?" said Mistress Miracle, and Heller waited a few

seconds before she spoke, as if she needed to say exactly the right thing.

"If I win . . . ," said Heller, and there was an overpowering hum because everyone in the arena knew this speech by heart and loved it and was murmuring the words right along with Heller. "No. This battle is not mine alone. I fight for all of us, for anyone who hopes and prays and dreams that goodness is possible. I fight for the Golden Lord, who has taught me, who has taught all of us, that the need for kindness and compassion and love, this need is always a struggle. I fight so that for perhaps a brief moment, the world can stop fighting."

There was a pause and then Mistress Miracle announced, "Round One—to the Chosen Winglet!"

Everyone, and especially me and even Wyatt, screamed, whistled and cheered, and all of the girls made heart shapes using their thumbs and fingers.

GO LYNNEA!!!! SO PURE AND SWEET LIKE
CUPCAKE OF GLORY!!!!!

CHOSEN WINGLET WILL BRING GOODNESS!!!!!

I AM LYNNEA ONLY HOTTER!!!!

DREAM ON KORTNEY

"Silence!" said Mistress Miracle. "The day is far from won! Round Two—a battle of commitment and allies. Who stands with Lynnea?"

Laser beams crisscrossed the mandala-covered floor like searchlights and then a corner of sand swirled into a tornado-like cone and when the sand settled there was Tallwen, standing a few yards from Lynnea. By which I mean there was Mills, who was visibly bruised and wearing ripped, stained linen because earlier in the day he'd been ambushed by Dastroids. He had wings but one of them was bent nearly in half. Most shockingly of all, Mills's hair was flat and greasy.

POOR TALLWEN!!! DASTROID HAIR!!!!

CAN HE STILL FLY???

DON'T CARE!!! WOULD STILL DO HIM!!! STELTERFOKKEN SO HOT!!!!!

EMMA SHUT UP!!!!!!!

"I am Tallwen," said Mills, his voice shaking, "of the Stelterfokken, who have nurtured the Winglet and watched over her. I am assigned to protect Lynnea from all foes and wrongdoing. I will stand beside her, unto my death."

"But if you die, who will protect her, oh brave and battered one?" asked Mistress Miracle.

"I will!" shouted Myke, and everyone in the arena swiveled their heads as a spotlight found Billy, hanging in a fiery cage high over the arena. Billy was wearing bits of shredded and dented armor that Myke had made from recycled coffee cans. Billy's arms and legs were manacled; in the books Myke is always getting kidnapped and beaten up and brainwashed so that Lynnea has to rescue him, usually when she's right in the middle of trying to defeat the Darkling Creeper. If he hadn't been so cute, Myke might have been annoying, like a little kid who keeps wandering off and getting into trouble.

"I am Myke!" said Billy. "I am but a humble potter and poet and leathercrafter from New Hampshire! I believe in Lynnea and all that she represents! I will stand with her at all costs!"

AM CRYING MYKE SO BEAUTIFUL!!!!

MYKE = LOVE EVEN IF SHORT!!!!!

WOULD FUK TALLWEN BUT MARRY MYKE!!!!!

U R DISGUSTING BUT RIGHT!!!!!!!

"Malestra?" said Mistress Miracle and everyone turned toward Ava, who smiled. She clapped her hands and from the blackness high overhead at least fifty children, all dressed completely in glittering black, with hoods, descended on ropes with silent, lightning speed, like special-ops ninjas or an exploding nest of spiders. Once they'd reached the floor these children all ran to Malestra and gathered at her feet, cackling and kicking the sand in order to demolish large sections of the mandala.

"My child army stands with me," said Malestra. "Their souls have been secured and they live only to serve. Children of darkness?"

At Malestra's command, all of the children tilted their

heads back and howled, and the sound was electronically magnified to become even harsher and more terrifying, like a pack of starving wolves who'd just come across a church picnic. As the howling peaked, each child held up a flare gun that shot purple flames high into the night, backed by the augmented sounds of machine-gun fire, and the arena was filled with smoke and chaos, as if the world was ending.

"Malestra's companions are mindless and enslaved," said Mistress Miracle over the din. "They will question nothing. Lynnea's companions are steadfast and free yet easily captured. Round Two—the victory is Malestra's!"

BOOOOOOO!!!!! HATE U MALESTRA!!!!!!

SO WORRIED ABOUT UNIVERSE!!!!!

MALESTRA EVIL BUT SO COOL!!! AVA THE BEST!!!!!!!

I WUZ MALESTRA 4 HALLOWEEN!!!!!

"The final round!" decreed Mistress Miracle. "A battle to the death! According to our Universium bylaws, flight, supernatural assistance and gunplay are not permitted. All else is allowed. Lynnea, Malestra—enter the circle of destiny."

The crowd hushed as the overhead lighting dimmed, while bulbs built into the floor outlined a circle at the very center of the mandala. Lynnea and Malestra stepped into this circle from opposite sides and Lynnea said, "Malestra, I wish you no harm. We can end this right now, simply by refusing to fight each other. Why can't we leave this circle together, arm in arm, as friends?"

"Agreed," said Malestra, and the two girls walked toward each other. Lynnea gave a special angel wave and then stretched out her arm, offering her hand in peace. Malestra grasped Lynnea's hand and then kicked Lynnea's leg out from under her, sending her sprawling.

"I'm not your friend," said Malestra. "I'm here to prevail!"

Lynnea leaped to her feet and crouched as she and Malestra circled each other like sumo wrestlers. Lynnea seemed to reach for Malestra but it was a trick. I'm not sure how she managed this but Heller soared over Ava's head, touching down right behind her, where she wrenched both of Ava's arms behind her back. Ava then sank her teeth into Heller's shoulder and Heller yelped in pain and let go.

"Did they rehearse all of this?" I asked Wyatt. "Because just now when Ava bit Heller, it looked like it really hurt."

"It's been completely choreographed and they've been practicing the whole thing," said Wyatt, who sounded concerned. "But I don't remember anyone biting."

Ava was now pursuing Heller, shoving and kickboxing her. From the darkness, outside the circle, someone tossed Lynnea her golden crossbow, but Malestra caught it and hurled it into the audience where at least ten Angel Warriors grabbed for what could become a very valuable souvenir, like a home-run baseball caught in the stands at a World Series.

"In the book, doesn't Lynnea catch the crossbow and use it?" I asked Wyatt.

"Of course Lynnea is supposed to catch the crossbow!" said Wyatt, who was looking around frantically for the security guards. "I don't know what Ava is up to, but they have to stop her!"

Heller was holding up her hands as if she was trying to surrender and stop the fight but Ava kept going after her, grabbing Heller's hair and landing what looked like a really painful jab right in Heller's stomach. I saw that Ava had either a dagger or a hunting knife tucked into her belt.

"WYATT?" I said, but Wyatt was gone to track down the guards. Because I was sitting so close, I could see that Heller looked genuinely terrified, but to the crowd it was still part of the show. I stood up and grabbed the railing in front of me, as the size of Madison Square Garden and the presence of so many people crashed over me. I felt like I was going to faint.

Focus on helping Heller. Focus on stopping Ava from hurting or even killing Heller. Do your job.

The girl in the seat next to me was wearing a homemade Dastroid costume with a knee-length black vest, a pointed helmet with a visor that covered half her face, and a sword, called a Lucifoil, where the blade ended in what was designed to look like two very sharp devil's horns.

"I'll give you ten dollars for your Dastroid outfit!" I told the girl.

"No way!" said the girl. "My mom made this! It took her a whole weekend!"

"Twenty dollars!" I said, which would use up a major chunk of the emergency fund that my dad had tucked into one of my extra pairs of rolled-up kneesocks. "And you can meet Lynnea in private after the show! Just do it!"

A few seconds later I was wearing the Dastroid outfit and I was standing right at the opening to the arena floor.

Save Heller's life. Trounce evil. Do your job, bitch.

Did I really just call myself bitch?

Heller and Ava were now wrestling on the ground and rolling in the sand and Ava was reaching for her knife. The crowd was screaming:

"KILL HER!"

"SAVE THE GOLDEN LANDS!"

"HERE COMES THE CREEPER!!!!"

I took a step into the arena and froze because I made the mistake of looking around, which made me feel completely exposed. Thousands of people were standing and yelling. The lights and the iron catwalks and other chunks of machinery dangled and swayed high overhead, as if they might fall at any second, and there was sand everywhere, swirling into clouds of choking dust.

I CAN'T DO THIS! I'm not a gladiator or a security guard or a special-ops ninja or anything useful! I started to shake uncontrollably, as if my skeleton was falling apart, and my newly acquired Lucifoil wobbled in my hand. I was having a massive panic attack.

SAVE HELLER'S LIFE!

"Catey!" said Heller, crouching on the ground. Catching

Heller off guard, Ava slammed Heller onto her back and strad-
dled her.

There was a microphone dangling from a wire a few inches
from my face. I grabbed it and yelled, so my voice blasted
throughout the arena: "I AM AVIANDA!"

Ava held for a second, with Heller pinned underneath her.

The crowd stopped yelling and began buzzing with questions: "Who's Avianda?" "She's not in the books!" "Isn't there an
Avianda in Lord of the Rings? Is she an Orc princess?" "Look,
she's got a Lucifoil!"

"BOW LOW BEFORE AVIANDA!" I howled. "THE
EVEN MORE EVIL DAUGHTER OF THE DARKLING
CREEPER! SPAWN OF THE CREEPER AND . . . THE
SUCCUBUS OF SARWELLIA!!!!"

"You're not Avianda!" said Ava, and I could finally see her
face and all I could think was—she really is a Killer Medium!
Even in her fancy custom-made Malestra outfit, Ava Lily
Larrimore looked like a seriously snitty, outraged girl who'd
gotten eliminated in the first round of a spelling bee and
who'd demanded a do-over and who'd still lost. She had nice
skin, beady eyes that were too close together and one of those
little upturned noses that some people call a button nose and
my brothers would call a pig's snout. She had too much smoky
eye makeup, which was supposed to make her look like Malestra
but instead made her look like a surprised panda.

"I don't know who you are!" said Ava. "But Heller Harrigan
is going to die!"

"Holy shit!" screamed Heller.

Ava swung her knife and Heller struggled and tried to yell but she was so scared that no sound came out. At the last second Ava leaned over and whispered something in Heller's ear that made Heller's face go white and she stopped struggling, as if it wasn't the knife that had defeated her but Ava's words.

"You know I'm right," I heard Ava tell Heller and Heller just stared up at Ava and nodded as if she was agreeing with her, which scared me more than anything else.

I screamed like a banshee even though I wasn't sure exactly what a banshee was or what a banshee's scream might sound like and I ran right at Ava Lily Larrimore and I used my Lucifoil to smack the knife right out of her hand. I dragged her off Heller, put my foot on Ava's chest and held my Lucifoil to her throat. I grabbed Ava's microphone and proclaimed to the arena, "MALESTRA IS DEFEATED! AND THE MOVIE IS GOING TO BE TOTALLY AWESOME!!!!!"

The crowd managed to scream even louder than all of their previous screaming put together. The security guards swarmed onto the mandala and surrounded Ava and led her away while she sputtered, "But I'm Avianda! I was going to post it on the website!"

I raised my head to watch the cheering, ecstatic fans and I am ashamed to say this but I felt fantastic; I felt the way people describe being on drugs or having sex or naked bungee jumping. I'd just championed the forces of goodness and saved Lynnea and maybe the universe. Maybe this would be the solution, to my panic attacks and my anxiety and the fact that I had no idea what I was supposed to be doing with my life. Instead of going to college I would travel the world, battling evil in all sorts of arenas as part of an *Angel Wars* ice show or an *Angel Wars* monster truck rally. I really was a hero because I'd won the day and I should call my parents and try not to brag about what a great job I was doing and about how their painfully anxious, socially backward daughter had just rescued Heller from an assault by a crazed stalker in front of thousands of cheering Angel Warriors.

Heller was going to weep for the terrible things she'd said and done to me, and she was going to bow her head as she asked for my help, and I was going to smile modestly and say, "Of course I'll help you, because I'm a servant of the Lord. Let's start with you writing an essay on the true meaning of friendship."

When I turned to help Heller stand up, she was gone.

Wyatt was on his phone. "She left," I heard him tell whoever he was talking to. "She ran out and she didn't tell anyone where she was going. Do you know something? I don't blame her."

twenty-one

A Dastroid in Times Square

Of course Heller hadn't bothered to thank me or hug me or see if I was okay. Instead she'd done what she always did: She ran away. Just the way four years ago after she'd almost gotten me killed, I'd never heard from her. Just the way she'd left New Jersey and headed to California to become a star, leaving everyone else—and especially me—behind to clean up her mess.

I'd saved Heller in the arena and I was going to track her down and not just make her behave, oh no. My job, and my confidence level, were way beyond that. I was going to find Heller and I was going to force her to finish promoting the movie, and then I was going to dump her, the way she'd dumped me. She was hopeless. She was beyond true salvation. I was going to do my job, as a righteous Christian, and then I would send her to Hades, where Satan would say, "Welcome home."

Only first I had to find her.

I ran, pushing my way through the mobs of Angel Warriors and up an escalator—yes! Even though escalators still scared me I didn't just grab the rubber railings and hope for the best— I took the escalator two steps at a time, while they were moving! I saw daylight and I moved toward it and then I was outside in the cool early evening air in the middle of New York City. On my trip so far I'd always been inside limos or vans or buildings, so for the first time I was facing the city itself.

People were hurtling in every direction and cars and trucks and buses seemed to be aiming right at one another as all of the drivers leaned out their windows to shake their fists and curse. Other people were riding bicycles and skateboards and weaving in and out of traffic on both the streets and the sidewalks, just to cause even more cursing.

New York City was everything that terrified me and it instantly triggered my shortness of breath and my brain frenzy. When I shut my eyes for a few seconds to eliminate at least one of my senses, I felt someone brush past me and reach inside my Dastroid tunic to either grope me or to see if I was carrying anything worth stealing. My eyes shot open and I ran, immediately crashing into three more people; the first one asked, "Are you okay?" while the second one said, "Excuse me" and the third one muttered, "Fucking tourists."

As my eyes darted everywhere and I could feel the panic rising in my chest and cutting off my supply of oxygen, I began to wonder if I was too young to be having a heart attack and I remembered why my parents had forbidden me to research extreme medical conditions online, because as my mom had said, "You'll either think you have them or you'll want to." I caught a glimpse of Heller's now grimy linen tunic from at least two blocks away. Heller was moving in what I was pretty sure was an uptown direction but when I yelled, "Heller!" she was either too far away and couldn't hear me or she'd heard me but I was the last person on earth she wanted to see. Which was too bad for her because I was going to catch her and I was going to make her see me. I was going to shove her against a wall and make her say, "Caitlin, I've been wrong about every-thing and you've been right. Blazers can be a powerful fashion statement."

I took off after Heller and the first thing I did was to get slammed by someone opening the rear door of a taxi. I fell backward toward the pavement but I managed to grab the taxi door and pull myself up.

I thought, Okay—I was just hit by a car and I survived. I'm still functioning. A terrible thing has happened and I haven't died. I stood up and said, "I'm really sorry!" to the guy getting out of the cab and I ran across the intersection, telling the pedestrians things like "I'm sorry! Excuse me! Coming through! I'm from New Jersey!"

Once I reached the opposite side of the street I stood on tiptoes and I saw a tiny bit of white linen in the distance amid a mob of people surging uptown. I kept going, trying to slide in between people or dance around them and I started thinking, This is what it's like to be a New Yorker. Maybe the reason why some New Yorkers get so angry is because they spend all their time trying to get the older people with canes and the younger couples who are holding hands to move out of the way. A wicked part of my brain wanted to yell at one couple, "I don't care if he's your boyfriend! You can tongue-kiss him all you want once you get home!"

I traveled a few more blocks, always trying to keep Heller or some identifiable part of her in view. I was closing in on her, I was only a few yards away, when someone grabbed my elbow and asked, "Can we get a picture?"

What was going on? Why would anyone want a picture of me? The woman who'd asked was dressed like my mom, in seersucker culottes, a fanny pack and a yellow cotton sweater with ducks on it. She was standing next to a man who reminded me of my dad except he had two cameras around his neck and was holding a folding map of the city. The man and the woman were surrounded by five kids from around four years old to their early teens and some of them were wearing green foam rubber crowns with spikes like the Statue of Liberty. The littlest girl had on a pair of oversized sunglasses. This family of tourists was staring at me as if I was the Empire State Building or a horse-drawn carriage in Central Park.

"Are you really a Dastroid?" asked one of the daughters, in awe.

"Kelli loves the *Angel Wars* books," said the mom—I knew that Kelli spelled her name with an i because that was how it appeared in sequins on her hot-pink sweatshirt.

"Can we get a picture of you with Kelli?" asked the dad. "Can you put your arm around her and look mean?"

I was still wearing the Dastroid costume that I'd bought from that girl at Madison Square Garden, including the tunic, the hat and the Lucifoil. I saw that I was standing in a section of Times Square. Within a few feet were people dressed up as Batman, Iron Man, Wolverine, a Teenage Mutant Ninja Turtle, Cinderella, Princess Jasmine, Mulan and at least three Spider-Men of very different heights and weights, as if there was a Spider-Man family like the Three Bears. Tourists were having their pictures taken with all of these costumed characters, who were smiling and posing.

"Oh, gee, I'm really sorry," I told the tourist family, "but I'm not really a Dastroid and I'm in a super-big hurry."

"Mommy, she is too a Dastroid!" said another daughter. "She has a Lucifoil!"

"Dastroids suck," said one of the girl's brothers. "Is there a Darkling Creeper around? I think I just saw Lynnea."

"You saw Lynnea?" I said. "Which way did she go?"

"I wish you were Elsa," said one of the really little girls. "She's pretty and she lives in an ice palace with a snowman."

"Please?" asked the dad, so I put my arm around Kelli and as the dad took the picture, the brother pointed and said, "Lynnea went that way."

"Are you going to kill Lynnea?" asked the littlest girl.

"No!" I said. "I'm really one of the Stelterfokken only I'm working undercover!"

"Here you go, thanks so much," said the mom, handing me a ten-dollar bill.

"Oh, no thank you and I have to go," I said because I couldn't accept money for just standing there and waving my Lucifoil around.

"I'll take it," said someone who was dressed as the Little Mermaid and she grabbed the money and shoved it down her seashell bra.

I looked where the brother had been pointing, and I saw Lynnea's tunic turning a corner half a block away.

"Stay golden!" I said to the tourist family, using one of the Golden Lord's favorite expressions as I squirmed past Captain America, who said, "Whoa, Dastroid. Nice kneesocks."

I raced across an open plaza, shouting "Heller!" and as I grabbed Heller's arm she turned around and said, "What? I'm off duty, asshole" and I realized that she was someone else wearing a Lynnea costume.

"I'm so sorry!" I said. "But Lynnea would never use the a-word!"

"Stupid Dastroid," the wrong Lynnea muttered as she took a bite of her bagel. I saw another Lynnea who looked more like Heller going down into the subway and I ran.

I'd never been anywhere near a subway so once I'd gone down the steps I was lost. I saw the other Lynnea using some sort of passcard to go through a turnstile so I tried to shove the credit card that my dad had given me for emergency use into a slot but it didn't work and I saw that up ahead Lynnea was waiting for a subway that was just pulling into the station. I did the worst thing I have ever done in my life. I boosted myself up over the turnstile and onto the other side.

I WAS A CRIMINAL! I couldn't believe it: Caitlin Mary Prudence Rectitude Singleberry had just jumped over a New York City turnstile without paying the fare! Like a thief or a murderer! Yes, I was chasing after Heller, so I had a good reason for my crime, but isn't that just what all criminals say once they've been apprehended? What was happening to me? What would I do next? Pick someone's pocket? Blow up a cash machine? And why, instead of having a pounding anxiety attack, was I feeling almost—exhilarated?

Then a uniformed transit officer said, "Hey, you! With the witch's hat! Fare jumper!" and came after me.

I told him, "I'm really, really sorry and I'm not a witch, I'm a Dastroid and I have to go! I'll mail you the money!" I ran over to the train just as Heller, or possibly some other Lynnea, boarded the same train two cars farther up. Since all the doors were about to close I leaped onto the car in front of me. The doors slammed shut and as the train began to move I saw the transit officer through the window shaking his fist and yelling something I was grateful I couldn't hear.

The car was jam-packed with every kind of person, including men in suits and uniformed waitresses and teenagers with headphones and moms with strollers that held babies and groceries. While I was smushed up against many other people, no one was looking at me or at anyone else. Everyone was lost in their own thoughts, their music or the video games they were playing on their phones. I knew that I should be passing out from anxiety especially because of all the germs I was being exposed to, but I wasn't. Then I remembered something from

my online searches about social phobias. Unless you're claus-
trophobic, being hemmed in can sometimes make anxious
people feel more secure and almost comforted. In fact, the
most modern slaughterhouses are designed to keep cattle
immobilized in padded spaces so they'll feel safer just before
they're turned into Big Macs and pot roasts.

I didn't have time to wonder if I was about to become an
entrée because I needed to squeeze through the car and locate
Heller. What was she about to do? Rip off her Lynnea outfit
and take a naked selfie? Dance in one of those places where
girls swing around brass poles? Get so drunk that she'd vomit
on a nun and laugh?

Goddamn her! Goddamn Heller Harrigan!

Heller had done it. Heller had made me take the Lord's
name in vain. She'd turned me into a fare jumper and a nightclub goer and a blasphemer. This wasn't just personal, not
anymore. This was a holy crusade.

We reached the next stop and the doors opened and half
the people in the car basically fell out onto the platform. I saw
that Lynnea had left her car as well so I got out and let the
crowd carry me, still following what I prayed was Heller's tunic
and hair, up a stairway, through a tiled tunnel and up a final set
of stairs and out onto the street. I tried to yell "Heller!" but I
didn't have much of a voice left so I stumbled after her as she
went through a set of revolving doors and into an older and not
very clean building.

By the time I got through the revolving doors I saw Heller
at the end of a hallway pushing open a wooden door. I ran down

the hall just as the door was closing and I slipped inside, where
I expected to find—what? A storeroom crawling with cock-
roaches where Heller would be buying drugs from a gang
member? A sleazy motel room where Heller was meeting Oliver
to have sex atop a bedspread bubbling with other people's sex
bacteria? Or was it something even worse, something so
immoral and putrid and revolting that I couldn't even imagine
it, because I wasn't Heller Harrigan!

I was in a small wood-paneled room with a few rows of
folding chairs facing a raised platform. There was a table off to
one side with a stack of leaflets, a pitcher of water, paper cups
and an open box of doughnuts, most of which were gone. There
were about fifteen people in the room, men and women, facing
the platform. Just like on the subway, these people were all
different: There was a woman in a designer-y looking camel-
colored skirt and jacket with a leather briefcase on her lap and
she was sitting next to a young guy who looked like a bicycle
messenger in spandex shorts and a little cap with a battered
canvas bag slung over the back of his chair.

Heller was standing at the front of the room in the tattered
remains of her Lynnea outfit. Her hair was a mess but she
looked more like her real self. She downed an entire cup of
water and wiped her mouth. Everyone else in the room was
quiet and no one was checking their phones or anything else.

"Hi, I'm Heller and I'm an alcoholic," said Heller.

"Hi, Heller," said everyone else in the room.

twenty-two

Kill Me Now

Oh my gosh. Oh my Lord. I wasn't positive because I'd never been to one before but I was pretty sure I was in a meeting of Alcoholics Anonymous. While I was incredibly relieved that Heller was here, I also felt embarrassed and ashamed because I knew these meetings were only for alcoholics and the anonymous part meant the meetings were supposed to be private. I had no business being here; I was a spy and an interloper and I should leave immediately, only I didn't want to call attention to myself by sneaking out. I decided to be honest and respectful.

"I am so very sorry!" I announced. "But I am not an alcoholic!"

Everyone was looking at me.

"I do not even enjoy grape-flavored soda!"

Everyone was looking at me as if I was insane.

"But I admire alcoholics! I mean, I admire alcoholics who have stopped drinking! I mean, I admire alcoholics who have stopped drinking alcohol! I'm sure there are many acceptable and delicious beverages that will not destroy your families and leave you rolling in the gutter!"

It was time for me to die.

"Catey, it's okay," said Heller, and then to everyone else, "That's Catey and she's my cousin and she's homeschooled."

Everyone said "Ah" and "Of course" and nodded at one another, as Heller continued: "If it's all right with everybody, I'd like her to stay for just a few minutes. I'd like her to hear this."

Heller was an actress and a star, so she was used to being watched by a lot of people, but I could tell this was different. While Heller couldn't stop being beautiful and magnetic and funny even if she tried, right now she was making an effort to be clear instead of performing.

"Um, okay," she said. "I'm an actress and for a while now I've been working on staying sober and not letting my job drive me crazy and not letting the whole scene make me want to drink just so I can—stop all the noise. I've been doing okay because I've been focusing on exercise and good habits and, oh my God, on being as boring as I possibly can.

"Today and this whole weekend have been kind of a test. I have a movie coming out so I've been doing lots of promotion, which is part of my job, and I'm grateful for the opportunity. About half an hour ago I was in the middle of Madison Square Garden surrounded by twenty thousand screaming Angel

Warriors and this other, fairly disturbed girl, and I'm putting that nicely; she had me pinned to the ground with a knife to my throat."

Heller grinned and said, "We've all been there, right?" and everyone laughed because Heller knew just how loony her life had become.

"Then something else happened. Something I didn't see coming, not by a mile, and I wasn't ready for it and I'm kind of a tough cookie. This other girl, the one with the grudge and the knife, she was operating pretty far into her own fantasyland and God only knows what else she was dealing with in her own life but she's smart in a satanic hall monitor sort of way and, well . . . do you know how we all have these triggers? These situations that we can get ourselves into and these things that other people can say to us that can really . . . well, they can really make a mojito or a cold bottle of beer seem like the best idea of all time, you know?"

Everyone nodded and I knew what Heller was talking about when she'd said triggers. I have more triggers than probably anyone else in the world. If I had to start making a list of things that trigger my anxiety I'd start with opening my eyes in the morning and soon I'd need a few hundred more legal pads.

"I'm lying on the ground in some very fancy Buddhist dirt and I'm all dolled up for a job that means the world to me and this girl, she leans over and she whispers in my ear, 'I talked to someone who saw your movie and they said you were terrible in it. They said you don't know what you're doing and the movie is going to be a huge bomb and it's all your fault.' Then she smiled."

Everyone in the room, and especially me, gasped. At that moment I hated Ava Lily Larrimore more than I'd ever hated anyone in my whole life. Maybe Ava had her reasons and maybe she loved the *Angel Wars* books just a little too much or maybe she was just nasty and vicious and jealous, but right then I didn't want to understand her or excuse her behavior or laugh the whole thing off. I wanted to kill Ava Lily Larrimore with my Lucifoil for telling Heller exactly the one thing Heller didn't need to hear. Because a part of Heller, a very important and vulnerable part, believed it.

"After that girl said what she'd said, I had two choices: I could grab her knife and cut her throat, which wasn't such a good idea because then I'd go to jail, where I'd have way too much free time to think about how untalented I am. My second choice, of course, was to find a liquor store and buy a bottle of Jack Daniel's in a nice brown paper bag and to head over to Central Park, where I could find a nice park bench hidden behind a nice oak tree where I could drink until I couldn't remember a single word out of that girl's mouth.

"Then something even nuttier happened. As I was trying to remember if the closest liquor store was in the train station next door or in the hotel lobby across the street, there was Catey. She'd been standing there, wearing the most absurd outfit, as you may have noticed—she looks like the love child of Darth Vader and the Wicked Witch of the West. Catey did something that wasn't easy for her because she's got some major demons of her own even though she thinks that nobody knows about them. But she put on that ridiculous hat and she pretty much saved my life. For which . . . I thank her."

I couldn't believe it. For the first time ever, Heller had said thank you. To me.

Everyone turned around to take another look at me and they all nodded as if they were saying, Gee, for a girl in a home-made Dastroid costume, you did a good thing.

"Which led me to a third choice, the hard choice and the disgusting, no-fun-at-all-in-any-way-shape-or-form choice. To not drink and to come here.

"For right now, here's how I'm trying to think. I'm trying to think that the girl who was so eager to hurt me, the girl who wanted so desperately to make me feel as bad about myself as I possibly can, well, just maybe, that girl was wrong. Maybe she doesn't actually know someone who's seen my movie because no one's seen my movie; hell, even I haven't seen my movie. Or maybe she's right and maybe I have no talent and maybe the movie will be the most catastrophic dud of all time, but you know what? She doesn't know that. I won't give her that power. I'm gonna try not to give anyone that power, to make me feel that terrible about myself. Thank you."

Everyone started clapping, and I saw Oliver sitting in the front row smiling at Heller and clapping harder than anyone.

twenty-three

A Really Long Day

Yeah, Oliver is my sponsor," Heller told me while we were walking back to the hotel. "Whenever things are getting truly dicey and I really want to drink, I call him up and he talks to me. Right after I left Madison Square Garden I called him and he used his GPS to figure out where the nearest meeting was."

"Is Oliver also . . . your boyfriend?" I asked. "Or . . . your husband?"

"Well, I can show you our sex tape," said Heller. "I'm kidding! But I will say this: You're never supposed to get physically or romantically involved with your sponsor. It's, like, a major AA rule. Of course I'm really good with rules."

"Heller!"

"Catey, it's been a really long day. Tomorrow's gonna be even more crazy because I have to deal with that little girl, the one with cancer who wants to spend the day with me. So right now because I'm not allowed to eat anything or drink anything or smoke anything, I should get some sleep. To prepare myself. To become Heller Harrigan, a deeply outstanding and super-sensitive role model for a dying thirteen-year-old."

I was about to scold Heller for her bad language and her poor attitude and especially for her mocking treatment of a sick child, but I stopped myself. Heller had been through a lot, although most of it had been her own fault, because she wanted to be a movie star. Only—she'd apologized to me, at least a tiny bit. It was a start.

As Heller's door closed I felt completely wiped out. I'd helped Heller get interviewed for media outlets from around the world, I'd seen her battle the forces of the Darkling Creeper in the Netherdome and I'd watched her almost get killed. I was a long way from Parsippany.

I shut my eyes and leaned against the wall, trying not to think about anything, especially not about Tally Marabont and AA sponsors and subways and Emily Dickinson. All of this was only increasing the ping-ponging of my brain, which was so loud and so nerve-racking that I'd never be able to sleep, ever again. I started touching my neck with my forefinger three times, which turned into thirty clusters of three times each . . .

"Catey?" said Mills as he stepped outside his own hotel suite, which was a few doors down from Heller's. "That scene at the Garden got pretty wild. Is Heller okay? Are you okay?"

I looked at Mills standing there in his sweatpants and his *Angel Wars* T-shirt with his hair wet from the shower he'd taken to get rid of all that mandala sand. I stopped counting. I walked over to him and I put my hands on his broad shoulders, which felt very nice, and I kissed him.

That was the exact moment, I have just decided while sitting in my jail cell, when I truly sailed off a cliff. That kiss. Up until then I'd been walking a tightrope. I'd lied to Tally Marabont and I'd swatted Ava Lily Larrimore with my Lucifoil and I'd jumped a turnstile. I could almost excuse all of that behavior because I'd been trying to do my job and save Heller's soul, or find her one. But kissing Mills Stanwood hadn't had anything to do with Heller. I'd kissed Mills because he was so handsome and because he was Tallwen and because I'd known that he had a crush on me and most shamefully of all . . . because I'd wanted to.

I wasn't just a criminal. And a liar. And an idiot. I was, and I'm just going to say it, I'm going to use a disgracefully hideous word because I deserve it, because I am . . . a FLOOZY. A TRAMP. I can't say this other word because it's too terrible and because I wish I didn't even know this word and because maybe I'm starting to use this kind of word as a result of being around Heller. But I have to say it because it's true. It's what I've become. I didn't just kiss Mills Stanwood. I LIKED kissing Mills Stanwood. I am a SLUT.

Here I am just one day later in jail and whatever is under that bandage on my arm is starting to throb and the magenta and purple dye from my hair is starting to drip onto my cheeks and—oh my dear sweet Lord baby Jesus sobbing his heart out in the manger. Something else on my body, on my face, is aching. I reach up and touch the left side of my nose and I feel—a HUGE METAL STUD.

I look down and I don't want to tell you what I see. It's too shocking. It's too evil. My name is, or at least it used to be, Caitlin Mary Prudence Rectitude Singleberry. I have raw, hacked off purple-and-magenta hair and at least one tattoo and what feels like a steel baseball bat sticking through my nose. I kissed Mills Stanwood and I'm not sure what else I've done or with whom or if anyone was filming it with their phone and will soon be posting it online so that the pope and the president and everyone in Parsippany can excommunicate me. While my hair and my tattoo and my nose piercing are all atrocious and shaming and a disgrace to my faith and my family and the entire Christian world, those things are nothing compared to what I just saw when I looked down at my left shin.

It was gone. My entire left kneesock was COMPLETELY GONE. NOT THERE.

I can't . . . breathe. My windpipe is closing. The cell walls are closing in and I'm going to scream while they crush me and pulverize me and grind my bones into dust. I need to wash my hands at least three hundred times and I need to fill out at least five hundred more college applications and I need to try and remember what sunlight looks like but none of this matters, nothing in my life is ever going to matter ever again for one simple reason.

I AM GOING TO HELL.

twenty-four

Sophie

The next morning as I sat beside Wyatt in the hotel ballroom I wondered what Sophie Schuler, the Make-A-Wish girl, was going to be like. I've never known anyone who had cancer, much less a thirteen-year-old girl, so the whole idea seemed sad beyond words: How could anyone deal with being that sick and with all of those complicated, painful treatments and with the thought of dying before your life had barely begun?

The Singing Singleberries had performed at benefits to fight different kinds of cancer as well as Alzheimer's disease, MS and ALS, that illness most people only know about through those videos where celebrities raise awareness by dumping buckets of ice water over their heads. We'd sung at hospitals where I'd met little kids who'd spent most of their lives undergoing treatment and we'd gone to nursing homes to entertain really old people in wheelchairs who'd seemed frail and barely awake but who'd always managed to smile and applaud. I couldn't claim to be friends with any of these people because I'd been more like a tourist stopping by their misery for a few minutes and a few upbeat songs. If I was being really honest, I'd have to admit that sick people, especially really sick people, scare me. I know that I'm not going to catch cancer just by being around someone who has it but the whole idea still makes me unbelievably nervous, even for me.

During our benefits I'd learned to control my breathing and I'd force myself to look everyone in the eye, even the kids covered in bandages or the old people with strange growths on their faces. My heart would be racing because I couldn't imagine being that ill or that old and I always wanted to magically cure everyone with a wand or a secret serum or a prayer, and I'd imagine everyone jumping from their beds and their wheelchairs and laughing and striding out of the hospital into the warmth of the sun and, of course, writing me thank-you notes with daisy stickers. I'd feel guilty because I'd get jolted back into reality and I'd know that while the sick people had to stay in the hospital I got to leave and escape.

My parents tried to prepare everyone in our family for these concerts by explaining how fortunate we were to be in good health and how it was our responsibility both to raise money and to let the sick people know that we cared about them and they weren't forgotten. My mom had also given me one of my favorite books ever, which was a young adult novel with characters who were sick.

The book is called *Arise All Ye Fools* and it's about a

sixteen-year-old girl named Ariel who takes a summer job as a volunteer health care aide in a hospital. She's thinking about becoming a doctor someday and she knows that volunteering will look good on her college applications. After her first day, when one patient vomits on her and a gunshot victim in the emergency room splashes her with blood, Ariel just wants to run out of there and never come back. Then Ariel meets James, who's eighteen and who has an inoperable brain tumor that he's named Sam. When Ariel and James first start to become friends, James warns her that Sam is always listening and that Sam is jealous and cranky.

Ariel and James fall in love and pretend the hospital is secretly an enchanted kingdom filled with what James calls "hidden pleasures and dreadful dangers," and just between themselves, they rename the staff things like Dr. Larry Lancelot of Rhinoplasty and Nurse Nostradamus, the Witch of Wart Removal. James's brain tumor starts to shrink and for a very short time Ariel and James allow themselves to imagine a life outside the hospital in what they call Fineville. On the day when James is scheduled to go home he collapses and dies in Ariel's arms and after finishing the book I couldn't get out of bed for three days and whenever one of my brothers or sisters would ask what was wrong, I'd just hold up my copy of the book and start crying again.

Even though this book had lots of details about being sick, I knew it was still a story and that really being sick would be very different and something I couldn't understand. Today I was trying to make sure I stayed extra pulled together so when

I met Sophie Schuler I wouldn't say or do anything ignorant or stupid and hurt her feelings, and I needed to firmly guide Heller because she'd be in the spotlight with Sophie. I was seriously worried about how Heller would deal with Sophie because Heller tended to ignore unpleasant things or make jokes, plus being a movie star was the opposite of being a sick little girl because movie stars get everything they want.

The Sophie Schuler situation was making me so anxious that one of my compulsions returned. Since I'd woken up and started thinking about Sophie I'd had this overwhelming need to knock on wood three times, because otherwise either I would get sick or someone I loved, someone in my family, would get sick and die. The only way I could stop this from happening was to find something made of wood, like a railing or the back of a chair or the top of a desk, and tap on it three times. The taps didn't need to be loud and I could use a fingertip so no one would catch me doing it. I couldn't stop.

My mom once asked me if I hear voices telling me to do my compulsive actions. She hadn't understood because anxiety isn't about having some nasty emotional gremlins living inside your brain and hissing at you to lick a doorknob or scrunch up your face. I don't receive instructions—I know things instantly. The goblins aren't giving me orders—I am. My compulsive thoughts aren't even thoughts, they're absolute certainties and obeying them isn't a choice.

The ceremony had started a few minutes earlier as a moderator introduced Tarelle Densmore, the woman who'd directed the *Angel Wars* movie; Sarah Smilesborough, who'd written the books; and the stars of the movie, including Mills and Billy, who both kept looking at me, which was easy because they were up on this little stage and I was in the front row of the audience. Mills and Billy kept winking at me and making faces and trying to get me to laugh. Last night after I'd kissed Mills, I'd immediately run right back to my room to concentrate on both pretending the kiss had never happened and trying to remember every second of it in case no one ever wanted to kiss me again.

The ballroom was filled with almost five hundred people, including the weekend's army of reporters, bloggers, tweeters and a batch of Angel Warriors, who hopefully weren't as homicidal as Ava Lily Larrimore. Wyatt had covered up Ava's behavior at Madison Square Garden by telling the media that everything had been preplanned. Ava herself was currently being examined by a psychiatrist in a private facility.

The moderator introduced Frank Markopoulos, who was the CEO of Omnisphere, the global corporation that owned the studio that had produced the movie and also owned the books' publisher and the chain of fast food restaurants offering the tie-in Angelicious SuperSnax for the full month of the movie's release. These SuperSnax included whole wheat doughnuts that the franchise was rebranding as Healthy Halos and chicken wings that were being called Angel Wings, which I thought was gross because I didn't want to think about angels getting their wings sliced off, breaded and deep-fried.

Mr. Markopoulos was all dressed up and making an effort to be super friendly by talking about "the *Angel Wars* family" and "the wholesome *Angel Wars* dreamscape." He introduced "our fairest Omnisphere angel of them all," meaning Heller, who was wearing a white-and-gold minidress with pleated, floating sleeves so she looked, as she'd told me, "like everyone's favorite angel who works at Hooters." Heller introduced Mary Straffords, a nice lady from the Make-A-Wish Foundation, who explained that the organization had been founded in Arizona in 1980 when a sick little boy had wanted to ride in a police helicopter and that ever since, Make-A-Wish had been granting requests for children all over the world with life-threatening illnesses. The Make-A-Wish people are amazing because they're like fairy godmothers or not-so-secret Santas for kids who can really use some happiness in their lives.

"A few months ago," Mary Straffords was saying, "we received a letter from the parents of Sophie Schuler." Sophie's parents came out onstage and I tried not to start crying because I didn't think I'd ever stop. The Schulers looked like anyone's mom and dad at a high school graduation or a talent night, where the dad would be shooting video and the mom would be giving him advice. They also looked worn down and as if they were trying extra hard to be cheerful and I began wondering about how my parents would behave if one of us kids got sick, and I knew they'd look just like the Schulers.

"Three years ago, when Sophie was first hospitalized for a biopsy," said Barbara, Sophie's mom, "she was very brave and very scared and the only thing that made her feel better was her brand-new copy of the second *Angel Wars* book."

"When she had to go back into the hospital two years later for her second round of chemotherapy," said Dave, Sophie's dad, "we made sure that she had the third *Angel Wars* book. By then she'd turned into our own little Lynnea, battling her own Darkling Creeper."

"When Sophie heard that her very favorite actress, Heller Harrigan, was going to be playing Lynnea in the *Angel Wars* movie," Barbara continued, "she was so thrilled that for a few minutes she forgot all about the tubes and the injections and the hair loss and the rest of it. Because while Sophie was in the chemo suite at Boston General for her earliest round of treatment, she'd be sitting in that big oversized chair with that IV drip in her arm and she'd be binge-watching *Anna Banana* reruns, one after the other, on her iPad. So in a way, so far, I think we can say that Heller Harrigan has helped to keep Sophie alive."

When Sophie's mom said this I thought it was wonderful, but I also looked at Heller because I knew she'd just been put under a lot of pressure.

"A few months ago," said Sophie's dad, "when things weren't looking so good, Sophie told me, and I'm quoting her, she said that the worst thing about dying would be that she'd never get to see Heller Harrigan in the *Angel Wars* movie. Sophie's condition has stabilized, at least for right now, and thanks to all the phenomenal people at Make-A-Wish and especially because of Heller Harrigan, today is going to be a very special day."

"Heller Harrigan," said Barbara, "I'd like you to meet our

number one daughter and your number one fan, Ms. Sophie Schuler."

Wyatt squeezed my hand, which I appreciated because all during this first part of the ceremony I'd started feeling frantic because the chair I was sitting on wasn't made of wood but some sort of metal, with an upholstered vinyl seat. Since I wasn't near anything else made of wood that I could knock on, my brain raced ahead and I could feel my thoughts fumbling for a substitution. I noticed that there was a wooden table at one side of the stage holding a display of the *Angel Wars* books and action figures and my brain made a deal with itself: If I could imagine myself knocking three times on that wooden table then no one would get sick and Heller wouldn't harm Sophie and everything would be okay. If thinking that way sounds crazy, it wasn't. Imagining myself knocking on that table was the only thing keeping me sane.

As everyone stood up and applauded, Sophie Schuler walked out onto the stage. She looked younger than thirteen and I don't know why this surprised me but she was a little plump. I'd always assumed that someone who'd been so sick would be skinny and delicate but Sophie was sturdy, with flushed round cheeks and a sort of squashed fishing hat covering her bald head. Sophie looked incredibly happy and unbearably nervous, which I'd noticed was the way a lot of Heller's fans looked—as if they couldn't wait to meet Heller but as if they were also on the verge of bursting into tears or running away to find a bathroom.

"Hi, Sophie," said Heller, opening her arms, and as she and Sophie hugged I glanced at the wooden tabletop, although now my brain was telling me that I couldn't keep using the tabletop because it was becoming too familiar and therefore useless. So my eyes darted all over the room, settling on a pair of double doors that I hoped hadn't just been painted to look like wood.

"It's so great to meet you," Heller told Sophie, with her arm around her. "Everyone's so glad you're here."

Heller was doing fine. She'd explained to me that when she'd met other sick children, she'd trained herself never to ask "How are you?" because it put the child in an awkward position. "I mean, what's the kid supposed to say?" Heller had told me. "I need a heart transplant only they still can't find a donor, but aside from that I'm just peachy?"

Heller handed Sophie a microphone, which Sophie clutched in both her hands while she turned to face the crowd. She started to talk a few times but she was overcome with nerves and excitement.

"Hi," Sophie finally said, which made the crowd laugh and applaud as Sophie smiled and bobbed her head. Everyone was rooting for Sophie. "Um, I just want to thank the Make-A-Wish Foundation for doing all of this," Sophie continued, at first in a whisper, but when Heller squeezed her shoulders, Sophie's voice grew stronger: "I want to thank my parents for coming here with me from Massachusetts and I want to tell Sarah Smilesborough that the *Angel Wars* books are the best books ever and I really mean it, and everyone who's ever read the books, which is probably everyone in the whole world, they all know it."

As everyone clapped, Sarah Smilesborough clapped her hands in Sophie's direction to thank her, and I could see that Sarah was smiling and crying at the same time, like most of the people in the room. This allowed me to relax a tiny bit and stop looking for other wooden surfaces to knock on because sometimes when I start feeling a different extreme emotion it can replace the anxiety.

"Most of all," said Sophie, "I just have to say one thing. Today is the best day of my whole life because of one person."

Sophie's voice had become a whisper again but then she said, in a cross between a railroad whistle, a blood-curdling scream and the sound of a thousand cheerleaders right after they'd had too much diet soda, "HELLER HARRIGAN!!!!!!"

"Oh my God," said Heller five minutes later in her hotel suite after Mr. Markopoulos had presented Sophie and the Make-A-Wish people with a huge, six-foot-long check for $100,000 and all of these white and gold balloons had been released from nets on the ceiling and the ceremony had ended. "That was surreal, even for this weekend. I mean, I couldn't even begin to process what was happening, between Sophie and the fried *Angel Wars* chicken wings and all of those balloons. It was like Sophie was running for president and then she won the Publishers Clearing House Sweepstakes and *Dancing with the Stars*."

"Sophie is so adorable," I said. "I couldn't stop sobbing. She's the cutest little girl I've ever seen."

"Which makes me feel so useless."

"But you're not! Sophie worships you!"

"Maybe she shouldn't. I'm just some ridiculous Hollywood jerk. I wish I was a doctor or a nurse or doing research or something that could actually help."

There was a knock on the door and Sophie came into the suite. Something was weird about her. She wasn't crying and trembling just because she was standing near her idol. She looked at Heller and then she looked at me as if she was sizing us up. She pulled off her hat and while she was mostly bald she had a samurai topknot tied with a rubber band sticking right up from the middle of her otherwise shiny head.

"All right, bitches," said Sophie. "Let's get this party started."

twenty-five

Sophie?

Heller and I looked at each other and turned back toward Sophie.

"What?" said Heller.

"Okay okay okay," said Sophie, and then to me, "You're the cousin, right? Catherine?"

"Caitlin," I said. "Catherine is my sister."

"Whatevs," said Sophie, looking at me as if I might be brain damaged, which I completely understood.

"Sophie?" said Heller.

"Nice," said Sophie, pointing at the suite with both hands. "Major. Five-star. Ginormous. Yeeps!" She calmed herself down. "Okay okay okay. First offs, I am a huge fan and I love the *Angel Wars* books and *Anna Banana*—YOW! And okay okay okay, I do have acute lymphoblastic leukemia, which has a survival rate of fifty-seven percent, which is fab except that in my case, after my first round of chemo and a pretty good year and a half, it came back. Ouch! Eek! Yay for leukemia! So I had like another round of even stronger chemo and now, yippee, I'm back in remission and my doctors, who I love and hug and kiss, mwah mwah mwah, they're saying, and this is the kind of word they use, right, they're all 'hopeful,' so yay for me! I love the Make-A-Wish people and my parents and whoever that dude was who handed me that big fat check and who I guess owns the entire world. But that's not why I'm here. No, sir! I'm here so I can spend the whole day with, oh my God, I can't believe I'm looking right at you, slap me and pinch me and make me scream—AHHHHHH!!!!!—Heller fucking Harrigan, who I fucking love, and I know I shouldn't be cursing but, number one, I'm a cancer kid so I can say whatever the hell I want and number two, sometimes I like to curse because it makes me feel JUST LIKE HELLER FUCKING HARRIGAN!!! 'Cause as far as I'm concerned, you are not just Anna Banana and Lynnea, which already makes you like, um, excuse me, the grand intergalactic wonder goddess of all time, I mean PLEASE, but you have also been through all sorts of crappy, yuck-o, butt-wipey stuff in your life and you still kick major sassafras Hollywood ass! That's why you're gonna help me! Yes! Yay! BOOM!"

Sophie grabbed a cushion from the couch and smashed it on top of her head and kept it there. Heller and I looked at each other, floored. For the first time ever, Heller was not the most outrageous person in the room.

"Um, okay, Sophie . . . ," Heller began.

"No!" said Sophie. "Please don't. Please please please don't start talking to me like you're a grown-up and I'm a baby, because you're not all that much older than me, okay?" She turned to me. "But you're really old, right?"

"What?" I said. "I'm not old! I'm two months younger than Heller!"

"Really?" said Sophie. "I guess maybe it's the way you're dressed or, like, your hair. 'Cause at first I thought that maybe you were, like, Heller's mom or her weird aunt or something."

"That's not true," said Heller. "Catey is more like my strange grandma who never leaves the basement because she's hiding from the space aliens and she needs to feed her imaginary cat."

"HELLER!"

"Nice!" Sophie told Heller as they high-fived.

"That was not nice!" I protested.

"I'm sorry, really and truly, maybe you have a disease too, like that one that makes little babies look a hundred years old, right?" said Sophie. "I'm sorry! I get all, I don't know, weirdy-bots and I just say stuff. I only have today and I know I'm supposed to hang out with Heller while she does interviews and a fashion shoot and makes a public service announcement for kids like me, which I will totally help with, look at me, I can stand next to Heller and make my eyes look really big and sad, like in those ads to get people to adopt abused puppies."

Sophie stood next to Heller and widened her eyes and made her feet pigeon-toed.

"Cool, right? I know that just spending, like, a regular day with Heller would be super amazing and super fun and that I'd get all sorts of fun free stuff, which I still totally want anyway, but—that's not what I need."

"What . . . what do you need?" asked Heller.

"Okay," said Sophie, putting her palms together and walking in a circle. "I've been thinking about this, like, a lot, like it's been filling up my whole brain and leaking out my ears, and it's the big secret reason why I did the whole Make-A-Wish thing in the first place—BOOM! My parents are great but if it was up to them, I'd spend my whole life in bed or on a couch with a blanket over my knees, right, just like looking out the window with a book of fairy tales in my lap, I mean, no. Ewww. It's probably 'cause they've already had to deal with me almost dying, like, twice, so they're scared shitless and beyond. They get all worried that if I go outside or jump around or eat anything that might actually taste good, I'll keel over right there in the living room and all of their worst nightmares will come true, which I totally get because having a sick kid is probably every mom and dad's worst nightmare, right?"

"They must be so concerned," I said, sounding like my own mom.

Sophie was staring at me as if she was trying to decide whether to shoot me or hand me the gun and let me do it myself.

"You read that book, didn't you?" Sophie said to me. "That *Arise All Ye Fools* book? This is so weird 'cause I'm, like, psychic or something, 'cause I can always tell when someone's read that book 'cause they get this sort of look on their face? You know?"

"What look?" I asked.

"Sort of half like you've just seen a unicorn flying over a rainbow, and half like you're constipated and really trying to pinch one off. All of these whack job girls at my school who read that book, they got all moony and drippy and oozy about how cancer is just SO SAD and SO DREAMY and then they read that book, like, twenty-eight more times while they're scarfing down a few more pints of that pistachio ice cream with the chunks of Oreos in it. Then they text their BFFs and they go, 'If I had a really cute boyfriend with cancer, I'd be SO NICE to him. I'd, like, play my guitar and sing him a special CANCER SONG. I'd write him a CANCER POEM.'"

"Sophie!" I said.

"She's right," said Heller. "When they made that movie out of *Arise All Ye Fools*, I auditioned for it, for what's that girl's name, Foxglove or Wind Spirit or Carburetor?"

"It's Ariel!" I said.

"Ariel, right," said Heller. "They asked me to read that scene where Ariel and James go up to the roof of the hospital and pretend that they're, what was it, King Skybutt and Queen Zithead?"

"King Skywards and Queen Zephyr!" I said.

"Fine," said Heller, "and I was doing a really good job, until I started cracking up. I mean, when Ariel had to keep calling that guy sire and milord, I just lost it, I was practically rolling on the floor. I kept apologizing and I told the casting director that I was having a reaction to my allergy medication but I don't think he bought it and I didn't get the part."

"BOOM!" said Sophie as she and Heller high-fived again. "CANCER BOOK BOOM!!!"

"I think you're both insensitive and heartless and disgusting!" I said. "Those books are beautiful! They're about people's souls!"

"My soul doesn't want to, like, call anyone my liege, okay?" said Sophie. "I'm just gonna say this, like, right out, but I don't know if my soul is gonna be, like, around for very long. And 'cause you're the most amazing and awesome and all-powerful Heller Harrigan—HELLER HARRIGAN, RIGHT IN FUCKING FRONT OF ME!!!"

Sophie reached out her arm and touched Heller's nose with her forefinger and then waved her arm in the air, howling, "YOW! BOOM! I TOUCHED HER! HELLER HARRIGAN DNA! ON MY FINGER!!!"

Heller and I exchanged a glance, wondering if Sophie might be genuinely crazy. Sophie caught our glance, nodded, and sat down, using a more straightforward voice.

"So I need you to help me do three things."

"You mean like a bucket list?" asked Heller.

"Um, NO," said Sophie, rolling her eyes, and I know this is a terrible thing to say but all I kept thinking was that for a girl with cancer, Sophie was being awfully sarcastic.

"I'm sorry if I'm sounding like a snot or a butthead or a mega-douche," she said. "It's just—there's stuff I need to do. It's not like on those bucket lists where really old people want to, like, I don't know, go to Paris or touch a pyramid or something. These are things I, like, really need to do, not 'cause I'm sick, or not just 'cause I'm sick. So it's not a bucket list—it's more like a jailbreak."

Sophie was looking at Heller and me with an openness, and a seriousness, as if she was trusting us. Sick people can't afford to waste time so they get right to the point. Although I had the feeling that even before Sophie got sick, she'd always been a very hyper and direct person.

"What do you need?" asked Heller.

Sophie sat completely still and looked both ways, as if government agents might be eavesdropping. In her most important, hushed voice, the sort of voice she might use on a witness stand, she asked, "Have you ever had Sweetcakes?"

"Excuse me," said Heller. "Of course we have. We're Americans and they're America's favorite cupcakes. When I was doing drugs I would live on them. I would hallucinate about them. I would have sex with them."

"I have only eaten one Sweetcake in my entire life," I said. "Strictly by accident."

"By accident?" asked Heller. "What, did someone tell you it was a new kind of communion wafer? With frosting?"

"No," I said. "My parents don't want us to eat processed sugary foods with lots of white flour, because they're not healthy and they make people go on rampages and do terrible things."

"Like what?" said Heller. "Smile? Lick their lips? Ask for more?"

"So how did you end up, like, eating only one?" asked Sophie.

"My sister Calico loves Sweetcakes," I confessed. "She

saves her allowance and sneaks off and buys them and then smuggles them into our room and hides them under her bed. Which is why we started getting mice in our room. When my dad came in to investigate, Calico panicked because she still had one of those double packages, so she shoved one Sweetcake into her own mouth and the other into mine."

"Like, didn't you LOVE it?" asked Sophie. "Didn't your mouth and your taste buds and your, like, whole everything just go BERSERK?"

"Did you come?" asked Heller.

"NO I DID NOT! All of that sugar made me jittery and . . . I'd just rather have some carrot sticks from our garden, or a nice crisp apple!"

"Are you homeschooled?" asked Sophie.

"Exactly," said Heller. "Sophie, you have to understand something. Catey is morbidly uptight and emotionally dead and she actually enjoys wearing those kneesocks, which are like leg condoms, but when it comes to sugar she's a pathological liar."

"I am not!" I protested. When I'd eaten that Sweetcake I'd been very conflicted because when my dad walked into our bedroom I'd had a mouthful of cupcake, which I'd had to swallow to protect Calico. Ever since then I've associated Sweetcakes with deceit and choking to death and mouse droppings.

"You just want us to get you some Sweetcakes?" Heller asked Sophie. "What, like a hundred packages?"

"No," said Sophie. "Nope nope nope. It's major. It's sort of like—majestic. When I was doing chemo, the chemo would take over my whole everything, right? They give you separate

drugs so you won't upchuck but you still end up with no appetite and total brain fog, and your whole body just feels like
it's been run over by a bus and like it wants to upchuck but it
can't. I totally hated not being able to eat anything because
I have a sweet tooth the size of Ho-Ho-Kus, New Jersey,
which is where the closest Sweetcakes factory is located. Which
is something I know because I've done a lot of research
into Sweetcakes production, I mean, a lot. I mean, I'm, like, the
Sweetcakes AUTHORITY."

Sophie had a gleam in her eye, the way my brothers do
when they talk about any video game that involves grizzled
mercenaries wearing eye patches, gang members wearing ban-
danas, melting zombies or preferably all three killing one
another. I was also starting to understand why even though
Sophie was sick she was still round. The more I thought about
it, maybe Sophie being round was an optimistic sign.

"Whenever my appetite would, like, finally come back,"
Sophie said, "I'd try to decide which is my favorite part of a
Sweetcake. Is it, like, the rich devil's food cake part—LOVING
IT—or the cream filling part—WANTING IT SO BAD I'M
GONNA PUNCH SOMEONE—or the smooth chocolate
frosting on top—ULTIMATE EXTREME TRIPLE YUM. I
made this chart and I rated every part of a Sweetcake on the
basis of texture, taste and visual appeal, right, and then I had
this little Olympic ceremony in my room and the gold medal
winner, like, on the podium, was . . ."

Sophie stood up and did an incredibly accurate impression

of the triumphant theme from the last summer Olympics. Then she said:

"The little white squiggle along the top of the cupcake! SWEETCAKES DEATH MATCH CAGE FIGHTING ULTRA-BOOM!!!"

She then did an incredibly accurate impression of a stadium filled with people cheering, as she waved her arms and sobbed and put her hand over her heart.

This squiggle was the Sweetcakes trademark, setting it apart from other cupcakes. Calico had told me that while other brands would imitate this squiggle, the wannabe squiggles were always blurry or haphazard. She said that when she got married she wanted her wedding ring to look exactly like the Sweeetcakes squiggle.

"I'm, like, propped up in bed," said Sophie, "Skyping my algebra class, only what I'm really doing is drawing that squiggle in my notebook over and over again like it was this Buddhist or Celtic or ancient Egyptian symbol for perfect happiness. Which it so completely IS. I tried to calculate how many individual squiggles you'd need to, like, go around the equator or from the earth's surface to the moon—I can show you. And don't judge me, 'cause it's my most favorite anything ever—I started to totally fixate on the machine that makes the squiggle. I found a picture of it online—it's this huge steel pastry-tube thing and it shoots the squiggles onto the assembly line of cupcakes. It's the coolest thing ever. 'Cause I kept thinking that, like, while some people were inventing nuclear warheads or barbed wire or chemical weapons, someone else was inventing this amazeballs machine that could make hundreds of thousands of perfect squiggles every day forever."

Sophie was looking at us like she'd just witnessed a miracle, with tears in her eyes, and very quietly she said:

"Boom."

"Do you want us to take you to the Sweetcakes factory for a tour or something?" asked Heller.

"No," said Sophie. "First of all it's Sunday so the factory is closed. Second of all I don't want a tour. Okay okay okay . . ."

She put her hands over her mouth and then lowered them.

"I want to put my mouth directly under the squiggle machine. I want to lie on my back on the conveyor belt and taste the squiggle. I told my parents and my mom actually emailed the Sweetcakes consumer outreach people and asked if the whole tasting-the-squiggle deal would be possible, but they said that the factory floor was, like, off-limits to visitors and that the equipment had to be kept spotless and sterilized, and that the idea was out of the question, and they sent me a coupon for ten percent off on my next Sweetcakes purchase, which was nice and all but come ON. Here's what I need: We gotta break into the Sweetcakes factory, turn on the machinery, shove me underneath the squiggle maker and then get the hell out of there before anyone catches us. Right?"

Sophie looked ecstatic and crazy and yearning. She looked like someone who was hopelessly in love, with a squiggle.

"Sophie, if you'll excuse us for just a second," said Heller, grabbing my arm and dragging me into the bedroom.

"We have to do this," Heller told me, once we were out of Sophie's earshot.

"Are you out of your mind? We can't! We have that whole schedule of interviews and that fashion shoot and the public service spot! I'm supposed to be keeping you on track! Especially after yesterday! Breaking into a factory is a felony and shoving Sophie under that squiggle thing sounds incredibly dangerous; she wants us to lie to her parents, and I'm sorry but I don't think that committing a criminal act and ingesting a squiggle that is most likely made out of toxic additives and artificial colorings is exactly what the Make-A-Wish Foundation had in mind!"

"Wyatt can push those interviews until tomorrow and I can tape that announcement whenever I want to. Thanks to you and your Glinda-the-pit-bull routine, I've been behaving myself this whole weekend, and it's killing me. I'm getting that horrible feeling again, that I'm being a good little soldier and a team player and a total Hollywood pimped-out phony. Sophie needs us, so she can do something that will make her happy, and it's something no one else in the world would ever help her to do. After what she's been going through, she deserves a completely wacked-out Sweetcakes sugar high. This is completely her Make-A-Wish wish. We have to do it."

"Heller, this is everything my parents and your mom warned me about. I'd be breaking my word and we could all end up in jail and I need to think about college and you need to stay sober and speak with a clergyman and tell everyone about the *Angel Wars* movie . . ."

"Stop it. Right now. Stop being you."

"What?"

"You think I'm selfish and thoughtless and spoiled. I'm try-ing to help Sophie. I'm trying to change. Isn't that what you want? You're prissy and snobby and scared of—pretty much everything. So stop it. You change too. Be someone else. Someone better."

"I . . . I . . . can't. I don't need to be someone else. I won't!"

"Just for the next few hours. Forget about how much you hate me. Forget about the last four years. This is about Sophie."

"You're confusing me! This is what you always used to do! You're trying to bully me! Don't you remember what happened?"

"I don't care about what happened! I care about Sophie! Catey, ask yourself . . ."

Heller grinned. I wanted to shut my eyes or hold up a cru-cifix to protect myself, to not fall under her spell and let even more impossibly horrendous things happen.

"Catey—what would Jesus do? If Jesus had a car?"

Before I could process what Heller had just said, let alone formulate a calm and logical and pious response, Sophie's head appeared at the bedroom door. "You guys? Just, like, a reminder?" she said. "I'm waiting. Oh, and I have cancer."

Then she grinned, and I knew exactly why she was Heller's number one fan.

twenty-six

Bonnie and Clyde and Heller and Caitlin and Sophie

We met Wyatt in the parking garage of the hotel ten minutes later. As he handed Heller the keys to April's van, he said, "I don't know why I'm letting you do this; I must be completely demented. Catey, you have to swear that you will stay in touch and that you won't let Heller get any more out of control than she already is. I've pushed everything on the schedule until tomorrow, but you still have to get back here by dinnertime or Sophie's parents will kill me. Sophie, I think you're insane but I won't tell your mom and dad where you're going so they can still think that you're spending a nice showbizzy afternoon with Heller. One more thing."

"Yes, Mr. Markowitz?" asked Sophie, who'd just switched to being sweet and innocent and well-mannered, just the way she'd fooled everyone at the morning ceremony.

"I want one of those cupcakes," said Wyatt, and then he muttered, "Kina hora," and pretended to spit on the floor.

"Why did you just do that?" I asked him.

"It's to keep the evil eye away," said Wyatt. "My grand-mother always did that. If she was here and she knew that I was helping you, she'd slap me."

Sophie programmed the van's GPS and with Heller driving we took the Jersey Turnpike to Ho-Ho-Kus. We followed a few back roads and I saw it: the Sweetcakes factory. There was a high chain-link fence surrounding a large, industrial-looking building, which was mostly dark with a towering SWEETCAKES . . . SO SWEET! sign on the roof. Heller stopped the van half a block away.

"There's a watchman in that little gatehouse," said Sophie, leaning over from the backseat.

"How are we going to get inside?" I wondered. "Should we just ask him politely?"

"Oh, Catey," said Heller and Sophie at the same time. I was shocked at how quickly they'd decided to gang up on me.

"You should just floor it and, like, blast right through the front gates," Sophie suggested. "So beyond cool."

"No," said Heller. "Watch and learn."

Heller drove the van up to the gatehouse and leaned out the window. "Sir?" she said, using her most respectful voice. "Oh, Mister Watchman Officer Security Person, sir?"

"What is it?" asked the uniformed watchman, peering at us.

"Sir, I'm so sorry to ask this," said Heller. "I was just here yesterday as a guest, and I left my purse inside. I was meeting with the president of the company."

"Harold J. Armbruster," Sophie prompted.

"With Harold," said Heller. "Who I totally adore. We're working on a promotional collaboration for my upcoming film."

"A what for your what?" said the watchman, not falling for it.

"It's for *Angel Wars*," said Heller. "I'm Heller Harrigan."

"Lynnea," added Sophie. "Like, LYNNEA."

The watchman's eyes opened very wide. "Oh my God," he said, and even though he was close to my dad's age, he instantly turned into a hyperventilating Angel Warrior. He held up a well-worn paperback copy of the third book in the trilogy and gushed, "I'm almost finished with the last one! Don't tell me what happens! I'm on Team Myke! I can't wait to see the movie, I'm going with my wife and my daughter to the first midnight show on Wednesday! We already bought our tickets online! When they hear that I met you they are gonna go nuts! Could I . . . oh no, I shouldn't even ask!"

"I tell you what," said Heller. "If you'll just open the gates, on our way out, I'll sign your book and we can take a selfie. We can call your wife and your daughter, if you'd like. What are their names?"

"Janice and Anabelle! They will go through the roof! Thank you so much! And you're doing something with Sweetcakes? That's so great!"

"They're making this special collector's edition premium batch, for the next month only," said Sophie, improvising. "They're called Angel Cakes!"

"I love that!" said the watchman as he pressed a button and the gates swung open. "I'll open the front doors electronically, but do you need me to come with you to find Mr. Armbruster's office?"

"Oh no, thank you, I remember exactly where it is," said Heller. "You need to stay out here to make sure that, you know, criminals don't get inside. You're doing an amazing job. We'll be out in just a few minutes. Stay golden!"

"Stay golden!" said the guard, who was already on the phone to his wife, saying, "Jan, I hope you're sitting down! Because Lynnea herself just told me to stay golden!"

"I can't believe that you lied to that nice man," I told Heller as she pulled the van right up to the factory's main entrance.

"Please," said Heller, "we're here for a good cause and we're going to take a selfie. When we get back to the hotel we'll send his family a truckload of T-shirts and power bars and those really expensive LED halos, not the cheap ones that set some guy's hair on fire."

"This . . . is . . . so . . . AWESOME!" said Sophie as we left the van.

The watchman had opened the front doors from the gate-house and Sophie guided us into a darkened hallway.

"We'll never find the right room," I said. "We should go back."

"Stop being such a Singlepain," Heller told me. "We're having an adventure."

"We're committing a crime!"

"That's what I said!"

"I'm leaving!"

"It's down here," said Sophie. "We can follow the smell."

Sophie was standing in the gloom, sniffing the air. Heller and I sniffed too.

"There it is!" said Sophie. "It's like perfume! If perfume had cream filling! Come on!"

Sophie charged ahead, with Heller and me struggling to keep up.

"This is so great," said Heller. "Maybe we'll find all sorts of secret formulas, or a dead body."

"I don't want to find a dead body!" I said. "Especially near food!"

I screamed because something had slammed into my head. "AHHH!!!!"

"Jesus, what is it? Why are you screaming like you just saw a naked picture of—anything?"

"Something attacked me! Stop laughing!"

"I'm sorry! But, Catey—it's a fire extinguisher hanging on the wall."

Heller was right and while I tried to stay upset, I started laughing too.

"It's not funny!" I insisted.

"We'll have the fire extinguisher arrested," said Heller as she disappeared around a corner.

"Heller? Heller, it's dark! Wait up! Where are you?"

"Cateeee . . . ," said a strange ghostly voice. "Caitlin Singleberreeee . . ."

"Stop it!"

"I am the ghost of the Sweetcakes factoreeee . . ."

"You are not!"

"I'm going to make you eat refined sugar!"

Something grabbed me from behind and I screamed!

"HELLER!!!"

"CATEY!!!" said Heller, imitating me, which made us both start laughing again.

"Come ON!" said Sophie from a few yards away. "Stop fooling around! I think I found the right door!"

There was a hissing noise and then a dim light appeared as Sophie opened a large steel door. Sophie was silhouetted in the light.

"Oh my God, oh my God, oh my God! This is it! We're here! If I didn't, like, have cancer, I would have a heart attack!"

A blaze of light flooded the hallway.

"I found the light switch! Get in here!"

"I can't! It's wrong! We're trespassing!"

"Catey," said Heller. "You can do this. I know you can."

Heller was grinning. She grabbed my arm and dragged me into the room. I made outraged noises but only because I was good at it.

Sophie was inside.

"Look at it!" said Sophie. "I can't believe it! It's like, like, just what I always dreamed of! Only so much way better! It's like, oh my God, maybe I just died and I'm in heaven!"

"But we're here too," I said.

"Maybe we all died in a car accident! Wouldn't that be AWESOME?"

"SOPHIE!"

I stayed near the door as Sophie and Heller explored the

room. Everything was very clean and impressive, with iron girders and catwalks and ovens the size of two-car garages, and there was a conveyor belt that was miles long winding all over the room, entering and exiting the different hulks of machinery.

"Over here are the baking pans!" said Sophie, as if she'd discovered gold. "You can tell by the different shapes—this one's for the Yumlogs, this one's for the LuckyPucks, and right over there, that's the bin where they toss the defective cupcakes!"

"What's a defective cupcake?" I wondered.

"Ava Lily Larrimore," said Heller.

"Over here," said Sophie, "oh my God oh my God oh my God—it's the Sweetcakes production circuit! With the rotating mixer!"

Sophie looked back at us, with her hands covering her mouth and her eyes bursting out of her head. Her topknot was quivering.

"Look at her," Heller said to me. "She's so happy."

"I guess in a way," I said, "this place is the opposite of a hospital."

"Hospitals suck," said Heller.

"I know," I said.

Heller looked at me, because we were both remembering the same thing: the weeks I'd spent in a hospital. Heller started to say something and I started to say something but we both stopped. The subject was still off-limits.

"You guys!" Sophie gasped. "There it is! Exactly where I thought it was going to be! This is, like, Mount Everest or the

Statue of Liberty or I don't know, the moon! No, it's way better than the moon, 'cause I don't wanna put the moon in my mouth! It's . . . it's . . ."

Sophie's voice dropped two octaves.

"It's . . . the SQUIGGLE CONE."

Heller and I joined Sophie as she stood beside a ten-foot-high mirror-bright silver metal cone-shaped device that tapered to a tiny hole at the bottom, where it hovered a few inches over the conveyor belt. Sophie was slowly examining the cone.

"See, I think the cupcakes go on this belt," she said. "Then, like, one cupcake at a time gets moved under the nozzle, which squirts the squiggle."

Sophie turned to us, speechless, waggling her head at the unspeakable wonder of the process.

"This whole cone thing is on springs," said Heller. "So it can move back and forth. Otherwise the squiggle would be just a straight line, like on a highway."

"That's right!" said Sophie. "That's incredible! That's, like . . . GENIUS!"

"Well, I don't know if it's genius," I said. "It's just a machine . . ."

"SHUT UP!!!" said Sophie and Heller.

"Okay," I admitted. "It is pretty amazing."

"And here you are," Heller told me. "Having an adventure. You're pretty amazing."

"So you guys aren't just cousins," said Sophie. "You're, like, friends, right? Did you grow up together?"

"We did," said Heller.

"Right here in New Jersey," I added.

"Did you have fun?"

Heller and I looked at each other.

"It's complicated . . . ," I began.

"We haven't seen each other for years . . . ," said Heller.

"My parents . . ."

"My mom . . ."

Sophie narrowed her eyes. "What am I missing?" she asked.

Heller and I looked at each other. We still couldn't talk about it.

"Okay!" said Sophie. "Have your little secret! We, like, don't have time for this! I think I know how the squiggle machine works, but we'll find out, I mean, unless something catches on fire or explodes."

"Sophie!"

"It's gonna be fine! I know it is! It's gotta be! Even if we die, I'd rather die in a Sweetcakes explosion!"

I was about to say something but Heller caught my eye and we both knew: When it came to dying, Sophie was in charge.

"Catey," said Sophie. "When I say go, could you, like, flip all of those red levers over there, the ones marked FULL POWER? So while all the machinery stuff is getting warmed up, Heller, you can get me up onto the conveyor belt."

I had a choice. I could refuse to go any further and I could put my foot down and force all of us to go back to the hotel, which was exactly what I would have done two days ago. So much had happened and now here I was, about to add another and far more serious criminal act to my growing rap sheet. I was about to do something that I could never explain to my parents or my pastor or to anyone except Heller, who'd already found a crate for Sophie to use as a footstool to get herself up onto the conveyor belt.

"Sophie," I said, "hasn't this gone far enough? You've seen the factory, and the squiggle thing, we can just head back . . ."

Sophie turned toward me and I saw her ridiculous, bobbing topknot and her shining eyes. Her shirt had come unbuttoned at the top and I saw something else, just below her neck.

"What's that bandage?"

Sophie looked down. "It's covering my port," she explained. "It's like, 'cause I've had so much chemo, the nurses have trouble finding a vein. So the doctor put this plastic thing in my chest, it's called a port, so they can just hook me right up."

"Catey?" said Heller. "Sophie asked you to do something."

I pulled the levers, praying they wouldn't work.

There was a *ka-chung* sound as the room's machinery hummed and clicked and whirred, as if an ancient, giant robot was waking up and looking around for his morning cup of ancient, giant robot coffee.

"I love it!" said Sophie. "It's going! It's on!"

"Catey, I need a hand," said Heller, and I ran over to the conveyor belt, which wasn't moving yet. Heller and I each took one side of Sophie and we hoisted her up onto the wide, well-used canvas belt and Sophie lay flat on her back.

"Are you okay?" Heller asked Sophie, who said, "I think so.

The lights are in my eyes but I'm going to concentrate on just thinking like a Sweetcake. Catey, I saw a button over there, where the sign says EMBELLISHMENT BELT. That's the official name for the squiggle, I read about it online, it's called the Embellishment, isn't that the best? If you push that button, maybe the belt will start moving."

I found the button and my index finger hovered over it.

"Ready?" I asked.

"Sophie?" said Heller.

"In a second," said Sophie. "I gotta do this just right, like I always dreamed. I wanna slide right under the cone and get squiggled, and then after that, Catey, you probably should turn the power switch off."

"Okay, but why?"

"I'm not totally sure about this, but, like, I don't want the cone to stab me to death."

"WHAT?"

"It'll be fine, Catey!" said Heller. "Just do it!"

"One . . . two . . . ," said Sophie. "Three! Do it! Start the belt!"

I pushed the button and for a few seconds nothing happened and I was incredibly relieved. "I'm sorry!" I called out. "Maybe it's broken or there's a safety catch or something! Sophie, we'll help you climb down!"

There was a grinding noise and a high-pitched buzzing and the belt started moving. I could see Sophie, on her back, getting closer and closer to the looming, menacing silver nozzle. There was another split-second pause and then Sophie's head began to slide under the cone. Frosting began to zoom out of the nozzle, first forming a perfect, looping squiggle along the center of Sophie's forehead and then onto her nose, and then the nozzle was right over Sophie's mouth, which she'd opened as wide as possible, and the squiggle zoomed inside.

I was mesmerized and then Heller yelled, "Catey! Shut it down!" My head jerked up and I lunged for the ALL POWER EMERGENCY OFF lever. I slammed it down and held my breath and all of the machinery in the room shuddered, made a loud belching noise and ground to a halt.

"Is she okay?" I asked as I ran back over to the conveyor belt.

"Sophie?" said Heller as we grabbed Sophie's feet and tried to ease her body out from underneath the nozzle without scratching her face. Finally her head was free and Sophie pulled herself up on her elbows, still on the belt. In only that short amount of time the squiggle had hardened, so that Sophie's face looked like a Sweetcake made out of a human head. A head that was smiling from ear to ear.

"BOOM!" Sophie said. "SWEETCAKES BOOM FOREVER!!!"

"That was pretty cool," said Heller.

"That was fantastic," I said.

"You guys," asked Sophie. "Do you wanna get squiggled?"

"Catey?"

"Heller?"

I remembered this sort of moment. Heller would grin and I'd get nervous and then we'd be off, climbing a tree or sneaking into a PG-13 movie or stealing one of my brothers' baseball caps and filling it with shaving cream.

"What if," said Heller, "we took off all our clothes? What if we got naked squiggled?"

"HELLER!!!!"

twenty-seven

Don't Even Think about It!

Once we'd turned off the lights and left the factory, without any further squiggling, Heller took a selfie with the watchman and called his wife and daughter and told them he was now an official Angel Warrior, and she invited the whole family to the premiere on Monday night. We jumped into the van and took off before the watchman could notice that Heller still didn't have a purse.

"You guys, thank you thank you thank you like infinity, that was so epic," said Sophie, who was sitting in the backseat and picking squiggles off her forehead. "Should I eat these extra squiggles or, like, save them forever?" she asked as she was already eating them.

"We got you squiggled," said Heller. "Sophie, you said that there were three things you need to do. What's next?"

"I think we've already done quite enough inappropriate and illegal activities for one day," I said. "We need to get back to the hotel so Wyatt doesn't get into more trouble than he's already in."

"I sent him a photo of Sophie with the squiggle on her face," said Heller. "He loved it. I grabbed him a bunch of defective LuckyPucks."

"I need to get a tattoo," said Sophie.

"Ink?" asked Heller. "Your first?"

"NO," I said firmly, and I knew that this time everyone was going to listen to me. "Just NO. NO WAY. ABSOLUTELY N-O. No one is getting tattooed. Tattoos are repulsive. God does not want us to disfigure our bodies, which are his sacred gifts to us, with graven images of skulls and dragons and Chinese lettering. A person is not a take-out menu. The only people who get tattoos are bikers and serial killers and strippers."

"Excuse me," said Heller. "But I have, like, eight tattoos."

"EXACTLY," I said.

"I know just what I want," said Sophie. "A pair of angel wings around my wrist, like a bracelet."

"That is so awesome," said Heller. "Maybe I'll get one too."

"EXCUSE ME," I said. "Why isn't anyone paying attention? This is a terrible idea. Sophie, you've just had all of those medical treatments, so it's not even safe."

"Yes it is," said Sophie. "I asked my doctor and he said, especially if it was small, a tattoo would be totally fine."

"What do your parents think?" I asked. "Wouldn't you need their consent?"

"They think it's just, like, some silly dopey notion," said

Sophie. "They keep waiting for me to forget all about it. Every time I talk about it they don't even hear me."

"My mom went with me to get my first tattoo," said Heller. "It was her idea. She wanted us to get matching Aztec sunbursts but I told her no, she could get a sunburst, but I wanted a devil having sex with Hello Kitty. Which is corny but come on. I was eight."

As Heller was about to tug her pants down to show Sophie this tattoo on her hip bone I told Sophie, "Please ignore Heller. She's a very bad influence. When we were little Heller tried to pierce my ears—while I was asleep."

"When she woke up," Heller said, "I was going to tell Catey that the ear-piercing fairy had done it. But Catey's a real light sleeper and she bit me."

"That's so cool," said Sophie. "I wish I had a friend like that."

"Like which one of us?" I asked.

"Both," said Sophie. "It's like you balance each other out. Heller is awesome and amazing and out there, and Catey's . . ."

"What?" I said.

"Awesome and amazing and insane," said Heller, laughing.

"I am not insane!"

"In a good way!"

I tried to decide if there was a good way to be insane but then I started laughing too.

"Sophie," said Heller, "when Catey and I were little I'd always try to push her to try new things and she'd usually start screaming. But if I could make her laugh I knew we were on the right track."

"But why do you want a tattoo?" I asked Sophie, changing the subject to less personal territory. "You're only thirteen and a tattoo is permanent. It's forever. Why do you want to do that to your body?"

"Okay okay okay. Here's the thing, right? It's like, I've been doing so much other stuff to my body," said Sophie. "I know that the chemo and the biopsies and the transfusions, it's all supposed to make me better and save my life and, like, hooray for that and blahdiddy blahddidy blah. That's what I tell myself, every time I go back into the hospital. Only all I keep thinking is: Hey, everybody, like for once, why can't I do something to my body that won't make me barf? You're totally right, a tattoo is forever, which for me might not be all that long. 'Cause I could live to be a hundred or I could get hit by a truck in five minutes and splattered all over the highway—BLART!"

"Sophie!" I said.

"Whatever happens," said Sophie, "you know what? It's, like, my body. It's my life. That's why I want a tattoo."

I still knew that Sophie getting a tattoo was a seriously bad idea, but it was hard to argue with her logic or with the determined look on her face. I knew she was serious because she hadn't said "BOOM!"

"The problem," said Heller, "is that I got all of my ink done on the West Coast, so I don't know any of the artists out here, and we want to use somebody really good. Wait a minute—I know who we can ask, because he lives here and he's got some amazing tats—Billy Connors."

"Billy has tattoos?" I said. During the yoga class I'd noticed something on Billy's chest peeking out from under the strap of his tank top, but I'd hoped it was a birthmark. My parents have always been very strict with us about tattoos, even when Castor, who's eighteen, asked about getting a musical note on the side of his neck. "You're of age," my dad had told him, "so I can't stop you. But I can start calling you B-Flat." So far Castor hasn't gotten his tattoo, but thinking about whatever Billy had on his chest was upsetting because it made me start thinking about seeing Billy with his shirt off, which made me think about either going to the beach with Billy or marrying him, because those were the only appropriate ways I could ever see him shirtless.

"I'm calling him," said Heller, pulling over to the side of the road. "Billy has this picture of two penguins and a zebra having an orgy, across his entire back . . ."

"WHAT?"

"I'm kidding," said Heller, dialing Billy. "Sophie, isn't it fun to make Catey scream like that? Like a teakettle in heat? It's my favorite thing in the world. Billy? It's Hel. You have to meet us on the corner of Eighth Avenue and 55th Street in twenty minutes. Wear a hat and a hoodie and don't tell anyone where you're going . . . No, you're not allowed to ask any questions . . . Yes, Catey's going to be there, and she says that she wants to have your two-headed baby and name both of the heads Heller, and that she wants to get started right now, in the backseat . . ."

"HELLER!"

By the time we'd driven into Manhattan, Heller had explained why we needed to kidnap Billy: "It's for his own protection, so he's not implicated in any of this and so he doesn't call Wyatt or Sophie's parents or anyone else who might try and stop us."

I looked out my window and there was Billy on the corner, wearing a baseball cap, a hoodie and sunglasses, all of which only made him look even cuter, like a nice, handsome, helpful boy pretending to be a tough guy or a gangster. I'd noticed that this was how all boys over the age of twelve, including my brothers, wanted to look.

"Get in," Heller told Billy as Sophie opened the door to the backseat.

"Hey, Catey," said Billy, touching my shoulder—why do I remember this? Why, even though I was wearing my blouse and my blazer, did it feel like he was touching my bare skin?

"Hey, Sophie," said Billy, and I knew that I'd become pure Godless evil because I was trying to decide if Billy was being nicer to Sophie then he was to me. I was jealous of a thirteen-year-old girl with cancer and a topknot.

"First, give me your phone," Heller told Billy.

"Why?"

"Just give it to me or I'll tell Catey you have gonorrhea."

"I do not have gonorrhea!" said Billy, handing Heller his phone. "Catey, don't ever believe anything Heller says!"

"I never do," I assured Billy, although I was also thinking about Googling gonorrhea on my phone, to make sure it was curable.

"Who did your ink?" Heller demanded.

"My ink?" Billy asked.

"I'm getting a tattoo, isn't that amazeballs?" said Sophie. "So are Heller and Catey!"

"SOPHIE!"

"It's such a perfect idea," said Heller. "I can get Lynnea chopping off Ava Lily Larrimore's head, and Catey can get the Darkling Creeper wearing kneesocks."

I debated opening the car door and jumping out onto the highway. Billy touched my shoulder so I decided to wait.

"I go to this amazing woman in Dumbo," said Billy. "She's the best, she takes her time and everything looks really crisp. She mixes her own colors. See?"

Billy lifted up his shirt and in the rearview mirror I could see an intricate design of interlocking circles and winding ropes along the side of his body.

"Catey?" asked Heller. "Are you okay? Why are you whimpering?"

"I am not whimpering," I insisted as I stared at Billy's tattoo and also at Billy's very defined abdominal muscles, which were something my brothers liked to talk about; they're always doing what Castor calls "ab checks" after they've had sit-up contests. Calico had once told me that Castor uses a magic marker to give himself even more defined abs and when I was doing the laundry there were marker stains on Castor's T-shirts. From what I could see, Billy's abs didn't need any help.

"It's a Celtic symbol for trust and global unity," said Billy.

"That is so cool," said Sophie. "I should get that one too."

"NO!" I said. "Even one tattoo is too many!"

"I've also got this awesome lizard, right here," said Billy, tugging down the collar of his T-shirt to reveal an extremely realistic lizard crawling across his collarbone. "You know what? I've never named my lizard before, but I'm gonna call her Catey."

I was now unable to move or talk because I thought that Billy naming his lizard tattoo after me was both the most disgusting and the most poetic thing that any human being had ever done for another human being in the history of the world.

"Catey can get a crocodile or a turtle tattoo and name it Billy," said Sophie as Heller held up her phone and told Billy, "Give me your tattoo person's number. You're coming with us."

Dumbo, it turned out, stood for Down Under the Manhattan Bridge Overpass, and by the time we'd found a parking space near Billy's tattoo lady, I was drumming my fingers on the dashboard. I was trying to act like it was just nervous energy, so no one would notice. I'd started by drumming exactly three times, but I had to reach thirty sets of three or a car was going to hit Billy. My phone buzzed. I answered it but no one was calling.

"It's an email," said Heller. "Don't you know you can get emails on your phone?" She turned to Sophie and Billy: "In Catey's village, they don't allow electronics. Or buttons, zippers or deodorant. That's why it's such a small village. Go on ahead, we'll be right in."

As Billy and Sophie got out of the van, Heller showed me how to read the email. It was from my mom: "More great news! You've also been accepted at the Torlington School of the Arts in North Carolina, with a full scholarship in Choral

Arrangement and Performance Studies! We are so proud of you!"

What? WHAT? My mind had been a million miles away from stressing out over where or if I might be going to college next year. Everything snapped back into place and I started drumming my fingers even faster, because now I had a choice. When I'd only gotten into Parsippany Tech I didn't have to worry about where I'd be living or what I would study. My future had been decided and I could accept that. But now—Torlington? And music? And best of all and worst of all—performing?

"Catey?" asked Heller. "Are you okay?"

"I'm . . . I'm . . ."

More than anything else I hate to stand up in front of an audience all by myself. When I'm singing with my family I feel surrounded and supported, but if I have to perform even a brief solo in the middle of a group number, I start to shake until one of my brothers or sisters holds my hand.

"Catey? What's going on?"

"Noth . . . noth . . ."

My parents had encouraged me to apply to Torlington because if I majored in Choral Arrangement and Performance Studies I'd be required to prepare solo pieces. My mom had insisted that this would increase my self-confidence. She'd said, "Caitlin, you have a beautiful singing voice but sometimes you sabotage yourself. You're too young to start shutting yourself down."

"Catey, you're shaking. And sweating. Is it Billy? Is this how you get ready for a big date?"

"I . . . I . . . I . . ."

"Catey?"

My hands fluttered, at shoulder height. My eyes darted in every direction, refusing to see anything. My brain lunged for every usual response, for counting or knocking on wood or repeating my family's first names, but I couldn't latch on; nothing was working. I slammed my hands on the dashboard as hard as I could, over and over again, trying to make them bleed, trying to replace all of my horrible thoughts with physical pain.

"Catey! Stop!"

Heller tried to grab my hands but I kept pulling them away, flapping them wildly as my head started to jerk, as if I could shake every terrible thought out of my brain. I was making sounds, not words, just high-pitched repetitive noises.

"CATEY!"

Heller threw her arms around me, like a straitjacket. She held me as tightly as she could while I kept spasming. I slumped against the seat, breathing hard through my nose. Heller released me but kept her arms a few inches from my heaving body.

"Catey, it's okay. You're going to be okay."

"I . . . I . . . I . . ."

"Don't try to talk, not yet. You're having a panic attack."

"Nnnn . . . no . . ."

"Yes, you are. You've always had them. I was there. Only not like this."

She . . . Heller knew? I'd always had panic attacks but I'd convinced myself that I covered them and that nobody noticed. They were my secret. My parents had taken me to a therapist but that was private. I was homeschooled. No one had to know.

"I know how bad they can get. It's okay."

"Not . . . not . . . no . . ."

"Let's try something, I think it might help. I'll do it with you. We're gonna hold our breath and count to three and then slowly let it out. One . . . two . . . three . . ."

I held my breath. I counted. I let it out.

"I saw that email. I think I know what's going on. North Carolina is far away. You'll be alone. They'll want you to sing. Of course you're scared. But this is me. I know you. And, Catey?"

I looked at her.

"You can do it. If you want to. You can do anything."

I tried to smile, but I couldn't. I was reaching for the dashboard.

"Catey?"

I was trying so hard, to pull my hand back. But I knew that my parents were going to die and it would be all my fault. I had to touch the dashboard, only I'd already done that, so I started to pound my fist on the window, in threes, hoping I could break the glass. Heller grabbed my wrist and I jerked around to see her face, and I knew she'd look fed up and disgusted, only she didn't. She looked frightened.

"Catey, this also helps."

Heller dug into her shoulder bag and found a plastic pill bottle.

I shook my head violently back and forth—no! That wasn't the answer! I tried to reach for the bottle to throw it out of the car, but my arm was too weak.

"It's not what you think, I'm clean and you know that. These are left over from when I was trying to quit smoking. They're called Heliotrex and all they do is calm you down, so you can function. You probably won't even notice. I'm just going to give you one."

Sophie and Billy were waiting. My parents were depending on me. Everyone was depending on me, even if I didn't know who they were.

Heller handed me the pill and a bottle of water.

I held the pill in the palm of my hand.

I didn't want to feel like this. I didn't want anyone to see me feeling like this. I wanted to make all of the terrible feelings and the compulsions and the shivering go away.

I swallowed the pill.

"Good girl," said Heller.

The tattoo parlor was in a storefront and the walls were covered with drawings of different tattoos. The possibilities included a tattered American flag, a skull wearing a pirate scarf and a hoop earring, tumbling dice, a woman in a leopard-skin bikini riding a lion, a peace symbol, and characters from *Star Wars*,

Avatar, Star Trek and every known video game, which made me wonder, Why would anyone want the Super Mario Brothers across their stomach? There was also Chinese calligraphy with English translations, for words like friendship, eternity, war, blood brothers, family and for some reason, "to vomit." There were also frillier designs of roses and lilies but these were surrounding hearts with daggers through them, dripping blood. There was a whole section devoted to stick figures, which at first looked like one of those charts on the wall of a restaurant that demonstrate the Heimlich maneuver, but then I realized that the stick figures were having sex with each other, in different positions.

"Billy!" said a woman emerging from behind a beaded curtain. I couldn't tell how old the woman was because every inch of her was covered in tattoos, including her face, which was patterned with tiger stripes. Her arms looked like comic books and she was wearing a tank top so I could see that her neck and shoulders had realistic pictures of smiling babies' heads; she was like a human grandchild bracelet. She had on tight, faded jeans with what I thought were patches but which turned out to be holes exposing tattoos that looked like patches. She had long jet-black hair and piercings along both ears, both eyebrows, both nostrils and her lips; her head was like a jewelry display at a street fair.

"Larinda!" said Billy, and as they hugged I began wondering if, once we were married, Billy and I would invite Larinda over for Thanksgiving dinner or on Saturday night for board games and mac and cheese.

"Larinda, this is Heller and Catey and Sophie. Sophie wants some ink."

"Welcome, one and all," said Larinda. "I love my Billy! Are we just talking about little Sophie here, or how about you girls getting in on the action?"

"I'm so there," Heller told Larinda. "I love your stuff." From what I'd glimpsed over the weekend, Heller already had tattoos of her mom's face, a smiling banana wearing a top hat, SpongeBob with his hand down his SquarePants, and the Statue of Liberty smoking a joint.

"Catey?" said Larinda. "Are you in?"

Ordinarily, right about now, I wouldn't be able to breathe or I'd be running out the door and trying to drag Heller and Sophie along with me. For some reason, and maybe it was the pill I'd swallowed, I was feeling incredibly serene and centered. The tattoos on the walls seemed very friendly, like a mural in a nursery with a dancing parade of Disney characters.

"Sophie, while I don't approve, I understand why you want to get a tattoo," I said. "As for me, I am the last person on earth who would ever, ever do anything like that. I just don't believe in doing anything overtly pornographic or reprehensible or trashy."

"You are the sweetest girl I've ever met," said Billy, which was when I grabbed him by the neck and started kissing him, only instead of like when I'd kissed Mills, this time I opened my mouth.

twenty-eight

Way Beyond over the Edge

The next thing I remember I was behind the wheel of a cherry-red convertible with the top down, going ninety miles per hour down a highway, singing along with a pop song on the radio at the top of my lungs, with Heller beside me and Sophie in the backseat singing even louder. I was feeling fantastic and when I glanced in the rearview mirror I saw that my hair had been hacked off and dyed at least five neon colors and there was a little silver post sticking through the side of my nose. I felt something on my forearm and I looked down to see a white bandage. Which was how I knew I wasn't wearing my blazer and that I'd ripped the sleeves off my blouse.

Heller had a bandage on her forearm too and Sophie's wrist was wrapped in gauze and her topknot was now hot pink, tipped in bright blue and orange, like a snow cone. As I was processing all of this information there was one central detail that stood out and stopped me cold: I was driving.

While I had a learner's permit, I hadn't used it for almost a year because I was terrified of driving. My parents and several of my older siblings had sat beside me while I'd taken very, very slow test drives on empty back roads, but on each trip I'd stopped after half a mile, convinced that I was about to careen off the road and slam into a nonexistent tree or house. I'd eventually stopped trying and my mom had comforted me by saying, "Driving isn't for everyone," and my dad had said, "You'll drive when you're ready," and my brother Callum had said, "Maybe you should practice driving while you're sitting at your desk, unless you're worried about ramming into a floor lamp."

I wasn't just driving, I was breaking the speed limit by at least forty miles an hour and I only had one hand on the steering wheel because I was pumping my other fist in the air, keeping the beat.

I yanked the wheel to one side and drove onto the shoulder of the highway and slammed on the brakes.

"What . . . what am I doing?" I asked.

"You were doing great!" said Heller.

"You're fucking amazing!" said Sophie. "You're my new hero!"

"Excuse me?" said Heller.

"My second new hero! My assistant new hero! You're both incredible!"

"But . . . but . . . I'm driving," I said. "My hair is . . . gone. There's something in my nose!"

I looked down at the seat beside me.

"I HAVE A GUN! WHY DO I HAVE A GUN?"

"Catey?" said Heller. "What's going on? Don't you remember?"

"Dude," said Sophie, "you were on fire! You were like . . . Lynnea! If she wasn't always so bummed about the end of the world!"

"What—what did I do? The last thing I remember is—oh my good Lord, I was kissing Billy Connors! Where's Billy?"

"You left him at the tattoo parlor," Heller explained. "He was running along behind us when you stole the car."

"When I WHAT?"

"She didn't steal it," said Sophie. "She, like, borrowed it. The keys were in the ignition, which means that whoever owns it, they wanted us to borrow it, right?"

I wasn't sure which was more horrifying: the things that Heller and Sophie were telling me I'd done, or the fact that I couldn't remember any of it.

"All right," I said, trying to keep my breathing and my heartbeat under control. "You have to tell me. Step-by-step. Don't leave anything out. What did I do?"

"Well," Heller began, "at the tattoo place you were a wild booty-humper. You were kissing Billy for a really long time— no, I would say that you were devouring him. All I could see were his feet sticking out of your mouth."

"Which at first I thought was kind of gross," said Sophie. "Because of all the slurping. And the moaning."

"Then you pushed Billy away," Heller continued. "You said, 'Thank you, William, and bless you,' and you said to Larinda, 'If your schedule permits, I would truly enjoy a tattoo.'"

"It was so great!" said Sophie. "You were like you, only, I don't know, wild! Because after Larinda did all our tattoos you said, 'Thank you so much and may I ask, what other services do you offer?' You were so, like, super polite, like you were ordering brunch or something, and when Larinda asked if you wanted to get your nose pierced you said, 'Might I?' You sounded, like, English or something! It turned out so awesome and it didn't bleed almost at all! I was gonna get mine pierced too but I decided to just let my parents kill me for the tattoo."

I looked in the mirror and gently touched the stud in my nose, which was throbbing. It looked like my nose had been in a construction accident.

"And then," Heller said, "I couldn't believe it, I was so pissed. Once we went outside, our van was missing. Gone. Not there. Some asshole had probably hot-wired it, and there weren't any cabs so I didn't know how we were going to get back to the hotel."

"Catey, you were so on it," said Sophie. "You just stood there and you looked around and you saw this convertible. You pointed at it and you said, 'The Lord provides.'"

"You looked up to heaven and you gave this little salute," said Heller.

"That's right, that's right, that's right!" said Sophie.

"You walked over to it," said Heller, "you found the keys and you smiled at us, and you said, 'It's such a lovely spring day. Let's put the top down. And perhaps I'll take mine off.'"

"Whoa!" said Sophie. "So cool! Billy was just staring at you, he was all like, what?!"

"We jumped in and you floored it, before Billy could get in," said Heller, "and you waved to him and you said, 'Ladies only, William! I enjoyed your tongue!'"

"I LOVE YOU!" said Sophie. "You should have your own video game!"

I couldn't comprehend any of this. I refused to. None of it was possible. There was simply no way that I, Caitlin Mary Prudence Rectitude Singleberry, could have performed any of the criminal acts Heller and Sophie were describing and cheering for.

This was all Heller's fault. She'd been planning this all along, to catch me at a weak moment and drug me. This was her evil triumph. She'd crossed the ultimate line.

The pill Heller had given me must have knocked me unconscious, or maybe the drug had changed my body chemistry in some hideous way. I'd once seen a TV commercial for an antidepressant that had shown a cartoon woman with a cartoon rain cloud over her head, and the cloud had followed her around until the woman had taken the antidepressant and then the cloud had turned into a bouquet of daisies with smiley faces. All during this commercial a voice-over had been saying, "Side effects may include dry mouth, a loss of sensation in the fingertips and toes, kidney failure, night blindness, stroke risk and intense homicidal or suicidal thoughts." I didn't understand why anyone would take that drug with all of those risks attached, so now I needed to know, what were the warnings on the pill Heller had given me?

"Heller," I said, trying to speak calmly and evenly. "What was in that pill you gave me? Was it a street drug? What are the possible side effects?"

"Nothing!" Heller insisted. "It's totally mild! On the bottle, it doesn't say anything about stealing cars or flashing people."

"Did you say . . . flashing people?" I asked, hoping against hope that by flashing, Heller meant blowing kisses or making a peace sign or maybe just waving.

"It was so stellar," said Sophie. "We're driving along having a blast, and this big tractor-trailer tries to pass us, right, and there's a dude hanging out the window and he's yelling stuff and he's being, like, so rude."

"So you say, 'Hel, could you please take the wheel,'" said Heller, "and I grab it while you pull your blouse open and you say to the guy in the truck, 'These belong to Jesus! But I'll pray for you!'"

"BOOM!" said Sophie. "I think that truck drove right off the road!"

I looked down to button my blouse back up, which I certainly would have done if the top three buttons hadn't been missing.

"And then, oh man, I love this part," said Sophie, "you see this hairstyling place called Tiffani's Happening Hairbomb. And you say, 'Ladies, I think I could use a little touch-up,' and you pull over."

"At first I was worried that you might do something that Kenz and Nedda wouldn't approve of, like a perm," said Heller.

"But you had a plan. You walked right into that salon and said, 'I would like to speak with Tiffani.' So Tiffani came over and you sat down in one of the chairs and you said, 'I would like the full Happening Hairbomb experience. Look at all of those marvelous bottles over there with so many different hair colors and rinses, and are those called cellophanes? Tiffani, I trust you.'"

"You were so fucking outlaw," said Sophie. "You shut your eyes and Tiffani got busy. And that, like, gave me courage, so I told Misti Ramona, who was one of the other stylists, to get goin' with my topknot. I told her to think parfait Popsicle on Mars. Do you love it?"

"It's . . . it's really colorful," I said, turning to look at Sophie, because that way I could stop staring at the active crime scene on top of my own head.

"Just when Tiffani had run out of colors and was finishing up," said Heller. "That's when we heard it."

"I got so scared," said Sophie.

"What? What did you hear?"

"Gunshots," said Heller, "from the Valu-Brite convenience store, which was right next to the Happening Hairbomb at the strip mall. Somebody was robbing it and everyone at the Hairbomb was all, 'Lock the doors! Let's hide in the back! Call 911!' But you were so totally together, you didn't even bat an eye, you just said, 'If everyone would please excuse me?'"

"We followed you," said Sophie, "but we stayed like a few yards behind you. You reached into the convertible, into the glove compartment, right, and that was where you got the pistol. You held it up in the air and you cocked it, like you'd been using a gun your whole damn life. Then you shut your eyes and you, like, prayed or something."

"And then, oh my God, I couldn't believe it, I was like, go, Catey, go," said Heller. "You marched into that Valu-Brite and we crouched down and watched you from the window. There were these two guys wearing ski masks, and one of them had a sawed-off shotgun and he was pointing it at the woman behind the counter, who was so nice, but she could barely speak English and she was shaking. The other creep kept telling her, 'Gimme the money from the registers or we'll splatter your brains all over the fucking breath mints.'"

"So I'm going, oh no, they're gonna kill that poor lady, and then they'll kill us," said Sophie. "But you walked in there and you pointed your pistol right at those two jerkwads, and you said, oh my God, it was so beyond badass, you said . . ."

"'I'm certain that you fellows hail from underprivileged and possibly abusive backgrounds, and I will do everything in my power to help you overcome those obstacles,'" said Heller.

"And then the guy with the shotgun turned toward you," said Sophie, "and he said, 'Overcome this, bitch.' And you said . . ."

"'I am not a bitch. I'm a good Christian girl and I'm gonna send you straight to Hell,'" said Heller and Sophie in unison.

"He dropped the shotgun!" said Heller. "He said to the other guy, 'She's scaring the shit outta me!' They both ran out of the store! And you told the lady behind the counter to call the police and to show them the footage from the security cameras, and the lady was so grateful and she kept thanking you and asking if there was anything she could do for you. You told her that you'd only done what any decent person would've done, and then you said . ..."

"'BUT I WOULD LIKE SOME SKITTLES,'" said Heller and Sophie, jubilantly high-fiving each other.

I looked down at my lap and there it was: an empty bag of Skittles.

"Did I . . . did I pay for the Skittles?"

"You tried to," said Heller, "but the cashier was so happy, because you'd saved her life, that she just handed them over. And she said that Tiffani did really good work."

"So what you're claiming," I said, "what you're telling me is . . . that I deep-kissed a boy I barely even know, then I got a tattoo, then I got my nose pierced, then I stole a car, then I exposed myself to a passing vehicle, then I got my hair chopped off by a person named Tiffani, then I threatened a stranger with a gun, and then I stole a bag of Skittles. You are telling me that I am an unstoppable one-person crime wave."

"You're a superstar!" said Heller.

"You're the baddest bitch on the planet!" said Sophie. "And you're still wearing kneesocks!"

I couldn't fathom, let alone begin to accept, any of this. I couldn't have done any of the things Heller and Sophie had just reported, even if I'd been drugged. Even if Heller had forced me to. Except—my hair. My nose. My arm. The convertible. The GUN.

I jumped out of the car. I stood there, turning in every direction, flailing, as if I could corkscrew myself back in time and reverse everything.

"Get in the car," said Heller, sliding behind the wheel. "I'll drive."

Should I run? Should I flag down a passing car and beg the driver to take me to a police station, where I could file charges against Heller? Should I lie down in the middle of the road so I could get run over?

"Get in!" said Heller. I pulled myself together. I had to take control. I would demand that Heller drive us back to the hotel, as a start. I would wear a scarf over my hair until it grew back. I would have the stud removed and pray that my nose would heal. As for whatever was under that bandage—I couldn't think about it, not yet. I got in the car.

"Catey," said Sophie, "totally thanks to you, we're, like, ready. To do the last thing on my list."

"No," I said. "Don't you dare. We're not doing anything else, ever. We're done. We are going back to the hotel. THEN WE ARE GOING TO CHURCH."

"Just one more thing!"

"No!"

"Like what?" asked Heller.

I tried to keep protesting but I was so upset I couldn't even form words.

"Okay," said Sophie. "Okay okay okay. Here goes. I did the squiggle machine and I got my tattoo. But all of that was kind of a warm-up. I need to do something, like, okay okay okay—dangerous."

Sophie took a deep breath and bounced up and down on the seat.

"Something that could kill me."

twenty-nine

Something That Could What?

Sophie," I said, trying not to scream. "If even half of what you and Heller just told me is true, then I think we've done more than our share of dangerous activities for one day. For one century. You're already dealing with a life-threatening illness—why would you want to get any closer to dying?"

"'Cause you're totally right," said Sophie. "I've spent, like, way too much time having cancer and almost dying all over the place. And yeah, for a while I was all like, why? Why me? Why would God, or whoever is pulling this stupid stuff, why would they give cancer to a kid? To any kid? Or even, like, to any grown-up? So I talked to my parents and my specialists and to a ton of therapists and to this online priest and my friend Julie's rabbi and to some Buddhist guy at the airport, and to other kids with cancer, and I always end up with, like, the same damn thing: No . . . one . . . knows. Boom. Total boom. Don't blame God, because maybe it's part of God's plan, or maybe it's out of

God's control, although come on, why would you want to believe in some ditz-ass God who keeps secrets, or who can't stop all the crappy stuff from happening? What kind of God is that, like, part-time? Is God like, what, some fucking unpaid intern, geeking off? Or I don't know, is it, like, my fault, did I get cancer 'cause I ate too much gluten, or not enough gluten, or because our house is too close to some high-tension wires, or because my mom used her cell phone while she was pregnant, although I figure that if using your cell gives you cancer, the streets are gonna be empty.

"So finally I just stopped asking, because, please, come on, like what did I expect? There is no answer. I even made up a word for it, like it's halfway between boom and crap: brap. Just brap. Like, deal with it. But while I was sitting there in that recliner, getting more chemo pumped into me, I don't know why, but I started thinking, like, what if cancer was a person, no, not really a person, more like a thing or a raptor or the bad guy in a movie, like Darth Vader or that bitch who tries to kidnap Coraline and sew buttons on her eyes? Only my cancer dude was, like, three thousand feet tall with green eyes and billions of sharp little teeth and he was from outer space like in the Alien movies, and all he wants to do is kill me.

"And once I got home I started drawing pictures of him and I started calling him the Cancer King. All I kept thinking was, How can I kill him before he kills me? I figure that, like, what I need to do is, I've gotta show the Cancer King that I'm in charge. Of, like, whatever's gonna happen. And no, of course I don't want to die, because dying sucks, and because someday

I might want to see if I could sneak into the factory where they make Skittles, or go to college and then drop out and invent something and make a billion dollars, or even have sex, which, I'm sorry, but I still think that sex sounds like bullshit, like it's two people pretending to like it while they're really thinking about Skittles. So I want to do something dangerous, or at least scary, but it's got to be something that has absolutely nothing to do with cancer. Something, like, totally Heller Harrigan, right? So that way I can tell the Cancer King, 'Hey, dickwad, watch this! Brap you!'"

I was going to scold Sophie about her language but she was already looking at me like, Really?

"I know what we have to do," said Heller.

"What?" I asked.

"The quarry."

thirty

The Quarry

No. NO! How could she? How could Heller even suggest going back to the quarry? For the past four years I'd spent most of my time trying not to think about the quarry. No, that's wrong. I'd been trying to pretend the quarry didn't exist.

Heller glanced at me in the rearview mirror as she pulled the car back onto the highway. Why was she doing this? Was she deliberately trying to hurt me? Had she been planning this all along? For all those years I'd hated Heller, but over the past two days my feelings had started to change. We'd shared things about our lives. We'd worked together. We'd laughed.

But now I wondered: Did Heller hate *me*?

I got very quiet. My mouth was dry. My hands were starting to flutter.

"The quarry?" asked Sophie, who knew she was onto something, and because she was thirteen, she wasn't about to leave it alone. "What's the quarry?"

Heller was still watching me, carefully, in the mirror.

"There's this incredible quarry, you'll see," she told Sophie. "It's practically the whole side of a mountain, only a mile from where Catey and I grew up. Up until fifty years ago it was still active and they used it for granite and limestone, tons of it; there used to be a sign saying that this quarry provided the stone for half of the civic buildings in Trenton, the state capital. But then, I don't know, I guess they'd chopped out all of the granite they could use or the company went bankrupt, because the mining operation got shut down. There's this underground spring, so over the years the whole quarry filled up with water, and it's really clear springwater so you can see right to the bottom. People started going out there, because it's so beautiful to look at and to go swimming and just hang out."

"Stop it," I whispered, because that was all I could manage. "Please stop talking about this. Right now."

"But this place sounds fantastic," said Sophie.

"Catey," said Heller, "we have to talk about it. This whole weekend it's been sitting there, in the corner, staring at us, and you've been like, oh no, everything's fine, everything's fabulous, except you haven't seen me or contacted me for four years. Until I became a big movie star."

"That has nothing to do with it," I said, trying to keep my voice as direct as I could. "I almost died. And you didn't care. You never care."

Heller matched my seriousness. "That's not true."

We were negotiating, and I wasn't about to back down.

"Fine," I said. "You can tell Sophie. After you tell her we

will never talk about it, ever again. Just the way that after this weekend we will never have to see each other, ever again."

"Oh my God," said Sophie. "This is like a dark secret that has haunted the two of you forever. Like if you went into an abandoned house and then murdered someone and ate them. Or if you got abducted by aliens and the aliens made you dance in front of them and then the aliens Instagrammed it to all the other planets, so that the entire universe was laughing at you. Or maybe you're, like, secretly eco-terrorists and four years ago you blew up a factory that manufactured those plastic diapers, and you didn't mean to hurt anybody but one of the diapers exploded and killed someone. This is the best day ever!"

"There's a chain at the quarry," Heller began, "and it's attached to this big mechanical arm, it's sort of like a crane, which was part of how they'd move the granite, because they'd wrap the slabs with rope and then attach the rope to this hook at the end of the chain and hoist the slabs up, and swing them over to where the trucks would be waiting. Even after the quarry shut down and got filled with water, the arm with the chain and the hook were still there. So people started daring each other to balance their feet on the hook and hold on to the chain and swing way out over the quarry and then jump off into the water, which is really deep. Over the years it became this thing, like right before the seniors graduate from Parsippany High, they do the chain, or guys would get drunk at a bachelor party and drag a keg out to the quarry and blast music and do the chain."

"But sometimes people would get hurt," I said, because Heller was making the whole thing sound like fun. "Someone even drowned, this sixteen-year-old girl."

"Whoa," said Sophie.

"Because she'd dropped acid and didn't know what she was doing," said Heller. "But after that the police put up a fence and warning signs and they tried to stop people from doing the chain, or even just going swimming or sunbathing on the rocks. Which meant, of course, that everyone in Parsippany was always daring everyone else to sneak out there. Especially Catey's brothers."

"Who never even went out there!" I said. "All they would do was talk about it and make plans but they'd never do it, because they knew that our parents would slaughter them and then ground them forever."

"Catey's brothers were always picking on us, and calling us babies and guppies and nice little sweetie-pie girly-girls."

"Which we were," I said. "At least I was."

"I couldn't stand it," said Heller. "As far back as I can remember, if someone told me I couldn't do something, or I wasn't allowed to do it, because I was a girl or because I was too young or because I was a scaredy-cat, well, watch out."

"Which is why I totally love you so much," said Sophie. "Like when I would play with my Anna Banana doll, I would make her dump all of my Barbies into the toilet and try to flush them. Which doesn't work, unless you just flush their heads and even then sometimes their ponytails still won't flush, they just sort of swirl around in the water."

"It was my thirteenth birthday," said Heller, "and I'm sorry, but in a whole lot of cultures that makes you an adult. I mean, in some places, thirteen-year-old girls get married or they go to work, to support their families."

I was going to tell Heller that because we lived in America, thirteen-year-old girls didn't have to do any of those things, but then I remembered that Heller had done most of them.

"I was getting all geared up," said Heller, "to become this big star, or at least to become something major, or at least to get the hell out of Parsippany. I wanted to mark the occasion. I wanted to get started on doing stuff that scared me. I wanted Catey to come with me because she was my best friend in the whole world, and because nothing really counted unless I did it with Catey."

Which was exactly how, four years ago, Heller had convinced me to disobey my parents and the law and common sense, and go with her to the quarry. I'd known every step of the way that what we were doing was wrong, but it had been Heller's birthday, which her mom had forgotten all about.

Aunt Nancy had forgotten Heller's birthday before and the next day she'd always feel terrible and she'd try to make it up to Heller by taking her for a special belated-birthday sushi dinner at a Thai takeout place, or she'd tell Heller that birthdays and parties and cake were just a westernized consumerist construct and that fully actualized beings didn't need birthdays. Heller would always defend Aunt Nancy and she'd try to act as if everything was fine but I don't think anyone is that fully actualized, especially about birthdays. My mom would always remember Heller's birthday and she'd remind Nancy, who'd still forget, maybe because celebrating anyone's birthday made Nancy feel older. My mom would always invite Heller over for cupcakes.

On Heller's thirteenth birthday my parents had been out of town because my grandma Peggy, who lives in Florida, had broken her hip. Catherine had been assigned to take care of the rest of us, but because there'd been so many kids, and because Catherine had been packing to go away to college, it had been easy for Heller and me to slip away.

"It was around four in the afternoon," said Heller. "We rode our bikes out to the quarry. It was such a gorgeous day; it was August, so it was still light out. The quarry was deserted so it was really peaceful and quiet except for the birds and the little waterfall. I guess I was feeling all full of myself, because it was my birthday, and I was trying really hard not to be mad at my mom. I knew that Catey was scared of a lot of things, well, of everything, so I thought it would be good for her, to do something wild. Well, wild for Parsippany."

Heller glanced at me in the mirror, daring me to correct her. I couldn't. But she was only telling her side of the story.

I'd been so scared because we were sneaking out and because we'd had to bike down a narrow path through some spooky woods to get to the quarry and because I'd never been to the quarry before. I'd felt as if we'd traveled really far, as if we'd left New Jersey, and I was relying on Heller to protect me and to remember how to get home.

"Once we got out there, I was dancing around," Heller

continued. "I was so excited to get away from all of my troubles at home and I just wanted to get started on my big new life. I grabbed that chain and I balanced my feet on the hook at the end of it. I felt like I was a pirate, setting sail, or like I was flying, or skydiving out over the ocean. I was swinging back and forth and all around and I was yelling, because it just felt so great. I swung all the way out and I let go, and it felt like forever, but it was really only a few seconds before I hit the water. It was summer so the water was warm and I started floating on my back looking up at the sky and at the granite cliffs, and I saw Catey standing near the edge, all the way up at the top."

"Catey?" asked Sophie. "What did you do?"

"I . . . I . . . I'd watched Heller jump, but she'd do anything, especially if it was dangerous. I didn't want Heller to think I was a scaredy-cat, and I wanted to be like her, and most of all . . . I didn't want to be like me. I don't really remember all of it. I thought that maybe I could change everything about myself, and maybe by the time I hit the water I'd be this brave, happy, cool new person. I grabbed hold of the chain, but I was clinging to it, because I was terrified. The chain was only moving a few inches back and forth but I was too scared to either jump back onto the cliff or swing all the way out, the way Heller had. Heller was shouting, 'Catey, come on! Catey, you'll love it! The water's so warm! Don't be such a baby! Quit stalling!' I tried to swing outward, to use my body weight, but I was so clumsy and I didn't know what I was doing and then my hand slipped. I tried to hold on with my other hand but I couldn't and so—I fell."

"Oh my God oh my God oh my God . . . ," said Sophie.

"I fell, I don't know exactly how far, but then I slammed into the rocks and then I finally dropped into the water, but by that time I was unconscious."

"I dragged Catey to shore," said Heller. "I didn't know if she was dead or alive. I started screaming to see if there was anyone around to help but there wasn't, so I called 911 and I sat with Catey and I tried to do CPR and mouth-to-mouth and finally an ambulance showed up and all these cop cars."

"I was in a coma for a week," I said. "They had to drain fluid out of my skull where it had built up, and I'd also fractured my arm and my pelvis. When I finally regained consciousness I had to stay in the hospital for another month because the doctors weren't sure if I'd have permanent brain damage. They finally decided that I was going to be okay and that everything would heal, and they let me go home." I rubbed my arms, because remembering all this was making me feel ice-cold. Sometimes my left arm still ached, because there was a steel pin in it.

"I never saw Heller again, or even talked to her. Until two days ago."

I'd never told anyone this story. Everyone in my family knew the details, so they left it alone. Although even now, every once in a while, I'd catch my parents looking at me with these worried expressions, as if they still weren't sure I'd survived. I know that telling a secret, or making a confession, is supposed to make you feel better, as if a weight's been lifted. I didn't know how I felt. I was trying not to look at Heller.

"We have to do it," said Sophie. "How far is the quarry?"

thirty-one

The Chain

By the time Heller had driven us out to the quarry it was late afternoon but there was still sunlight. I wasn't sure what I'd expected to find but everything looked just the way I remembered. The quarry was both beautiful and intimidating, like a picnic spot on the moon. You could see where the miners and their machines had sliced through the rock, but trees and grass and vines were reclaiming any area with soil and even sprouting through cracks in the granite.

There wasn't much of a breeze and there was no one else around so the surface of the water was smooth, with glinting sunbeams; the quarry was too small to be called a lake but much wider and deeper than a pond. The fence was still there although it had rusted and there were scraps of yellow crime scene tape fluttering from the corners. I wasn't sure if this tape had remained from what had happened four years ago or if there had been other accidents since then.

"Come on," said Heller, leading Sophie around the fence and onto the flat layer of rock that overlooked the water.

I needed to stop this. We'd told Sophie the story. We'd seen the quarry. Heller knew this was the last place on earth I wanted to be. Why was she torturing me? Why did she want me to relive the worst moment of both our lives? Why couldn't we get back in the car?

Then I knew why. Heller wanted to convince herself that nothing was her fault. Heller wanted to prove that she was still braver and stronger than me.

"This is like . . . where an asteroid hit," said Sophie. "Or where the Loch Ness Monster stays when he comes over here for a visit."

"I love it here," said Heller, looking out over the water. "You can still see clear to the bottom."

I didn't want to get any closer to the water to check if this was true, and I didn't want to go anywhere near the crane, which was still hanging over the quarry itself, with the chain and the hook attached. The arm had rusted even more and the green paint was faded and peeling. I didn't know why the police hadn't removed the whole rotting mechanism—maybe it was too solidly anchored to its cement base.

"We shouldn't have come here," I said. "We have to leave. Right now."

"Catey, it's okay," said Heller. "You don't have to do anything. This is just for Sophie, and I'll show her how to do it."

Heller looked at me but I couldn't read her expression. Was she challenging me? Ignoring me? Or was it something else?

Did she almost look—like she wanted me to understand something?

Heller and Sophie took off everything except their underwear. Sophie's pink-and-blue topknot looked even more bizarre when combined with her round white body and her neon lime-green bra and panties, with a pattern of black bunny heads with Xs over their eyes, as if they'd been electrocuted.

"Okay, Sophie-toons," said Heller, "the trick is to get some momentum going, to swing back and forth, and then, when you're ready, you let go, once you're all the way out there."

"I think I get it," said Sophie, who was shivering, although I couldn't tell if this was from fear or being almost naked.

"NO," I said, as forcefully as I could. When I heard my own voice I was shocked by how determined I sounded.

"Catey, I told you," said Heller, "you don't have to do anything. You can just watch."

"Excuse me?"

"This is about me and Sophie."

"Heller," I said, and my voice was shaking with rage. "Do you really think this has nothing to do with me? Is that what you really fucking think?"

I couldn't believe I had just used an f-bomb, but I'd needed it. Heller cursed all the time so her swear words barely meant anything. My using an f-bomb had startled Heller and Sophie.

"Catey?" said Heller.

"Are you okay?" asked Sophie.

"No, I am not okay," I said, which was something I would ordinarily never admit. I was the girl who would never complain. I was the girl who my parents and everyone else would say was a blessing and no trouble at all. I was the girl who was always okay, or who would lie and pretend to be okay. Until now.

"I almost died here," I said. "I was unconscious for a week. Because of you. AND YOU NEVER CAME TO SEE ME. YOU NEVER EVEN CALLED. MY BEST FRIEND NEVER EVEN CALLED."

"I wanted to! But I wasn't allowed to talk to you! Your parents wouldn't let me! My mother wouldn't let me! It wasn't my fault!"

"It wasn't your fault? Did you really just say that? Heller, EVERYTHING that happened here was your fault! I never would've come out here if you hadn't made me do it! I never would've jumped if you hadn't kept calling me a coward and a pussy and fraidycat Catey!"

"I WAS TRYING TO HELP YOU!"

"BY ALMOST KILLING ME? Sophie, you can't listen to her. This is exactly what Heller always does. She puts herself in charge of everything and she makes everyone else feel like they're tiny, like they're nothing compared to her. She makes everything seem like fun, like a wild crazy adventure, until it's not. Until someone gets hurt. Until someone almost dies!"

"Shut up, Catey," said Heller. "You don't know what you're talking about."

"I know exactly what I'm talking about! I know everything about you! I was here, four years ago! I listened to you!"

"AND YOU SHOULD HAVE!" said Heller as she took a step toward me. "You're exactly like you always were! You're such a fucking good little girl! Just like everybody always says, everybody you spend your entire life sucking up to! Just so they'll say, Look at Catey! She's so smart! She has such perfect manners! Her parents are so proud of her! But you're still scared of EVERYTHING! Is that what you want? To be terrified for the rest of your life? Is that who you are? Is that all you are?"

"Guys?" said Sophie, who sounded really worried. "Please don't fight. I mean, you were friends, right? Like best friends?"

"Were we?" said Heller.

"I don't know! Don't friends love each other? Don't friends try to find each other, no matter what's in the way? Heller, I loved you so much and I kept waiting. For something. Anything. But you were too busy. Because you were a star. Which is why you don't have any friends, not real ones. You have fans and followers and haters and stalkers, but you don't have a single real friend."

"Heller?" said Sophie. "Like . . . is that true?"

Heller stared at me in a way she never had before. She stared at me as if she wanted to kill me. Which didn't make me panic but it did make me shiver. It made me incredibly sad, sad in a way I'd never been, even in the hospital. Heller was right. I was going to be sad and scared for the rest of my life. And alone.

"I'll go first," said Heller. She stood next to the mechanical arm, in her expensive black lace bra and panties.

Heller stood with her bare feet spread apart and her arms raised as high as they could go. In her most booming, actress-y voice she announced, "I am Heller Harrigan, Daytime Emmy Award nominee and People's Choice Fresh New Face First Runner-Up! In the names of Anna Banana, Lynnea, and wacked-out chicks everywhere, I will conquer this quarry! Because I'm not afraid of anything!"

She grabbed the chain and wound her legs around it, balancing one foot on top of the hook. Even when she was little Heller had always behaved as if she was in a movie, with the cameras and millions of people watching. Heller was a really good actress, but since she was born, Heller had been a star.

Heller howled like Tarzan or like somebody who'd just won the lottery or like someone who was determined to use her voice to drown out everything else in her life, and she swung all the way and then she started showing off by making the chain spin her around really fast so she became a blur, and then she centered herself and swung so far that her body was almost parallel to the water. She let go.

As Heller dropped she grinned and waved her arms to prove that she was reckless and free, but when she hit the water she got a surprised look on her face, as if she'd forgotten the water was there. She disappeared for a few seconds and then a few more, just long enough to make Sophie and me worry that something had gone wrong and to make me worry that she was trying to drown herself just to get back at me. To prove some sort of impossibly self-destructive point. To have the last word.

Then Heller shot out of the water with her hair plastered down her back.

"YOW!!!" Heller yelled. "It's warm, but not that warm! But it's good! It's fabulous! Sophie, are you ready?"

Sophie looked at me and then she ran over and hugged me, which I wasn't expecting. She was a little sweaty and smelled like oranges and lilacs.

"I am so scared. I'm scared of dying. I'm scared of having to go back into the hospital. I'm scared of having to watch my parents watch me barf. I'm scared of everything. But I don't want to be."

"Sophie, you don't have to do this. I don't know if jumping will make you any less scared. It might just make you cold and wet and you could get really hurt. Even if you don't jump I'll still think you're the bravest girl I've ever met."

Sophie thought for a moment and then she said, "No, I want to do it. I have to. Kids with cancer never get to do this."

Sophie shrieked, like someone in a horror movie getting stabbed by a pitchfork. She ran over to the chain, stared at it and grabbed it. She wound her leg around the chain, imitating Heller, and she shoved herself off the edge with her other foot. At first she couldn't manage to swing out very far or very fast; she was moving in slow motion.

"Momentum!" yelled Heller, who was floating on her back. "Back and forth!"

Sophie started to swing a little farther each time by shoving her body forward. She wasn't as graceful as Heller but she was getting the job done. Her foot slipped and I gasped, but she had a firm grip on the chain so she didn't fall. She managed a wide loopy swing, then the chain bent into an L shape, and she yelled, "Brap you, everything!" and let go. As she dropped, her arms and legs pinwheeled in different directions so she looked like a cartoon rabbit trying to run really fast in midair. She grabbed her knees and curled her body inward, hitting the water with a loud noise and a major splash.

"Classic cannonball!" yelled Heller. "Sophie rules!"

Sophie popped up almost instantly, sputtering, with her wet topknot glued to the side of her head. She raised a fist in the air as Heller hugged her.

"Yay!" Sophie yelled. "I did the chain! And I still have my underwear on!"

Before this weekend I'd had an idea of myself, or at least a goal, of the sort of person I'd wanted to be. I'd be a Girl Scout crossed with a nun and a headmistress, with a collection of Good Conduct medals and Headed for Sainthood trophies, all of which I'd be too modest to accept. I'd go to Parsippany Tech and get perfect grades and I'd not only do my family's taxes, I'd travel to underprivileged countries as a member of Accountants Without Borders. I'd be exactly what Heller said I was: a priss-pot in granny panties. I'd spend my entire life keeping my head down and behaving myself and trying desperately to never secretly congratulate myself on being so perfect, because the second I did that, the second I tried to be happy, or proud of myself, or weird, or different, that was when my own personal

Cancer Kings, which were my Anxiety Monster and my Guilt Goblin, would come roaring out of their subterranean caves, looking for me and cackling.

Now those monsters had me in their jaws for a gleeful tug-of-war, as I felt my chest tighten and I could hear every vicious, taunting thought rushing into my brain, telling me that I was worthless and useless and worse. My throat was starting to contract and my fists were clenching and I began looking around wildly for trees to count, or license plates without the dreaded number 9 on them, or a bathroom where I could wash my hands again and again, only not a public bathroom because the germs would swarm over me and eat me alive.

It was me or those monsters and it was a fight to the death. I told my legs to move, to power me right over to that crane. Four years ago the chain had been damp, which had made my hand slip. I kicked off my shoes and I peeled off one of my kneesocks and I tugged it over my hand like a protective mitten, and I used that mitten to get a tight grip on the chain. From below I could hear Heller and Sophie calling my name as I placed my foot decisively on top of the hook. Once I had both of my hands on the chain, I shoved, using my whole body, and I swung out over the water. I could hear the mechanical arm creaking and I could feel the cool air rushing past me as the setting sun blinded me.

I swung back and forth with the distance growing higher and longer with each swing. I felt like I was swinging so far out that I might leap off and land on my feet on the far side of the quarry. For better or for worse—and since it was me, for worse was more likely—I was doing this.

I was doing the craziest, most defiant, most irresponsible thing I could think of, not because Heller had dared me and humiliated me but because I wanted to. I had to. I had to stop hating Heller and hiding inside my blazer and worrying myself into a fate way worse than drowning. I had to save my own life. Or end it.

I swung all the way out. I let go of the chain and as I started to drop I heard a splintering crunch, and I saw that a few yards above my head the mechanical arm had broken off, wrenched by my weight from its cement base, and that hundreds of pounds of rusted metal were plummeting right toward me as Heller and Sophie screamed.

I hit the water, I was under the water, and just inches away, the mechanical arm crashed into the water beside me and I could feel a jagged chunk of metal brushing against my elbow as the water churned and bubbled, making it impossible to see anything.

My head burst out of the water as Heller and Sophie each grabbed one of my arms and began dragging me toward the shore. The mechanical arm and the chain and the hook were far below us, sinking to the bottom of the quarry. As far as I could tell, while I was wet and dyed and pierced and gasping for air, I wasn't hurt.

I heard the police sirens, more than one, wailing and getting closer and closer.

thirty-two

Guilty of Everything

ere I am in my jail cell where I belong. I don't know where the police brought Sophie and Heller. I intend to plead guilty to whatever I'll be charged with, to avoid an unnecessary trial and so I can begin serving my most likely lifetime sentence in a prison far away from New Jersey because I don't want my family to feel obligated to visit me and so I can stop embarrassing them with headlines about Convict Caitlin, The Shame of the Singleberries, or Crime-Crazed Caitlin: Parsippany Punk.

Since I won't be attending college anywhere I've decided to spend my prison term in the most humble manner possible, maybe by scouring the prison bathrooms on my knees with a toothbrush, or maybe every morning I can make all of the other prisoners' beds without being asked to. I can become part of a ministry-behind-bars where I can teach arsonists to make flameproof holiday wreaths, and I can be used as a

scared-straight example to visiting at-risk high school students;
I can show those students just what happens when a person
makes one wrong and sinful decision after another. I've also
decided that for the rest of my life I'm only going to wear one
kneesock as a sign of remorse and repentance, and maybe in
the prison crafts room, I'll even carve simple wooden crucifixes
where Jesus is wearing only a single, drooping sock.

"Whatcha in for?" asks the girl in the sleeveless biker vest.
"Jaywalking? Overdue library book? Cheatin' at Scrabble?"

"Ms. Singleberry?" says a uniformed guard. "Will you
please come with me?"

I'm sure that the guard is going to fingerprint me and
take my mug shot, which, with my ragged hair and the stud
through my nose, can be used in one of those ads to stop people
from smoking or doing drugs. Instead he takes me down a hallway and into a conference room with a long table and folding
chairs. My mom and dad are here along with Aunt Nancy, Dave
and Barbara Schuler, and Wyatt. Sophie and Heller are sitting
off to one side wrapped in blankets, although I've insisted on
wearing my still-sopping skirt and what's left of my blouse,
because that's all I deserve. When I see all of these people I
don't know who to apologize to first. I run over to my parents,
who hug me while I blubber, "I'm sorry, I'm so sorry, I'm
the worst person who ever lived . . ."

"Hush," says my mom. "You're safe, everyone's safe and in
good health, and that's all that matters . . ."

"Are you worse than Hitler?" my dad asks, smiling, which
confuses and even irritates me because I was trying to confess

and apologize and accept my punishment, so I say, "Dad! I'm much worse than Hitler! Look at my hair!"

"The Honorable Judge Henry Bryce Drandower presiding," says a bailiff. "All please rise."

Everyone stands as Judge Drandower enters the room from another door, although he isn't wearing his judicial robes. He's a little older than my dad, and he doesn't look happy to be here, especially on a Sunday. I hear Aunt Nancy mutter under her breath, "Fascist hatemonger," which is something I've also heard Aunt Nancy mutter at a waiter who didn't bring her enough bread, at a crossing guard who asked her to please wait for the light, and at a lady who'd overcharged her for gourds at a farm stand.

The judge looks at everyone, scowling. He stares at Heller, who looks especially bedraggled and shrinks into her blanket.

"Sit," says the judge sternly, and as everyone sits, he says, "This is a preliminary hearing so I can decide which charges should be brought and against whom. Attorneys won't be necessary just yet, although sometimes I wonder if attorneys are ever necessary. I would now like everyone to laugh because I just made a little joke and you want me to like you, don't you?"

He glares and everyone laughs dutifully as Aunt Nancy mutters, "This is why the terrorists hate us. Patriarchal pig."

"Is there a problem?" the judge asks Aunt Nancy.

"No, Your Honor," she says meekly.

"As I understand it," the judge continues, "we have three young ladies present. Or perhaps three young criminals who need to be taught a lesson. Could they come forward, right now."

"Your Honor," says Heller, standing up, her voice shaking. "I'd like to say something."

I know what's coming. Heller is going to blame me for everything. She's going to explain that she never asked me to come to New York, and that I'm pushy and dim and annoying. She'll be earnest and charming and everyone will believe her. Which is fine. Even if Heller manages to sweet-talk her way out of all the trouble she's caused, I still deserve to be punished. Even if I didn't, Heller is a movie star so she'll get off scot-free, because that's how things work.

"Your Honor," says Heller, "this is all my fault. I forced Catey and Sophie to take off and spend the day with me and I wouldn't let Sophie call her parents and I gave Catey drugs . . ."

WHAT? What's Heller doing? I get it—she's taking the blame, but she's also taking center stage. She's tossing her wet hair and she lowered her voice on the word "drugs." She's being selfless and noble and everyone's eating it up. As Wyatt would say, I smell Oscar.

"No!" says Sophie, standing beside Heller. "I did it! I blackmailed Heller and Catey into doing everything I wanted, because I have cancer! They were, like, my hostages! And . . . and . . . I did that stuff to Catey's hair!"

"Which is a serious offense," says the judge, looking at me as I stand up. He's staring at my hair as if it's something repulsive that he's just stepped in.

"Your Honor," I say, "if anybody has a Bible I would really like to place my hand upon it, especially that part of the Old Testament where the Lord smites evildoers . . ."

"Just tell the truth," says the judge. "If you can manage that, with that car antenna through your nose. And I'll be happy to smite you myself."

"Your Honor," I say, "I was the person in charge. I was supposed to make sure that we followed the guidelines and the schedules so that Heller could promote her movie and so that Sophie could spend the day with us, and I'm the most incorrigible and violent . . . and . . . and unlawful criminal mastermind who's ever lived. I messed up everything and I disgraced my family and my country and my faith and . . . and . . . my right to ever enjoy a cupcake or anything with frosting ever again. I should be punished to the full extent of the law and even further, and even though I know that New Jersey doesn't have the death penalty maybe you can make an exception . . ."

I shut my eyes and hold my arms straight out in front of me.

"What the hell are you doing?" asks the judge.

"I'm ready. For the handcuffs."

"I'll be the judge of that," says the judge, and he chuckles in this dry, creepy way, which makes everyone in the room chuckle obediently. "First of all," he continues, "you're correct, New Jersey doesn't have the death penalty, because we are a humane and compassionate state and if we had the death penalty all of our Real Housewives would be gone. But let's attend to the matter at hand, which seems especially reprehensible. I'm told that over the course of a single afternoon these three delinquents have . . ." He puts on his reading glasses and studies a document that the bailiff has handed him. "They have stolen a sports car, brandished an illegal handgun, trespassed on government property and endangered the welfare of a minor. These are all activities that can incur substantial penalties, including incarceration, especially if these young felons are charged as adults. I am also told there is video footage of all or most of these activities."

The bailiff activates a flat-screen TV atop a nearby rolling cart and there it is: grainy but still completely identifiable surveillance video of me jumping into the convertible. Of me waving my pistol at the guys wearing ski masks in the Valu-Brite. There's me, Heller and Sophie, one after the other, dangling from the chain and dropping into the water at the quarry. As the mechanical arm wrenches apart and tumbles into the water, missing my head by inches, everyone in the room gasps, including me.

"Oh my Lord!" says my mom. "Caitlin!"

"That was so rad!" says Aunt Nancy, who likes to use slang that even I know is years out of date.

"This is like my favorite Heller Harrigan movie ever!" says Sophie.

"Oy vey iz mir," says Wyatt. "To the max."

"This footage is heinous and irrefutable," says the judge, "and can easily be used as justification for a grand jury hearing."

I glance across the room at Heller and even she looks nervous. No, more than nervous—she looks scared. Good. Finally. She's worried because there isn't a Golden Globe category for

Best Performance by an Actress Currently Serving Twenty Years Upstate.

"However," says the judge, again consulting his documents, "I'm also informed that the owner of the convertible in question has refused to press charges, owing to the fact that he was in possession of an illegal and unregistered firearm. Employees of both the Valu-Brite and a neighboring establishment called, I believe, the Happening Hairbomb, have told local law enforcement, quite vigorously, that these young women were in fact thwarting an armed robbery. We have a statement from one Tiffani Del Glorioso, who contends that, and I'm quoting, 'That Caitlin girl was a super-sick effing mindblaster. She saved everybody's butt and she looked hot doing it!' Unquote."

"Caitlin?" says my dad, sounding both surprised and impressed.

"I brought you a hat," my mom whispers to me.

"Which leaves us with the remaining charge of endangering the welfare of a minor," says the judge.

"Your Honorship?" says Sophie, waving her hand ferociously. "Can I talk now?"

"And you are . . . ?" asks the judge.

"I'm Sophie Schuler and I have cancer. I'm in remission but it's my second time around, so, well, super brap . . ."

"Sophie . . . ," says Barbara Schuler, squeezing Sophie's hand.

"Okay okay okay," says Sophie. "I asked the Make-A-Wish people, who are beyond awesome, if I could spend a day with Heller Harrigan, who's only my most favorite everything ever. They said go for it and so that's what I did. I just want to tell everybody, including Your Honor-Person and my mom and dad, that—it was the best day of my whole entire life! 'Cause I didn't just get to meet Heller, and her fucking amazing cousin Caitlin, I'm sorry, I know I shouldn't curse, but I forgot, shit, fuck, I did it again, but, Your Honor, no one endangered me. They saved me. They made me so happy. Your Honor, in, like, conclusion, I would like to remind the court that I'm only thirteen years old and . . . I have cancer."

Sophie lowers her chin, which trembles, and she stands pigeon-toed and looks up at the judge and I could swear that she somehow widens her eyes to twice their normal size. Out of the corner of my own eye I see that Heller, while still keeping her hands at her sides, is offering Sophie a surreptitious thumbs-up and mouthing the words "Way to go."

"You're in remission," Sophie's mom whispers to her, trying to be comforting.

"Shhh!" Sophie tells her mom.

"Well, goodness gracious," says the judge, "that is extremely persuasive testimony. Sophie, you are one adorable little girl and please know that the court's heartfelt prayers are with you. I suppose that Ms. Singleberry has demonstrated a certain degree of misguided and yet very real valor, in protecting both her companions and the staffs of the Valu-Brite and the . . . Happening Hairbomb."

"Your Honor?" says Heller, raising her hand politely. Here it comes. Sophie was great so Heller has to top her. Heller has to out-act a thirteen-year-old girl with cancer. Heller's going to claim she has a brain tumor, or diabetes, or that she has a multiple personality disorder and that Erin, one of her other personalities, committed the crimes. Heller is shameless. Duh.

"Yes?" says the judge, who stares at Heller, consults his papers and then asks, "Are you Heller Harrigan? *The* Heller Harrigan? From various television programs and supermarket tabloids and other assorted media?"

"Yes, Your Honor," says Heller, looking shy and demure, which makes me want to strangle her. "I've also appeared as a teenage prostitute on an episode of *Law & Order: SVU*, in which I was treated more than fairly by the esteemed judge on the show, who was played by a ruggedly handsome older actor. But that doesn't matter, even though that episode also won a Peabody Award for Excellence in Responsible Broadcasting. Because, yes, I am an actress, and a celebrity, and I do have over one point three million followers on Twitter, many of whom would love to visit Parsippany and enjoy . . . the scenic wonders, contributing perhaps millions of dollars to the local economy. But that doesn't matter either. What matters is that this weekend I have been tempted to do terrible and unholy things. I mean, seriously fun stuff, are you feelin' me? But I didn't do any of those things, thanks to one righteous and trustworthy and God-fearing human being. She's standing right there, wearing that one wet, filthy kneesock, and her name is Caitlin Singleberry. Your Honor, there is only one thing more important than the life-affirming decency that Ms. Singleberry teaches us all."

Oh my Lord! Heller is unbelievable! She'll say anything! She's dabbing at her eyes! I know she's pretending to defend me, but is anyone buying this? Especially when Heller talked about decency and put her hand over her heart?

"What might that one thing be, Ms. Harrigan?" asks the judge, and I really want to hear Heller's answer. In fact, the whole room is leaning toward Heller. What does she consider the most important thing? A single piece of candy corn? A push-up bra? Eyeliner?

"Your Honor?" asks Heller. "Do you have any grandchildren?"

"Why, yes, I do," says the judge. "I have three spectacular little girls. There's Katniss, who's just turned five, Bella, who's seven and the apple of my eye, and Hermione, who's all of nine. They are the prettiest, smartest, sweetest girls you'd ever hope to meet and I can't get enough of them."

"Well, Your Honor," says Heller, "do you think that your wonderful granddaughters might like to attend the gala premiere, as my guests, of the big new *Angel Wars* movie?"

thirty-three

Free at Last

The judge decides to dismiss all the charges, especially after Wyatt comes forward holding three collector's edition Lynnea Action-Bots complete with wings, crossbows, halos and a microchip that allows the Action-Bots to say phrases like "Stay golden!," "Wings up!" and "Death to the Creeper!"

This is followed by at least half an hour of hugging, lecturing, sobbing, more hugging, scolding, a group debate over teenagers and curfews and cell phones and then even more hugging, by everyone in the room. My mom and dad tell me that they've been worried sick about me, they've been furious at me, they've prayed for me, they are so proud of me, and they love me more than I can ever know. My dad says he is also gratified that someone has finally demolished that infernal mechanical arm at the quarry and my mom passes me a cupcake in its own little plastic container, which she's smuggled into the conference room inside her purse.

My mom and Aunt Nancy talk for longer than they have in years and the most shocking part is that they agree on everything, especially about how out of control their daughters are, and how concerned they are about this heedless, spoiled, entitled new generation with its tech gadgets and Twittering and secret languages involving semicolons. The Schulers inform Sophie she's grounded, which Sophie says is fine while rolling her eyes, and then the entire Schuler family poses for selfies with Heller and I see Heller giving Sophie five of her most private cell phone numbers and email addresses.

Heller, in this polite and totally phony voice, asks everyone if "before we go back to the hotel, can I just have a minute alone with Catey? I promise that we won't drive anywhere or swallow anything or shoot anyone."

Once everyone is out of the room, Heller shuts the door and stops smiling.

"All right," she says. "We both just handed that judge fifteen trillion barrels of steaming horseshit so he wouldn't put us in jail. Once we leave this room, we'll never have to see each other ever again. And after everything you said to me at the quarry, I really should rip your smug little Christian face off."

"I'm sorry if you feel that way," I say, using my most proper, talking-to-an-older-person-or-our-pastor tone of voice.

"Cut the crap, Sister Mary Turdface. There's something I need to tell you, just so we're clear. So if you decide to gossip with all of the other Singlesnitches, you'll at least have a few facts."

"Facts? About what? Your fifty-eight houses? Your five

thousand ex-husbands? Your thirty-eight million assistants? Because if I want to know about any of those things I can just read a magazine at the dentist's office. Right next to the pamphlets on gingivitis and root canal."

Heller turns away so she won't hit me. She turns back. "First of all, pisshead, my four houses? They're all mortgaged, and when I'm not there, they get rented out. The studio is paying for all those assistants, and once the movie opens, they're gone. I'm still broke."

Broke. Only Heller could use that word before going home to her personal chef, her yoga instructor and her racks of custom-made designer gowns.

"I'm going to tell you something I swore I would never tell anyone. It's completely private. You'll think it's bullshit or a joke or just another disgusting chapter in the life of your cousin Satan. Here goes: After I shot the *Angel Wars* movie, I was completely exhausted, I mean, I was roadkill. I'd tried so hard just to get cast in the damn thing, and then I'd worked my ass off; everyone on the movie worked unbelievably hard, in Morocco and Wyoming and on soundstages in Albuquerque, because we wanted the movie to be fantastic, because there was so much riding on it."

"I really don't care about how incredibly hard it is to be a big movie star. It must have been so difficult for you. What happened—was your trailer the wrong color? Wouldn't the studio match it to your nail polish?"

"Once it was over," says Heller, refusing to acknowledge

anything I said, "I thought I could take a breath. I thought, People will hate me or they won't, but no one can say I didn't do my best. Instead I dove right off the deep end, even for me. I couldn't sleep or eat or sit still. I just kept going over and over the movie in my head, and agonizing over everything I could've done better. I decided that the haters had been right all along and that I was contaminated rat puke and that once the movie opened, everyone would know."

I'm about to make another nasty remark but I don't. Heller has a strange, blank, defeated look on her face. The same look she had at Madison Square Garden after Ava Lily Larrimore hissed that hatred into her ear.

"I started drinking again and doing meth and hanging out with the kind of people who can get you anything you want, as long as they can stay an extra two weeks or two months or two years in your guest cottage and have their friends from Brazil stay over and let you pay everyone's cell phone bills. I went with it because it's like, when you work that hard, when you pour everything you've got into those five concentrated months of filming, you need something to replace it, to keep yourself up there, spinning and shooting off sparks. Finally I crashed. I woke up one morning, or actually it was three in the afternoon, and for the first time in forever, I was alone. Which I hated more than anything because then it was just me and my I-suck-so-much-I-don't-deserve-to-live thoughts. I noticed that my flat screen was gone and my laptop and all of my jewelry, including my mom's turquoise ring, which she'd always said could ward off evil spirits. Then I get a text from someone telling me that my phone had been hacked and that if I didn't wire this insane amount of cash to some account in the Cayman Islands, then naked pictures of me were going to flood the Internet, which would fuck up the movie and whatever reputation I had left, and my life.

"I knew exactly which pictures they were talking about because I'd sent them to this jerk, he's a rock star, or he thinks he is, and I thought I was in love with him and I'd wanted to show him that I was all grown up. I didn't pay the hacker, and when those pictures were everywhere I tried to think, Fuck it, who cares if other people, if the whole world, sees me naked? Still—the whole world. Staring at me. Sending the pictures to their friends, and everybody laughing, and saying all the things people like to say, about how that stupid slutty little Harrigan bitch got what she deserved."

I'm more glad than ever that my parents never allow me to spend much time online. I never want to sound the way Heller sounds right now, hollowed out and sad and empty. I almost reach out to touch her arm or take her hand but I can't.

"I turned off all the lights and I sat in my bedroom and I lit a whole mess of candles, because this was LA and if you're going to kill yourself there have to be candles, right? I mean at least sandalwood and green tea, with maybe a few sticks of vanilla-infused cinnabar incense in a hand-thrown mug."

"Heller . . . ," I begin, although I have no idea what to say. I can't tell how serious she is. About killing herself.

"Here's how I was going to do it. I was going to smoke some weed, and I had all of these pills, which I lined up on my little Buddhist altar, and I was going to swallow them with some white wine, it was sort of like the menu for a suicide buffet, or an LA kid's birthday party, if you added a clown who'd bring flourless brownies and soy milk. I was planning to crawl into the tub, which I'd filled with warm water and lavender oil, with floating camellias, which I thought would sound romantic online: 'Heller Harrigan, dead at seventeen, amid candle-glow and camellias.' I wanted everyone in the world to sob their guts out, and forget all about those naked Anna Banana screengrabs."

The awful thing is, I can picture the whole thing. The even more awful thing is, I'm starting to understand it.

"As I start downing the pills, slowly so I wouldn't barf them right up, there's someone pounding on my front door. I assume it's my dealer, or someone who's left their monogrammed bong at my house, or even the cops, but there's no way I'm going to answer it. I hear the door getting pried off its hinges and whomped open and I start to get scared. Because excuse me, I want to kill myself, not get murdered, so Mister Serial Killer, don't you dare upstage my story line. I hear whoever it is getting closer and closer and I decide that I don't care if it is a serial killer, as long as I end up dead. A serial killer, especially if he's wearing, like, a Darkling Creeper mask and carrying a bouquet of rotting roses, it might be a nice twist: 'Heller Harrigan, dead at seventeen, the Creeper wins.'

"The bedroom door opens and—it's Oliver. I hadn't talked to him for weeks and I'd stopped going to meetings and he'd been texting me like mad and so he'd figured, well, he'd figured that I might be doing exactly what I was doing. Do you know the weirdest part?"

I shake my head because I'm having trouble believing that Heller's story can get any weirder or more upsetting. Since it's Heller telling the story, she's making it entertaining and even funny—for Heller, even her own suicide attempt is like the exciting trailer for the blockbuster movie of her death.

"The weirdest thing was that Oliver didn't try to stop me. He just sat on the edge of my bed and he said, 'Go ahead. If that's what you want to do. If that's how you want everything to end. If you're in that much pain, or if you're that kind of coward.' I started crying, and Oliver held me. We've never had sex. Later on, people sometimes thought we were married because we wore these matching silver rings. He just stayed with me until the sun came up, and then you know what he said? He said, 'You need Caitlin.'"

"What?"

"I'd told him all about you, the whole story. He said, 'Hel, everything you've ever done, it's all been either to make Caitlin proud of you, and forgive you, or to make yourself fall so far down the rabbit hole that Caitlin will finally have to come looking for you.' I said, 'Whatever, fine, and I'm not saying you're right about anything, but Catey won't talk to me or come anywhere within a million miles of me. She hates my guts for a very good reason. I almost killed her.' Oliver smiled and he said, 'You'll think of something. Come on, you're Heller Harrigan.'"

I'm not sure why but I'm starting to smile. And cry.

"I did think of something. Eventually. This whole weekend, and your coming here to be my chaperone and my warden and my nanny, it was my idea. I told Wyatt about you and he talked to my mom, who decided that the whole thing was her own idea, and then she called your mom. I had my fingers crossed the whole time and I was praying to whatever god I believed in that week to let this happen. To let us be together. I guess it was maybe the worst idea I've ever had and I'm really sorry. I'm sorry about everything. I'm sorry about four years ago and I'm sorry I listened to our parents and didn't go to see you in the hospital or call you or at least FedEx you some Percocet. It's just—I thought I'd be the last person you'd ever want to hear from. I thought our parents were right."

As soon as Heller says this about our parents she yelps: "I KNOW! What was I thinking? And I'm sorry about this weekend and I'm sorry about today and I'm sorry that I'm the worst friend anyone's ever had. I'm like the anti-friend. The nightmare friend. But, Catey, there's one last thing I have to tell you . . ."

Heller is looking right at me and I think, Oh my Lord, she's seeing a drowned rat with a rainbow haystack on her head and a cuff link through her nose. She's seeing someone who used to be so organized and so punctual and so on top of everything and who's now a hopeless, one-grimy-kneesock, sniffling mess.

"Catey—take the bandage off your arm."

I'd completely forgotten about my tattoo. What is under that bandage? A devil-worshipping pentagram? Elmer Fudd with an erection? A musical note vomiting? I gingerly peel off the surgical tape, holding the gauze in place. The skin underneath is puffy and red and slathered with a clear antibiotic gel. The tattoo is simple and beautifully drawn. It's a heart with the words "Caitlin and Heller Forever. God Help Them."

Heller is holding up her own forearm, which has the same tattoo with the names reversed.

"Oh, and Catey, one more thing—that pill I gave you? It wasn't an antianxiety med or a pill to stop smoking or anything hard-core. It was a baby aspirin."

What? WHAT? I have broken so many laws and disfigured myself and almost died, because of a BABY ASPIRIN?

"Why?" I wail. "Why did you give me a baby aspirin? Why did you tell me it would help?"

"Because I wanted it to. Because you couldn't move. Because I hated seeing you tied up in knots. Because I know that anxiety and panic attacks are real and I hate that you have them. Because you deserve so much better. Catey, you're a really smart, beautiful, talented girl but you don't believe it. So the panic always wins."

"Not always," I say. "Not when you're here. I'm so sorry I never called *you* and I'm sorry that you had to go through so many terrible things all by yourself and I'm sorry I wasn't there. I'm a terrible friend too—no! I'm not just a terrible friend! I'm much worse! I'm a bad CHRISTIAN!"

Heller turns her head toward heaven and asks, "Did you hear that?"

"HELLER!!!"

Heller opens her arms and I hug her so hard that our tattooed arms rub together, which really hurts.

"OWWW!!!" we both howl but we don't stop hugging.

"Ladies?" says Wyatt, at the door. "I'm glad this all worked out and that neither of you are going to jail, at least not until your next little crime spree. We still have a problem. A big one. That surveillance footage? It's all over the web. Everyone has a different theory about what Heller was up to and what she was high on and how badly she's lost her mind at the most pivotal moment in her career. I've been trying to spin the whole thing, to tell everyone that you were making an independent student film, but I don't think anyone's going for it."

Wyatt slumps in a chair with his head in his hands and when he looks up I see that he's crying. "I'm so sorry," he says. "I just want the whole world to know that even if Heller is certifiably nuts, she's still an amazing actress and a seriously good person. I want them to forget all about rehab and those naked pictures and people holding up convenience stores. Hel, I don't know what to tell you. I love you, and I'm a great manager, and I want the *Angel Wars* movie to be an international phenomenon, but I'm done. I can't find a way out of this."

Heller stares at Wyatt and I can see that she's falling apart too. She's worked so hard on *Angel Wars* and it's her last chance. Then she says, "Wyatt, don't you dare apologize! You're the best manager and the best person ever! This is all my fault. You and

Catey tried so hard to help me, but I fucked up this whole weekend and the whole movie and everything else! I'm the only thing that's worse than a bad Christian—I'm a bad MOVIE STAR!"

Heller hurls herself into another chair, hanging her head. She looks even more lost than Wyatt.

"Bubbelahs," I say, using another Jewish word Wyatt has taught me, "I have an idea."

thirty-four

Reputation Rehab

All it had taken was a baby aspirin, swallowed under false pretenses, to turn me into a wild, lawless, deranged creature—into Heller. We need to turn Heller into me.

On Monday at noon the Singing Singleberries are scheduled to perform at a shopping mall in Parsippany to raise money for our local children's hospital. Wyatt spends the morning alerting the paparazzi, network and cable TV news crews, every possible website and Twitter feed and everyone else he can think of about an upcoming surprise event that may or may not involve Heller Harrigan, the once again notorious star of the upcoming, much-awaited *Angel Wars* blockbuster. He's using #AngelAppearance, #HellerBlast, #JerseyBabe and #OMGHeller!!! An hour before the concert is set to begin, April drives Heller, Wyatt and me out to New Jersey.

By noon the central plaza of the mall, the place where they

do things like setting up a three-story-high Christmas tree, is packed, with more people hanging off the railings of the mall's second and third levels. Thanks to Wyatt and his staff, everyone is buzzing, although no one's sure exactly what's about to happen. There are rumors that the president is planning a surprise speech and will use Heller as an example of youth in peril; other people are claiming that precisely at noon Heller is going to ring a bell and millions of dollars in cash is going to be whooshed into the mall through the air-conditioning vents so shoppers can dive for the money and get into nasty, greedy brawls, as part of Heller's new reality show. There's also the strong possibility that other big stars, maybe Taylor Swift or Katy Perry or a hot new English boy band, will make an appearance in support of Heller, and the boy band option is already causing mobs of tween girls to scream and faint, or scream and pretend to faint, so that Chadwin or Brock or Niall will try to revive them, preferably with kisses, autographed collarbones and selfies.

At 12:05, Sophie walks out onto the small stage that has been set up, which is ringed by security guards.

"Yo, I'm Sophie," she says, and there's some grumbling from the crowd because Sophie isn't Heller or any other recognizable star.

"Shut up, I have cancer, you douchewads," Sophie continues, taking off her baseball cap to reveal her topknot. "I'm one of way too many kids who are getting sick, but thanks to Saint Anthony's Children's Hospital some of us are doing okay, or even better than that. The doctors and nurses at Saint Anthony's are amazing, but they need our help to pay for equipment and salaries and research."

"Where's Taylor Swift?" yells someone from the crowd. "We want Taylor!"

"Taylor isn't here," says Sophie. "I love Taylor but we got someone even better, so shut your piehole, you ass-clown. Right now I wanna introduce a totally major group of people, who spent a whole lot of time raising money for Saint Anthony's and for kids like me. I know, like, at first you're gonna think they're a bunch of hopeless mall dorks and you're gonna start texting your friends to see if they want to hook up for pizza, but don't do it. These people are secretly awesome and if you just stop getting all scrantsy and antsy, there's also gonna be a very spe-cialicious guest star and I'm not gonna say her name, but she's like the biggest star out there, I mean, she's like the person Beyoncé texts and is, like, dying to hang out with and eat microwave popcorn with and go shopping with for big designer purses to put their tiny little dogs in . . ."

The crowd starts to buzz and everyone is saying Heller's name and everyone has an opinion, and I hear the words "slut," "bimbo," "gorgeous," "alkie," "druggie," "Anna Banana" and "major hot mess with a side order of train wreck."

"Dudes!" Sophie shouts over the chatter. "You think you know this person but she's not what you're thinking. Today she's raising tons of money for Saint Anthony's and making a totally massive personal donation and you're gonna be really surprised, you're gonna be all like, 'What?' But first I want you to meet— the fabulously fabulous Singing Singleberries!"

There's almost no applause as the Singing Singleberries walk
out onstage, all nine of us plus my mom and my dad. We're all
wearing our Singleberry uniforms with the boys in their burgundy
blazers with embroidered musical notes on the breast pockets,
and the girls in blazers, pleated skirts and kneesocks with the
burgundy and gold stripes at the top. My dad and mom wear
the burgundy sweaters that my mom has knitted with a pattern of dancing musical notes. Caleb has his guitar, Calico sits
behind her drum set and Corinne is at her electronic keyboard.

I stand in the middle between Carter and Catherine. As I
look at my family I feel so proud, because once I left the police
station all of my brothers and sisters had been waiting outside.
Everyone hugged me like crazy and asked all about my big
weekend and Calico whispered, "You can tell Mom and Dad
the PG-13 version but I want the hard R." I told everyone about
my plan to rescue Heller's reputation and everyone agreed to
help out. They'd missed Heller too.

My dad gives us an opening note from his pitch pipe and
we all match the pitch. We start singing something that Castor
has written and it's become our theme song: It's called "The
Singleberry Stomp" and it begins with Carl, who's twelve and who
has the most beautifully pure tenor voice, singing all by himself:

I'M SITTING IN THE DARK
I DON'T KNOW WHAT TO DO
I WANT TO SING A SONG
WHO SHOULD I SING IT TO?

Then Calico, while keeping a light but steady beat on her snare drum, joins in with Carl:

> *IF YOU'RE ALL ALONE*
> *YOUR SONG JUST GOES TO WASTE*
> *SOMEONE NEEDS TO SING ALONG*
> *EVERY TENOR NEEDS A BASS*

Callum joins in because he's got one of those freakishly wonderful, super-deep bass voices, as if his chest has its own echo chamber, and the three of them sing:

> *WHEN I HEAR ANOTHER VOICE*
> *I KNOW I HAVE A FRIEND*
> *WHEN WE START TO SING*
> *OUR SPIRITS START TO BLEND*

The rest of us join in for the first chorus:

> *SING WITH ME AND I'LL SING WITH YOU*
> *WHEN WE SING TOGETHER, THERE'S NOTHING*
> *WE CAN'T DO*
> *SING ME INTO JOY AND I'LL SING YOU INTO HOPE*
> *SING ME AS WE CLIMB AND I'LL SING YOU UP*
> *THE SLOPE*
> *SING ME THROUGH THE STORM AND WE'LL GIVE*
> *THE CLOUDS A SHOVE*

SING ME INTO SUNSHINE
I WILL SING YOU INTO LOVE!

As we sing, our voices wind around one another, pushing the song's energy higher and higher. At first the crowd is skeptical, especially because of our outfits and our scrubby-clean faces, but as we sing and Callum adds his underscore of deep-voiced bop-bop-bops, and Corinne, Calico and Catherine move into a girl-group dance routine, the song gets hotter, more complicated and jubilant. People get caught up in the swirling counterpoint and start to clap along with the rhythm and some people even start to dance, which is just what I'd had in mind when I figured out the vocal arrangement for the song. I wanted the song to begin simply and then gradually explode, as if our voices are challenging one another and finally blasting into a combination of a gospel choir, a pop song and the booming, hands-in-the-air finale of a big Broadway musical.

Ever since I was little I've been fascinated by what voices can do, as if each voice is a separate color that can be used as an accent or in bold contrast, or overlaid with the other colors to create something brand-new. Over the years my dad has taught me how to write down my ideas, to annotate them, and to create arrangements for our concerts. I've done this so much it never feels like work, especially because I have so many wonderful voices to use. That's why I've always worried about a college major in choral arrangement, let alone performance studies, because getting credit and a degree for having that much fun would feel sinful.

As the song keeps building, Heller walks out onstage, wearing her own Singleberry blazer, skirt and kneesocks, which Catherine and my mom pulled together overnight. Heller's hair is tugged back into a neat ponytail and Kenz has done her makeup so that Heller looks like a ten-year-old schoolgirl who's not wearing any makeup at all. Heller stands next to me and she weaves her voice into the melody, without trying to stand out in any way. As I'd told Wyatt earlier: "If we want people to think that Heller is a nice person who would never take drugs or kidnap anyone or have sex, let's turn her into a Singleberry."

Heller has a great singing voice and she harmonizes expertly with my family as we sing:

WHEN YOU'RE FEELING DOWN AND GLOOMY
I WILL SING AWAY YOUR FEAR
WHEN I'M LOST AND FEELING FRIENDLESS
IF YOU SING I'LL KNOW YOU'RE NEAR
WHEN THE WORLD CAN'T GET ALONG
WHEN EACH RIGHT HAS GONE SO WRONG
WE CAN HEAL IT, WE CAN FEEL IT
IF WE SING EACH OTHER'S SONG!

As the crowd realizes, one person at a time, that Heller Harrigan is not only singing onstage but that she's a Singleberry, the mall goes berserk, as everyone grabs their phones and starts forwarding Heller's picture and live-streaming the song—Wyatt has taught me what all of these things are. The teenage girls are screaming Heller's name and the teenage boys are rubbing themselves and moaning and then punching one another on the shoulder, and Wyatt has made sure there's a group of nuns right near the stage, smiling and bobbing their heads in time to the music.

As we keep singing, something strange happens: I start singing by myself. At first I'm confused because this part of the song isn't supposed to be a solo. As I keep singing I turn both ways to look at my family and I see that Heller has her arms spread wide, cuing everyone to take a step back, and she has a forefinger to her lips as a signal for everyone except me to stop singing.

For a second I pause in midnote because I don't like to sing by myself. When I hear my own voice it embarrasses me. Not because I can't sing or hit the notes but because the whole idea of singing by myself seems prideful, as if I'm showing off and saying, Hey, look at me, I'm such hot stuff, I'm better than everyone else. But right now as I keep singing I give myself permission: to go for it, to enjoy the moment and to let the world hear my voice.

Here's my darkest and most precious secret: While I'm singing, I never feel anxious. Before I open my mouth I can get nervous and even frantic but once I produce that first sound, a sound that pleases me and a sound the world might like to hear, I'm golden. It's not that I get lost in the music; in fact it's the opposite. I find myself. When I'm singing I feel like I'm exactly where I'm supposed to be and until the end of the song, the demons and the twitching nerve endings and the paralyzing fear can't touch me; there's no room for them. The music always wins.

Thanks to Heller, I know which college I'm going to choose, or which college I will dare to choose. I'm going to Torlington even if the idea terrifies me. Maybe because the idea terrifies me. I don't want to try and become a star like Heller because I could never stand that kind of pressure and because I don't have Heller's huge personality and her need to make the whole world pay attention every second, or else!

Maybe I can be my own kind of star. Maybe I can sing just because I love music and because why would God give me a voice if he didn't want me to use it? If I'm being selfish and prideful, well, next month I turn eighteen years old, so maybe being selfish and prideful comes with the territory. I don't have any of these answers, but at Torlington, maybe I can start to find them.

I grab Heller's hand, and Carter's, and I glare at them, at my whole family, to force them to start singing again. That's the other reason I love music: It's something everyone can share. Music doesn't have to cost money and while people are making music together they have a harder time, at least for a few minutes, hating or killing each other. I don't think that music can solve the world's problems but it usually feels like a step in the right direction. Sure, I know that sometimes soldiers march off to war to the jaunty tunes of a military band, but that's not what's happening right now at the Parsippany Tri-State All-Weather Shopping Destination.

Something else is happening. Uh-oh. Oh my dear sweet baby Jesus hide your tiny blessed eyes or maybe take a bathroom break. Heller is starting to unbutton her blazer and now she's tugging the rubber band off her ponytail and shaking out her hair. I don't even think she realizes she's doing it, but she's turning back into Heller. She's starting to sing:

I FEEL IT, IT'S SO REAL
THAT I'M SINGIN' WITH MY PEEPS
WE'RE PRAYIN' AND WE'RE SAYIN'
THAT OUR MESSAGE, BITCH, IT'S DEEP

Then Heller's voice gets low and soulful:

FUCK ME, I'M A SINGLEBERRY
GOOD LUCK TO ME, I'M A SINGLEBERRY
I'M GONNA ROCK
EACH KNEESOCK
FUCK ME, I'M A SINGLEBERRY!

There's a pause as my whole family stops singing and the crowd holds its breath. I tap Heller on the shoulder and she looks around and remembers what she's supposed to be doing. She grins, which can pretty much fix anything, and we all swing right back into the song:

IF YOU SING WITH ALL YOUR HEART
I WILL SING WITH ALL MY SOUL

IF WE SING WHEN WE'RE APART
OUR SONG WILL MAKE US WHOLE
IF WE SING THEN I WILL PROMISE
WE WILL FIND OUR HARMONY
OUR SONG WILL SING US STRONG
BUT ONLY IF YOU'LL SING WITH ME!

thirty-five

Premiere

My idea works and Wyatt is beside himself. "Catey!" he says that night while I'm waiting with Heller outside the movie theater right before she's about to walk the red carpet. "You're a born publicist! Thanks to you the whole world believes that Heller is really just a nice girl from New Jersey who loves helping others and singing uplifting songs and wearing hideous polyester clothing. She broke Twitter, because #kneesocks has been getting so many hits that the system had to shut itself down for over half an hour. Look!"

Wyatt shows me a Tumblr feed on his phone of people all over the world wearing kneesocks. There are pictures of pre-teen girls in Finland carefully lined up in a kneesock rainbow; tall, scary-skinny models on a runway in Milan wearing knee-socks with their zippered leather miniskirts; gang members in California wearing kneesocks in their gang colors, yanked up over the legs of their pants; and soccer teams, who'd been wearing kneesocks anyway, but were now being photographed by fashion magazines as trendsetters under headlines like "On Your Knees!" and "Needsox!"

"And, Catey," adds Wyatt, "Omnisphere tripled its donation to Make-A-Wish and Heller pledged her salary if they make the next *Angel Wars* movie!"

I'm so excited that for the first time in my life I attempt a fist bump, with Wyatt, although I miss by a few inches.

"We'll get there," he says.

For the red carpet Heller is wearing a strapless golden designer gown and Nedda has talked me into a silvery gown with a thankfully higher neckline, and underneath she's given me matching silvery kneesocks with rows of tiny pearls along the tops. Kenz has dyed my hair back to its regular color and styled it to look, as he put it, "Short and sweet." I've removed the stud in my nose, although I've saved it as a keepsake, and I've taken off my bandage to feature my tattoo. "You look fantastic," Heller tells me. "We look like the world's most glamorous salt-and-pepper shakers."

"I'm so nervous but I don't know why," I say, although I'm feeling a better kind of nervous, instead of my usual free-floating if-I-don't-check-to-see-that-I've-locked-the-front-door-five-times-the-house-will-be-robbed anxiety. I'll probably always have panic attacks but I'm determined to keep them under control, as snuffed-out flickers rather than five-alarm blazes. This past weekend has helped because so many painful and life-threatening things have happened, and I've survived. From now on when I start to feel anxious, instead of surrendering helplessly I'm going to tell myself, "Catey, remember—you stole a car and a gun. You jumped off a cliff. You have a tattoo. Calm down!"

"I know why I'm nervous," says Heller. "It's because after tonight everyone's gonna know if the *Angel Wars* movie is any good and if I'm any good, and if we're gonna be allowed to make the next three sequels. It's like facing a firing squad, only the executioners don't have guns, they have Twitter accounts. Death by hashtag."

We hear a noise coming from inside a nearby tent where guests have been picking up their screening tickets and party passes. There's cursing and someone gets shoved into the side of the tent, which bulges out and almost rips.

Heller and I investigate and we find Mills and Billy, both in tuxedoes, having a fistfight. Mills's hair is messed up but not in its usual, deliberate way and Billy has the beginnings of a black eye.

"I saw her first!" says Mills.

"Nobody cares!" says Billy. "I helped her get a tattoo!"

"What are you two idiots doing?" asks Heller.

"He tried to switch our tickets!" says Mills. "So that he can sit next to Catey!"

"Because he'd already switched them!" insists Billy. "Catey doesn't want to sit next to that douchebag! She'll get a gallon of hair gel all over her dress! She'll smell like knockoff body spray! Mills covers himself with something called CrotchRot!"

"At least I took a bath!" says Mills. "Billy's afraid that if he stands under hot water he'll get even shorter!"

Mills pretends to look around the tent, asking, "Billy? Has anyone here seen Billy Connors? Everyone look down!"

"Catey?" says Heller. "You're going to have to choose between these two morons. Or you could just become a lesbian, which is a much better idea."

I can't believe this is my life, with two handsome actors fighting over me, or at least over their seating assignments. Heller had warned me to beware of actors and I know that after tonight Mills and Billy will most likely head off to other countries to shoot other movies and kiss other girls. But right now I feel like Lynnea, when she's torn between Tallwen, her stalwart Stelterfokken protector, and Myke, the small-town poet and potter with the cowlick and clay under his fingernails. In the books Lynnea finally settles down with Myke because he needs her more and because he writes her a poem that rhymes Lynnea with hooray-ah. In so many YA books the heroine, who's just a regular girl, has to choose between two dreamboats who are both, for no particular reason, madly in love with her, which is probably why these books are labeled fiction. For my big moonlit night I'm going to do Lynnea one better.

"I don't need to choose," I announce. "Mills can sit on one side of me and Billy can sit on the other."

"A three-way!" says Heller. "That's so hot!"

As I'm about to say "HELLER!" Wyatt approaches us, saying, "Time to meet the public, Hel! Wings up!"

"Not without Catey," says Heller, grabbing my hand.

"I am not going on the red carpet!" I say. "Nobody knows who I am! No one cares!"

"I know who you are," says Heller.

"I care," say Billy and Mills at the same time, which makes them scowl at each other and then start trying to step on each other's expensive shoes.

"Get out there," Billy tells me. "If it wasn't for you, Heller might not even be here."

"You have no choice," says Wyatt. "I'm going to tell the media that you're an actual angel, taking a break from your heavenly duties because Heller needed you for research."

"Oy vey iz mir," Wyatt and I say together.

I only last a few seconds on the red carpet because the lights are blinding and the noise and the shouting get too intense. Heller soaks it up because she's used to this degree of over-whelming attention and she's good at it—she grins and poses and knows all her best angles, and she flirts with the photographers and the fans and the world. I love finding out what walking the red carpet is like but I think that people should earn the spotlight through hard work, the way Heller has.

I wonder: Did I do my job? Did I save Heller's soul? I'm not sure, but I have witnessed a miracle: Heller has admitted she's been wrong, about all sorts of things, and apologized to me. I've admitted that I'm a slut and a sinner and that I'll never be perfect. We're even. No—it's so much better than that. I've got my best friend back.

I'd assumed that Heller and I would have seats in the first few rows of the theater, but instead we get seated right in the center because, as Wyatt explains, "This way all the people in the back will stand up to get a look at you and all the people down front will spend the whole movie trying to wrench their necks around." Before the movie begins I take a moment to let everything sink in. My family fills the row right behind us and my mom and Aunt Nancy are gabbing away and I even hear my mom use the name Ecstasy. My brothers and sisters are giddy and Calico is in heaven because she keeps spotting celebrities and then she tells Callum who they are and who they're supposedly sleeping with; this reminds me of a game my family plays on long trips where we lean out the windows of our bus and compete to see who can spot the most out-of-state license plates. My dad is trying to stay dad-like and keep everyone in their seats but he's looking around too and nudging my mom whenever he sees anyone major.

Sophie and her parents are sitting further down in our row and Sophie has circled her topknot with a twenty-four-karat golden halo from Tiffany, a gift from Heller. The Schulers are really excited and it's great to see them at an event that has nothing to do with illness or worry. Sophie waves to me and pulls a defective Sweetcake out of her purse and holds it up as a trophy.

Speaking of Sweetcakes, Heller came through: The security guard from the factory is sitting right in front of us with his wife and daughter, next to Judge Drandower and Hermione, Bella and Katniss. Heller has obliged with one selfie after another and the judge can't stop beaming.

Oliver is sitting on the other side of Heller, and with his

dark hair and dashing white forelock, he looks as if he was born in a tuxedo. He smiles and nods at me because we understand each other. We're both on Team Heller.

Wyatt is sitting right behind me and as the lights go down he squeezes my shoulder and whispers, "You did good, Catey. You're the pride of Parsippany."

I almost can't watch the movie because I'm so nervous for Heller and since I'm also a passionate Angel Warrior I'm concerned that the movie will leave out something important or mess everything up and betray the spirit of the book. But after the first few minutes I'm completely caught up in the story, even though I know everything that's going to happen. The weirdest thing is that after the earliest scenes, I forget that I'm Heller's cousin and that I've spent the weekend with her, and that up until a few hours ago I wanted to kill her. I only watch Lynnea.

Along with everyone else in the audience, I'm thrilled when Lynnea's wings grow large and strong enough for her first flight and I clutch Mills's arm when Lynnea almost crashes into a mountainside. I sigh when Lynnea kisses Tallwen, and then Myke, even though in real life in the movie theater, Mills and Billy keep trying to flick each other's ears behind my head.

When Malestra challenges Lynnea in the Netherdome I'm so involved that I gasp and say, "Oh no!" and "Watch out, she's right behind you!" and "Use your golden crossbow!" I wonder what Ava Lily Larrimore will make of the movie, if she allows herself to see it. Will she automatically hate it because she hates Heller and because nothing could ever measure up to her expectations and her demands? I feel bad for Ava because she's backed herself into a corner, where nothing will ever be good enough. But I never want to become Ava, sitting at home with her arms crossed, sneering and judging everyone else, ruling from her iPad and never taking a risk or daring to enjoy herself.

When Lynnea finally faces the Darkling Creeper the audience goes crazy, cheering for the ordinary small-town girl who's trying desperately to save the world. Of course since this is only the first of the four projected *Angel Wars* movies, the story just sort of stops with Lynnea almost dying but vowing to return and realizing that she now commands a ragtag Angel army. The movie ends with a lot of pounding, soaring music and Lynnea in midair silhouetted against a blazing sun. There's a pause and then the entire audience jumps to its feet, with everyone cheering and clapping, and when the words "Prepare Thyself for *Angel Wars II: Devil's Dominion*" appear on the screen, I think that the theater's roof will blow off because the audience is screaming so loudly.

During the noise I lean across Mills's lap and grab Heller's hand and I say into her ear, "It's really good and you're absolutely amazing." Heller looks at me and I can see how nervous she still is, and scared, but that it's starting to dawn on her that everything might just be okay.

She holds up her forearm so I can see her tattoo and I hold up mine. She grins at me, a grin filled with relief and happiness and even, oh my dear Lord, a hint of some new, dangerous and thrilling adventure because Heller is already restless and eager to upset me in some horribly wonderful new way. I don't mean to do it and I know I shouldn't and I'm positive that I will absolutely regret it, but I can't help myself and I grin right back.

acknowledgments

I would like to thank my editor, Rachel Griffiths, for her many astonishing skills, which include her infinite patience, her superb guidance, her joyous enthusiasm and her ability to chat on the phone for extended periods, about both my book and everything else we can come up with. Prior to writing *It's All Your Fault*, I made a few attempts at other books, and Rachel was always wise and supportive, and once I'd abandoned those misbegotten tales, she never asked "What were you thinking, you fool?"

I'd also like to thank everyone at Scholastic, the most wonderful home any author could hope for. Everyone at Scholastic is always smart, imaginative and a treat to hang out with, and they include Kelly Ashton, Lori Benton, Ellie Berger, Bess Braswell, Lauren Festa, Sheila Marie Everett, Tracy van Straaten, David Levithan, Rachael Hicks, Gabriel Rumbaut, Elizabeth Parisi, Lizette Serrano, Emily Heddleson, Antonio Gonzalez, Elizabeth Whiting, Alan Smagler, Annette Hughes, Jacquelyn Rubin, Alexis Lunsford and Duryan Bhagat-Clark.

I'd also like to thank David Kuhn and his staff; the fine folks who manufacture yellow legal pads and Mallomars; and booksellers everywhere, for insisting that, while movies, music, television and the Internet all are perfectly valid pursuits, they're really just minor distractions from the glorious pleasures of reading a book.

As always, I must thank John Raftis, for his impeccable driving, his spectacular gardens and our shared love of IHOP.

Above all, I would like to thank my readers, for allowing me to write. It's all your fault.

about the author

Paul Rudnick is a novelist, playwright, and screenwriter. His screenplays include *Addams Family Values* and *In&Out*, and he's written for *Vogue, Entertainment Weekly, Vanity Fair*, and the *New Yorker*. His plays have been produced both on and off Broadway and around the world and include *I Hate Hamlet* and *Jeffrey*. His first young adult novel was *Gorgeous*, which Libba Bray for the *New York Times* called "a wicked good time." Under the pen name Libby Gelman-Waxner, he is also the world's most beloved and irresponsible film critic. Paul lives in New York City.